Finding FIZZ

JULIE HODGSON

ISBN 978-91-88045-15-7

Chave.co.uk

CONTENTS

CHAPTER ONE

S am had no idea how long he had been there; it could have been five minutes, it could have been his whole life. It was definitely peaceful, there was no disputing that, but the peace, the beauty, didn't reach him. It were as if he had landed in paradise twenty seconds or twenty years ago, but his body was inside a bubble and he would never know what it would feel like to breathe in this air, an air that skimmed in off the rainbow surface of the lake, which twisted and turned into the distance and a permanent, golden sunset. He knew it was permanent, as if the gods had spent an eternity selecting the most beautiful, compelling and affecting view of the sky to have descended over the world and cast a spell of solidity over it so the people of this strange land could always feel the emotions that it provoked – a deep sense of peace, satisfaction, comfort. Yes, everything would always be all right under this sun. But Sam felt immune in some way. He idly dipped a finger in the lake and when he pulled it out it was coated in every imaginable colour. At the same time, the far bank became home to an elegant, grazing creature whose mane reflected every one of those colours into the sky as its single horn glowed with a light so pure it could almost be heard. Sam wiped his finger, ran a hand through his golden curls and stood up. If

1

he had been looking at the scene in a book in his homeland he would have been more affected by it than being here in person; he knew this. He knew that it was powerful and sensual and beyond the magic of anything he had seen in his life, but still it made no impact on his senses. A fog inside of him kept away the wonder of this world and every enchantment caused his skin to buckle and churn with dread. If he didn't get away from this place soon it would surely make him ill.

Just as his tears were about to spill all over the glowing, emerald grass, Sam heard a noise behind him – a familiar noise that halted all sense of self-pity. Crying. A woman crying. Although he didn't feel quite himself, he knew that the tears of a woman took precedence over his own. He turned to trace the noise and could see no one amongst the choir of flowers or the mesmerising twisting, turning, dancing leaves in their burnt autumn shades of red, orange and yellow. As he rose to his bare feet, he realised that the only place this woman could be hiding was behind a tree, or perhaps it was a pair of hands rising out of the ground to radiate their warmth onto the small scurrying creatures all around.

'Hello,' he whispered gently, and cautiously moved towards the weeping, which turned to snuffles as he spoke, as if the person crying was trying to hide her distress but was clearly unable to stop the tears however hard she tried. 'Hello,' he repeated even more softly this time and was able to peep behind the hand-tree for the first time, revealing a young woman slumped against the winding wrist-trunk, hugging her knees into her chest and watering the grass with her tears. When she looked up at Sam it was with eyes like two sparkling emeralds, so vivid, reflecting an old soul with wisdom and peace. Her lips were lush and pink and he could only imagine the dazzling smile that transformed her face when she was full of joy. Her hazel tresses were the colour of buttered rum and as she shifted to meet his gaze, he could see shades of sepia, amber, honey, fire and coffee. He had never seen hair like this. He had never seen beauty like this; there was something ethereal about the way she looked, her enchanting face was luminous and mysterious, and he knew it should have taken his breath away, but still he felt nothing.

She turned to him with breath-taking grace and said, 'Do not look upon me, Sam. I have let you down.'

'How could you let anyone down?' he asked, kneeling beside her, trying to feel the words coming from his heart, but feeling only emptiness. 'What can be so bad to make you cry like this? You are the most beautiful creature in existence; such beauty can surely not be overcome with life's trivialities.'

The young woman sniffed back her tears and almost smiled then said, 'You would not be so nice to me if you knew the truth.'

As she spoke, feelings washed over Sam for the first time since he had arrived in this strange place, as if he were at home, a small child, and being cared for in a most unbelievable way. He then reached out to take her hand, believing himself to be comforting her, but this small touch gave him immense peace as if someone had put ointment onto his open, bleeding wounds.

'You are a healer,' he told her, although the words seemed inadequate. 'You are healing my soul.'

'If only I could, Sam,' she said and dropped his hand. Rising to her feet, he could see the full extent of her dress, which might have been made from thousands, millions, of butterflies tickling her flesh with their delicate wings. All at once he could see them clearly, gracefully flapping to conceal her modesty, and then they merged into glistening layers of fabric that lived and breathed with the contours of her pure, white flesh. As she broke contact with him and moved away, his empty hopelessness returned. He fell back to seat himself against the tree and gripped his knees with almost as much despair as she had shown.

'But we are connected,' he told her.

'Yes and no.'

'You are the solution to my woes.'

She shook her head sadly. 'I am the problem.'

Suddenly Sam was on his feet again. 'So tell me, please. Where am I? What is this place? Why do I feel this way surrounded by such beauty? Who are you?'

'I am your guardian angel, Sam, for all the good it has done you.'

'So it is true then,' he said and slumped again against the tree. 'I am dead.'

'I cannot lie to you. Yes, you are dead.'

As the reality settled into Sam's mind he realised that it didn't trouble him quite as much as he thought it might. Other issues were more pressing. 'Why do I feel this way? If this is heaven – a feast laid out for a man with no sense of taste – I stagger to imagine a hell.' And then something else occurred to him. 'And why can I not remember anything?'

'This is all my fault,' the guardian angel repeated sadly and buried her head in her hands.

'I am not interested in who is to blame. I simply want to know the truth.'

She peeked up and could see from the open expression on his face, which was also beautiful, with its wide, innocent, blue eyes and uncorrupted, youthful features, and of course those tight golden curls, that he was speaking the truth. He simply wanted to know what was going on.

'Let us start with your name,' he said softly.

'My name is Athena.' She looked down at her bare feet as she spoke, not quite able to meet his eyes for longer than a few seconds at a time. 'You were my first, Sam. I have not been doing this long and it would seem that my skills as a guardian angel are not quite as accomplished as I had hoped.'

'This, I do not understand. Why do I even need a guardian angel? I have never felt you with me before.' As soon as he said this, though, he knew it to be untrue.

'Everyone has a guardian angel, Sam, to look after and protect them.'

'Protect them? And here I am dead. Your success was limited with me, Athena.'

Athena dropped her face in her hands again and Sam could hear the deep sobs spilling out of her.

'Please don't cry. I did not mean it,' he said softly – although he kind of did mean it. 'I just want to know what happened.'

'You are not here because of me,' she eventually told him, 'but I have added to your woes and now you are in this place unable to move forward, not yet detached from the earth and the love you have found there.'

'Fizz!' he suddenly said, finally remembering something of his life. 'I love Fizz. It is so.' He took a deep, quenching breath at the thought of her and then the sadness struck him. He was dead and she was not here with him.

'I was told,' Athena began again. 'The elders told me that you were not long for this world. It had been written that you would pass to the next phase before your twentieth birthday.'

'Before my twentieth birthday? But why?'

'This I do not know.'

'But it is so unfair.'

'This is exactly what I thought,' Athena told him, 'and this is how I let you down, Sam, so badly.'

Sam rose to his feet to move closer again to Athena, and sat down beside her. Once again the warmth of her presence undid the knots inside of him. He simply looked into her emerald eyes, calmly, showing forgiveness and letting her know that she should continue.

'I intervened, Sam. You were going to die and I saved you.'

'I remember!' he spat suddenly, another memory slowly returning. 'It was you in the water that day. I remember now.'

'Yes, Sam. You were supposed to die that day, but I just couldn't let it happen. You were so young and full of promise. You were so happy. You didn't deserve to die so young.'

'And yet here I am.'

'Yes,' Athena pursed her lips together as if deciding how much she should tell him. 'You died eventually, before you were twenty, as was written, and it was ten times worse than it would have been had I not stopped it the first time. And what came after was my fault too.'

'The love? That I love Fizz? How can you say that? I would die a thousand deaths for a single moment of the love I have experienced with Fizz.' This he knew in his heart without having to recall the details of his life and his final moments.

'But now you are stuck here. Your heart is circling the earth, desperate to find your soulmate. You cannot move forward, Sam, and this is my fault. You will never be at peace.'

Sam paused for a moment to let the magnitude of the words settle inside of him and then he was on his feet again, moving away from Athena, back to the lake. He needed to be alone. He needed to think. He dropped down onto his knees at the water's edge and peered into the rainbow water where no reflection of him could possibly exist. Again, he poked his finger into the cool and stirred this time. He watched as the colours merged and swirled into a dirty, brown goop.

'I can't stay here forever,' he shouted over to Athena and when he turned back to her he saw that she was closer than he thought, sitting amongst the creatures on the grass beside him. 'This place is warped.'

'It is your idea of heaven,' she told him and looked thoughtfully into the horizon. 'It is a poet's view.'

'But it is sickly and inhabitable. I cannot stay here.'

'Everyone begins in their vision of a heaven – some land in clouds with harps playing, others on sunny beaches with a sun that never stops shining. The land then morphs around them as their desires change and they see that these things do not make a perfect world. A perfect world is made of the people that are loved and the simple things in life. So most people end up in a kind of common heaven that is not dissimilar to their own life. They even still face struggles because the bad is necessary to make us all appreciate the good. There are many lessons to be learnt in the construction of heaven and then the soul can move onto the next stage.'

'Which is?'

'I have no idea. I am very junior around here. Nobody tells me anything. But your heaven, this place, will never change because your heart is no longer with you.'

'So why would you want to stop me from dying? My heaven would have been a good place to be.'

'Your own life would have been better.'

Neither spoke for a moment.

'So this is it then?' Sam asked, feeling his despair rising inside of him. 'I have to stay here for … for how long?'

Again Athena remained silent, telling him all he needed to know, but then she added, 'Look, there is a solution.' She looked around herself to make sure no one else was listening, although they were clearly in a private world of Sam's own making. 'I can send you back.'

'Really? This is a possibility?' Sam beamed and then his shoulders sank. 'Wait just one moment. How would you be able to do that? You are a novice guardian angel and not a very good one. How am I to believe you can accomplish anything? And I cannot just come back from the dead anyway. It would be the devil's work. But …' Thoughts of Fizz filled his mind again. 'And what of Fizz?' he asked, picturing her face. 'Where is she now? Did she survive me? And what happened to me?' The questions were firing out of him, as his mind darted in one panicked direction after another.

'It all started the day of your first joust,' she began and then waved her hands in front of her face as if erasing the picture she had started to create. 'But none of that matters now. All I can tell you is what I have been taught, that love is the power of the universe; there is nothing stronger. At the moment it is the force that will condemn you to this limbo, but if you can find Fizz, both of your souls can be laid to rest.'

'I …' He just didn't know what to say.

'You have two choices, Sam. You can stay here for all eternity and try to make a life for yourself, amongst the hollow poetry and fragrant stench, or you can be reborn and search for your beloved.'

'Reborn as … as what? Can I have my life again?'

'No, this is not possible. You may be reborn into a new body, but your spirit will be driven by one thing alone – finding Fizz. She too will be reborn and you will both find peace when you are reunited.'

'But the size of the world is beyond the boundaries of my imagination. How will I ever find her?'

'This will not be the problem,' Athena told him.

'There is more?'

'Yes, your death will follow you, hungry for your flesh, and you will not be free until you have passed your twentieth birthday.'

'So, to make this clear in my mind, Athena. I am to wear the skin of another from birth, find my beloved and battle death until I am safely into adulthood.'

Athena nodded solemnly. 'Yes, and you will do it as many times as it takes to get it right.'

'So I am stuck in limbo or purgatory?'

Athena gave her thin smile again and waited for him to reply.

'I cannot stay here,' he told her, taking far less time than Athena had imagined he would need. 'I will be reborn and I will find my beloved. Make it so.' He stood tall and proud in the final moments of his existence as Sam, waiting for Athena to sprinkle magic dust in his direction or wave an implement of sorcery or speak enchanted words. Instead, she told him to close his eyes. And at the moment of his eyelids touching, he simply ceased to exist.

9

Athena sat alone in Sam's unchanging heaven. It had a definite appeal: the colours, the smells, the scampering animals and wondrous lake. It was simply beautiful, breath-taking, but it couldn't sustain all the needs of a soul for long. In that moment she could only hope and pray that Sam succeeded in his mission to find Fizz. She had broken all the rules by giving him these chances and now it would be she who would take his place in limbo until he succeeded. It would be she who was condemned to this twisted paradise for all of eternity. She looked around herself, taking in the full view, and let out a long, lingering sigh …

Chapter Two

Within the picturesque grounds of Mardridge Castle, which had stamped its mighty stone feet into the landscape long before the birth of all those present and was determined to stand tall for all time, a trumpet sounded – a deep, parping toot, sending birds flapping overhead in all directions. Lord Mardridge rubbed his mighty hands together. He had waited a long time for this. He sat forward in his seat and squinted over to his son across the green. How he wished the sun was slightly less imposing, but the fact that it had made an appearance on such an important day, when the spring flowers had barely made the decision to pop their heads up into the world, was a definite good omen. Just the week before, the jousting had been cut short by a thunderous storm, the ferocity of which he hadn't experienced since his boyhood, when he would secretly tremble in his bed chamber and sometimes even cry, but he never went running to his mother and father. No, he knew from a very young age what it was to be a man. He knew that however scared and sad he was, he could never show it to another living soul. Eventually, the secrets he kept – of petrifying storms, terrifying dreams and monsters in the dark – fell away in the night until he was able to laugh in the face of fear. Pretend anything for long enough and it becomes reality. Pretend not to be afraid and the demons eventually get bored. Turn yourself to stone and you will become immovable. Yes, he knew what it was to be a man and to lead other men. He was less sure, however, of how to impart this information to his son.

'Stop fidgeting, m'lord.'

But Lord Mardridge couldn't sit still, nor could he take his eyes off the imminent action to acknowledge his wife. She expected no less. He had been speaking about Sam's first joust since the boy was born and he wasn't about to miss a moment of it. He had waited so long already. Nineteen years old was too old in his opinion. If he had his way he would have slipped a lance into the boy's hand before his tenth birthday, but Lady Mardridge had other ideas.

'Seriously, m'lord, you will wear holes in your hands.'

This time Lord Mardridge turned to Lady Mardridge. He hadn't noticed how he had been wringing his hands and now it would have been a relief to stop, but he couldn't let her know that.

'And you, m'lady, will wear out that tongue, but it does not stop you flapping it in my direction.'

This silenced Lady Mardridge, but she pulled the kind of face that made her husband instantly regret his harsh tone. Her bottom lip was gently comforting the top and her eyebrows had delicately shuffled a little closer to each other and a little higher. It was all very subtle, but Lord Mardridge knew every wrinkle, every dimple and every movement of his beloved wife's face; he had paid as much attention to memorising the outline of each feature and its strategic positioning as he had the twists and turn of the maps he used to steer his knights to victory. And so he knew that this particular face – framed as it was by long, coarse hair, which had once been red and luscious and was no less

13

appealing now it had paled into autumn shades with a lightning strike of white powering back from her left temple – wasn't real anger or hurt, but a gentle reminder that she was his beloved and he should always treat her as such. Slipping into the role, Lord Mardridge lowered his head respectfully, but he had no time to linger on his favourite sight in the world – that body, those curves, although no longer as firm as they once were, driving him wild beneath the long, embroidered, scarlet velvet of her dress. This day was about their son and he turned back to the green just in time to see the dust kicked up by the hind legs of the horse, as both horse and Sam came to life and powered down the course.

'He was born to it!' Lord Mardridge beamed heartily. And this seemed to be true as he watched his son's proud, upright command of the horse, although restricted by the training armour in which he – and all those who had worn it before him – could barely walk. But he wore it well, as a nobleman, as his father's son. His headgear, tapered at the front in an animal-like moulding that had been the trademark of the Mardridge Knights for generations, completely covered his face, but Lord Mardridge focused on the blonde curls peeking from the bottom and could picture his son easily within it – smiling wildly at the adventure of it all, finally embracing the life of a knight. Lord Mardridge had seen his son ride a horse many times as a young boy, but this was the first time he had seen him as a man, the first time Sam had allowed it, and he had exceeded all of his expectations: this was a man who would lead armies and win wars; this was a man to whom other men would look for guidance; this was a man who more than deserved to call himself a Mardridge.

On Sam galloped, the powerful legs of the horse blurring into a slew of limbs as he gripped the lance and braced for impact. From the other direction his competitor – a young man of equal age, but one whose experience far exceeded Sam's – was gathering similar speed, although Lord Mardridge would later comment that he appeared, it would seem, to be riding without a spine compared to the grace displayed by his son. All around the green, knights and noblemen had gathered, along with their families, to enjoy the day of games and in this moment, as the momentum, speed and anticipation grew, so did the noise from the crowds; a slow handclap started the proceedings, which slowly gathered pace until it was a full applause accompanied by the whoops and wails of the excited masses. This was always the way with the joust and especially so today as the mettle of their ruler's only son would be put to the test for the first time.

'Come on, boy!' Lord Mardridge shouted and Lady Mardridge silently gripped his arm, comforting him, comforting her, although as the riding began she had a feeling that she had nothing to worry about. No harm would come of her beloved son – on this day at least. She looked up to her husband and the bright red, bobbly cheeks that she lived in fear foretold poor health. She had heard of excitable men such as he dropping down dead in the throes of such exertion and this was on her mind as he practically jumped out of his seat. His mouth was throwing out all sorts of wild words of encouragement in the centre of the unruly beard that he thankfully allowed her to cut every so often, but it was still white, overgrown and as fluffy as the clouds in the sky. Everyone else in the royal enclosure – a handful of nobles and a sprinkling of servants – focused on the jousting and tried not to catch his eye. His unpredictability was legendary and they all feared being the first face he saw should his son lose. Who knew what would happen? Would he start lobbing dignitaries into the air, out of the curtained seating area – he was as big and round as he was unpredictable after all?

Would he take up his own weapon and begin a cull of those he saw as dispensable to vent his frustration? There was no way of knowing, so as he became more and more excitable, leaping to his feet, his magnificent, purple, embroidered robes swishing around him, those around him tried to remain as impassive as possible.

'Ride like the wind, my boy!'

And, as if Sam had heard his father, he seemed to gather even more speed and now impact was imminent.

Although this was training and they used only hollow, blunt lances, it was not without risk. The losing knight would be thrown from his horse and there was no way to predict on which body part he would land. The armour would, for the most part, ensure that the knight survived, but more than one knight in Sam's lifetime had been left unable to move his body after landing awkwardly, twisting his neck, condemned to the life of a statue.

'Go hard, lad!'

And again Sam followed his father's advice, although there was no way he could hear it. He leaned forward in the saddle, renewing his grip on the lance with one gloved hand and drawing the reins ever closer to him with his other. And then, quicker than a commentator could explain what had happened, collision, and Sam's competitor had somersaulted backwards off his horse like a pinwheel and crashed to the ground, while Sam was riding away punching the air, untroubled by whatever impact his armour had taken – the victor. And as the magnificent figure of Lord Mardridge shook the royal enclosure with his victory dance, those around him let out a collective sigh of relief and were able to join in the celebrations. But then Lord Mardridge looked over to the course and saw that his son had not stopped to enjoy his own victory.

'Where does he think …?' the rest of the sentence drifted into thought as he watched his son become smaller and smaller, riding into the distance.

'He is a gentle soul, m'lord,' Lady Mardridge assured him tenderly. 'It is not difficult to imagine that he would now like to spend some time alone away from the excitement of the crowds.'

'But–'

'But he has done exceptionally well, m'lord,' she interrupted his roaring outburst. 'And we have much to be proud of on this fine day.'

Lord Mardridge hesitated and took one last look at the tiny figure of his son, now a dot in the distance and about to disappear at any moment. 'I suppose your words hold truth, m'lady. Everyone!' he then boomed, addressing those around him, joyfully forgetting his woes. 'A banquet to celebrate in the morrow!' And even more whoops erupted. It was only Lady Mardridge who eyed the figure of her son until he disappeared. She knew exactly why he had made such a hasty retreat. She knew from the moment he appeared on the green.

The appearance of the sun that day had not only surprised Lord Mardridge; it was on Sam's mind as he looked out over the horizon. It had come out just for him on the day of his first joust, or so he imagined, which made him smile – perhaps for different reasons to those in his father's mind. Such a sun was unseasonal and told of the great summer ahead, but with the trees still bereft of leaves and the springtime creatures still slumbering against the big chill, it had little warming power and as if in time with the thought, Sam could no longer suppress a shiver that had been teasing the underside of his skin. He rubbed his arms and moved away from the open lookout of the barn – if that was what it was. It was an old, dilapidated animal house of some kind that he had discovered with Robin when they were children and it had been their place ever since: a place of adventures and intrigue, a place of excitement and daring, and sometimes, although he didn't always tell Robin, it was a place of poetry, where he would come and silently contemplate the world, buffered by the endless fields around him. Sometimes he would spend hours there by himself simply listening to all of the sounds presented by nature that others would mistake for silence: the ever-changing symphony of the elements as the winds sang to the leaves, the snows tapped their rhythmic feet or the rains commanded overwhelming solo performances; he would absorb the commentary of the creatures – squeaking, squawking, buzzing and tooting; the flapping wings of the birds soaring overheard; and sometimes there were sounds that Sam would never be able to identify, although he tried, as if the world were being held in a giant hand, the fingers of which would tap at times, as if impatient, or gently squeeze, or caress the skies with loving fingertips. He tried to make sense of it all and when he knew that he couldn't, he would compose poetry and it eased his soul just a little. On this day, he would have liked to write a few stanzas describing the unseasonal sun, but he had not brought his quill. Instead, he allowed words to flirt in his mind, greeted each other, showing their finest aspects in the hope of a successful union, until he had phrases, which might later slip sweetly into verse. All the time he looked out over the view and just a few minutes into his idle composition, a horse and rider appeared in the distance. They were a blur at first, but he instantly recognised Pinecomb, his beloved horse, whose mighty, powerful muscles were such a contrast to his gentle nature, and Robin on top, as upright and regal as the finest knight in the country. As his friend came into view, he could see that he was still restricted by the armour, but was carrying the helmet under his arm along with the lance. He could also see that he was smiling. Sam immediately ran out of the den to meet his friend and grabbed Pinecomb's reins as he slowed to a trot before him.

'Your smile gives you away, Robin. Our plan is a success.'

Robin awkwardly manoeuvred inside the armour to drop down to the ground. Before he landed he had somehow managed to throw a curly wig in his best friend's face. Sam couldn't control the laughter as the vile smell of the court entertainer hit his nostril, from whom they had 'borrowed' it.

'Well?' he asked, and dropped the wig in the grass. It would pass as his own hair only at a distance or if viewed by a blind man, but he hoped that the small curls protruding from Robin's helmet would have fooled all of those watching the joust.

'Well what, Sam? Do you really need to ask? Am I not the best jouster in the land? Would I let you down?'

'No, but do you think my father believed you?'

'I think people believe what they want to believe. I stumbled a little in the middle to make a show of it being your first time, but wearing your armour, riding your horse with your hair and insignia was all it took, my friend. People do not like to think if they can help it.'

Sam took the helmet and lance from his hand and stood them beside the dilapidated, rotting wood of the barn as Robin began to remove the armour. His plight was hindered by the fact that he was a little taller and broader than his friend – his natural athletic ability sculpting his body. He was also hot and sweaty from the exertion, but clearly happy to be freeing himself from the ill-fitting metal suit and uncomfortable binding that had concealed his own long, dark hair.

'I'm not sure that I agree,' Sam told him. 'People have more in their minds than you credit them.'

'I credit people think about when it is they will next eat, sleep, drink, make merry and make love. Beyond this, people have very little cause to worry themselves with thoughts.'

Sam tried and failed to hide his embarrassment at the reference to making love. 'Just because these are the only thoughts troubling you, Robin. Other people have more depth.'

'Yeah?' Robin playfully squared up to his friend as he answered, the big smile revealing the dimples that drove women wild, and Sam didn't withdraw.

'Yeah!' he replied and soon Robin had him in a headlock and his face was down in the cool, long grass.

'Your own thinking needs to be challenged if you think me stupid.'

Sam, wiry as he was, twisted his body so that he was easily freed and pushed Robin face-first into the grass. 'If you are so clever you should have seen that coming.'

'And you this,' Robin shouted and took out Sam's legs with a flick of his own. They wrestled each other for supremacy as they had done since they were children and then both lay panting on their backs, the moisture in the ground dampening their clothes, until Sam spoke seriously, his mind returning to the events of the afternoon.

'Thank you,' he said solemnly. 'I do not know what this will change, but it might hold him off for a short while. Failing that, you might have to actually teach me to joust.'

'You? In combat? I would stand more chance teaching a butterfly to hold a sword.'

'Thanks, friend!'

'It is not an insult. I just wish your father had open eyes in your direction.'

'It would not change a thing. I am supposed to be a knight, Robin; it is written. I can only hope that the respect of today's victory will afford me a little space.'

'And then what?'

'And then …' Sam sat up suddenly and said, 'I have absolutely no idea.'

'I was wrong, you know,' Robin said seriously, pulling himself up and beginning the change back into his own clothes. 'Not everyone has no time for thought.'

'Oh?' Sam said idly, his mind still chewing over the problems he had with his father.

'We would have to do more than put on a wig and stumble a little to fool your mother.'

'How do you mean?'

'I mean that she will see straight through all of this.'

'Do you think?' Sam now began to undress, ready to take the weight of the heavy armour and ride back to the castle, victorious.

'Sam, your father would be looking only at whether you won or lost. Your mother would know from the subtlest turn of my head or movement of my hand that I wasn't you.'

'Great, so we are in trouble.'

'No, my friend,' Robin beamed, throwing the helmet into his friend's chest. 'You are in trouble.'

'Great!'

'But first things first – you owe me!'

CHAPTER THREE

"Two nil! Two nil!'

'Shhhh!' Noah told his friend, but he knew he stood no chance of silencing him. It was so rare for Mardridge to beat the Botans that he would still be singing about it for weeks to come. 'You'll wake the whole village.'

'Could not give a shit!' Thane sang out and then continued his victory chant as the two of them staggered through the dark, cobbled streets with what must have been at least a barrel of beer in their bellies between them, past the quaint, overhanging Tudor houses and shops that made the village such a popular tourist attraction – those and the castle, which Noah had always found a little creepy, up on its hill, keeping the village under permanent, stony surveillance.

'Why do you even care about the football? It's hardly the Premiership.'

Thane stopped suddenly and stood before his friend. The meagre street lights meant Noah could see the full extent of his sudden seriousness, his dark, bloodshot eyes and the beer he had spilt down the front of his pale blue shirt. 'Where's your sense of local honour?'

'I'm not from here, Thane.'

'That's beside the point.'

'And neither are you?'

'But we are currently residing in this village.' He was putting on a posh voice now for some reason that Noah couldn't fathom, because he had never met anyone less posh than Thane. 'We have chosen to pursue education in the shadow of centuries of history, all of which have led to this great game of football and the defeat of the Botans.' He was holding his arms aloft as he spoke, but the grand gesture was let down by the drunken slurring of the words.

'There's so much wrong with what you just said that I don't know where to start,' Noah told him. He was less slurry and naturally well spoken, but he was every bit as drunk as his friend. 'Education? You're studying catering, Thane.'

'And the ladies! I'm studying catering and the ladies.'

They had both stopped now and were leaning against the old sweet shop window, in which they had spent so much time during their first week in Mardridge, rediscovering cola cube, sherbet dips and chocolate tools, but the novelty had soon worn off.

'You're an idiot!' Noah laughed and ran his hand through his curly, blonde hair. It was getting late. In fact, it was much later than he had intended to stay out. He had an exam in a little over a month and was supposed to be spending every second studying. 'Cakes and ladies, that's quite a curriculum.'

Now they were both laughing and then Thane said, 'Well you can't eat a book – or shag it for that matter.'

'What are you talking about?'

'You and your daft literature course. Whoever got anywhere by reading books?'

'Er … I'm not even going to answer that.'

They stood in the dark and laughed as only good friends can – friends who would have normally known each other for years to be so in tune with each other, but Thane and Noah had only met during freshers' week. However, it was a strange meeting; an instance camaraderie existed between the two of them and their differences meant little to either of them. They had both approached the Student Union table at the freshers' fair at the same time and just started talking as if the beginning of their conversation was a continuation of a much longer conversation that neither could remember having.

'Hey, Noah!' Thane's tone was suddenly conspiratorial and a sense of dread fell over his friend.

'Whatever it is – no!'

'Don't be that way.'

'I have to go home, Thane. It's nearly two in the morning.' How it had got so late he had no idea.

'I heard a rumour that the landlord of the Sir Robin's Head sometimes gets so drunk that he doesn't bother locking the back door.'

'Who cares!' Noah shrugged and continued their walk, now at a more determined pace.

'I care!' Thane called, catching him up. 'And you should care too. Do you know what this means?'

'It means I have to go home.'

Thane stopped suddenly and scratched his head, which was closely shaven to the skin. 'How can it mean that? You're not even trying. How can the open back door mean you have to go home?'

'I just mean I have to go home.'

'I see.' The familiar finality of his tone forced Noah to turn suddenly.

'Don't start this again.'

'No, Noah. I completely understand. You take yourself off home. I'll be fine. I wouldn't want to stand in the way of true love.'

'This again?'

'I'm saying nothing.'

'You already have.'

'I'm saying nothing, but you've changed, Noah. You would have leapt at the chance of free booze before you met her.'

'Her name is charlotte.'

'Charlotte Smarlotte!'

'What does that even mean?'

The two of them had suddenly taken the appearance of an odd couple airing their dirty laundry in the street at the tops of their drunken voices. And this wasn't the first time they had had this conversation.

'It means you've changed.'

'But I don't even want any more booze. Someone would have to physically give me money for me to want to drink more beer and make it my job.'

'That's shit! You might not be able to drink any more regular beer, but this would be free beer.'

'I don't care if it's one hundred carat, gold-plated beer with a rainbow surface and little polar bears dancing in it.'

'Oooo!' Thane beamed. 'Where can you get that from?' When Noah didn't smile he continued his offensive. 'You said having a girlfriend wouldn't change things, Noah. And now look at you; it's only two a.m. and you're already dicking out on me.'

'I'm not dicking out on you.'

'Then come with me.'

Noah was thinking about it.

'And I won't mention Charlotte ever again.'

'I find that somehow difficult to believe.'

'All right. I won't mention her for the rest of the week.'

Again, Noah paused for thought. 'So when I go and see her I'm not going to have to put up with how she's taken me away from you and all the rest of your girlie shit?'

'One hundred percent. Come with me tonight and I won't have a bad word to say about her until next week.'

Noah held his hand out for Thane to shake and the fact that he agreed to the deal showed just how much the rift had been troubling him. Even a week of peace would be worth the trouble. The problem was that his meeting with Charlotte had been every bit as strange as his meeting with Thane. They had kissed within minutes of meeting each other – and not in a drunken nightclub kind of way. They were in the university careers office, both investigating potential routes for after graduation and all it took was the meeting of their eyes – Sam's intense and sky blue, Charlotte's seriously fixed on her subject and lightening when she spied Noah. With no words spoken, they had gravitated towards each other and their lips had joined in the most magnificent kiss either had experienced. They had spoken about the moment since and tried to explain the magnetism, but words failed them. Noah was as powerless against the relationship with Charlotte as he was his friendship with Thane. In fact, from the moment he arrived in

Mardridge he knew deep down that something had changed, that this was a deeply affecting place and his life would never quite be the same again. He initially assumed that it was the historical nature of the village – its Tudor roots – that gave him a feeling akin to unworthiness, combined with the humbling effects of his literature studies. He was growing through his studies with every day that passed and the dramatic physical and emotional landscape that Mardridge offered him served only to make his time here all the more mysterious.

Within minutes, Noah and Thane had arrived at the Sir Robin's Head. It was a funny little pub, which had apparently been in contention for the title of the oldest pub in the country, but had been beaten by a little ale house up north. They had no way of knowing if the ivory and teak-coloured beams and panels were original or restored, and neither of them considered finding out a priority as Thane gave Noah a leg up onto the fence and then pulled himself over and they stood before the back door.

'Fiver says it's open,' Thane said.

'Shhh!' Noah whispered. 'You'd be a shit burglar.'

'You'd be a shit wrestler but I don't go on about it. It stinks back here.'

'Shhh, Thane! You'll get us sprung.' Then they both fell silent and communicated using their eyes alone. Noah indicated with his eyebrows that Thane should try the handle, and Thane very slowly reached out his hand. Noah couldn't quite see the movement in the darkness, but when he saw the beaming smile on Thane's face he knew they were going in. He watched as the darkness beyond the door was slowly revealed and Thane took one last look back to him before stepping into it. Noah sighed heavily before following him in; he knew he shouldn't be doing it, he knew that no good would come from it, but somehow here he was, following his friend into yet another stupid situation.

Noah clicked the door gently shut behind him and when he turned back to his friend he was lit up by the glowing screen of his mobile. He then managed to operate the mobile phone torch and the deserted bar came into view. They had arrived in a back corridor that led straight through to every student's dream – free beer on tap.

'Sit down,' Thane whispered, finally observing the need to speak quietly. 'I'll grab us a couple of beers and bring them over.'

'But–'

'We won't stay long. Just one drink. One last drink before I lose you altogether.'

'You promised you wouldn't–'

'Relax. I'm joking. Just sit down would you.'

As quietly as he could, Noah dragged a stool out from under a nearby table and planted himself down onto it. He could feel his heart pumping through his navy shirt and the slightest noise turned him in knots, including Thane arriving beside him with the drinks.

'Calm down, Noah.'

'That's easy for you to say. You're used to this kind of thing.'

Thane placed the two beers on the table. 'Are you calling me some kind of criminal?'

'No, breaking in here is all perfectly legal, I'm sure.'

They both silently sipped their beers and although Thane talked a big job, he looked every bit as jumpy as his friend, but he was determined that sitting in a deserted pub in the darkness with his friend was the most normal thing in the world and he made every effort to keep their conversation as normal as possible too – just two guys enjoying a chat over a drink.

'Did I tell you about my green scones?' he asked, wide eyed.

'Yup!' Noah nodded.

'I'm going to be interviewed on the university website about them.'

'I know. You told me. It's awesome, mate. Have you considered letting them publish the recipe?'

'Never! It's top secret. They taste good though don't they?'

'Well, they taste interesting.'

'What's that supposed to mean?'

'Nothing. Hey, do you know why this place is called the Sir Robin's Head?'

The sudden change in conversation worked a charm and Thane shook his head, suddenly interested. He loved to hear stories connected to the village and Noah had them in abundance.

'In the late sixteenth century – you've heard of Lord Mardridge?'

'Only in the way that the village is called Mardridge and I've heard of that,' Thane whispered, moving closer and sipping his beer.

'He had a son, Samuel Mardridge, and according to myth he was slain by his own best friend, Sir Robin. Sir Robin was beheaded for the crime; hence, the Sir Robin's Head.'

'They were all at it then, though, Noah. Everyone was killing everyone. It didn't mean the same as it does now.'

'On the battlefield maybe, but this was different. He was killed in a rage of jealousy. Sir Robin had fallen in love with Sir Samuel's true love, Lady Felicity, and he slaughtered him in cold blood right up there on the roof of the castle on the day before Samuel Mardridge hit twenty years old.'

'Is that right?' Thane mused, but the thoughts swirling in his mind were suddenly interrupted by a crashing noise out back. 'What the–?'

Noah brought his finger to his lips, silencing his friend and they both listened without moving as the crashing and lumping continued.

'You stay here,' Thane whispered. 'I'm gonna go and check.' He was on his feet and creeping towards the door and then he disappeared and Noah was all alone. He looked all around himself in what was now pitch darkness as Thane had taken his phone with him. As his eyes became accustomed to the black, ambiguous shapes began to form in the shadows before identifying themselves again as the things he recognised – tables, chairs, pumps, the bar.

'Thane!' he whispered when he could no longer hear either his friend or the crashing that had originally spooked them. 'Thane!' but he said it so quietly, in a whisper-shout, that the sound could have travelled no further than a few feet. He wrung his hands in his lap and his leg began to jig uncontrollably beneath him as his mind chewed over the options. Thane had told him to stay put, but this had little bearing on what he would eventually do. The crashing had stopped, so maybe he should just stay there and see what happened, but then why hadn't Thane returned? No, something was happening and the last place it was safe for him to be was inside a deserted, dark pub on his own. He was suddenly on his feet. For reasons known only to himself (because he certainly didn't need it), he downed the last of his pint and then slowly felt his way across the bar. He had been in the pub often enough, but finding his way in the dark was more challenging than he could have imagined and when he gathered confidence and speed, he ended up tripping on a stool and sending himself and a whole table flying. 'Shit! Shit!' he cursed and now scrambled to his feet, feeling like a character from a horror film. 'Get it together, Noah!' He set off once again in the direction of the door, but before he could reach it he heard the same crashes and thuds once again. He stopped deadly still, but decided against hiding. It was dark after all and at least he had the advantage that his eyes had adjusted. However, this was a decision that he would live to regret as the lights suddenly flashed on.

'Police! Stay where you are! You're under arrest!'

Sam was a sore thumb in the middle of the pub and easily grabbed by the young police officer on the night shift. He had no idea where Thane had suddenly gone, but he was going to have serious words with him when he found out.

CHAPTER FOUR

M ere hours had passed since Sam's jousting victory and there he was, standing guard outside his own bed chamber, trying desperately to unhear the noises from within. The laughing he could cope with; Robin was a funny and charming young man and he could see why all women found him so attractive. It was the other noises that made him want to run away or at least force sharp objects into his ears – the oohing and ahhing, the deep sighs and the guttural groaning. But he owed Robin; there was no way he would have the nerve to race at speed towards an opponent on the jousting green; there was even less chance he would be able to win and present himself as the kind of man his father wanted him to be. So, although he could feel his face reddening at every carnal sound he heard, he was happy to allow Robin the use of his chamber. What woman wouldn't be impressed by the prospect of being romanced in the castle? And although Robin's parents would be blind not to know that their son was not only on the wish list of every woman in the land, but was successfully working his way down a list of his own, they did not want him to bring shame upon their dwelling. Originally, Sam had been willing to accommodate the occasional liaison at the castle, but his own parents had become suspicious, so the dilapidated animal house became home to Robin's passions when it was not accommodating Sam's poetic ponderings. However, Robin didn't miss a single opportunity to throw Sam into his debt and the joust provided a perfect opportunity. So here Sam was once again, sentry to his own room, unable not to hear noises that were as mysterious to him as they were annoying.

His dwelling was at the very top of the castle, so the only people coming up the stone steps would be those looking for him or those on their way to the roof, who were real sentry soldiers and had more pressing things to concern themselves with than the notches on Robin's bedpost. Despite this, the sense of deception stirred panic in Sam and the prospect of being found out made him pace up and down the steps.

To take his mind off the sense of foreboding and the noise and the fact that he would have to sleep in that bed just hours later, he thought back to the moment he had arrived back at the castle after the joust. He had never seen his father so animated and full of pride – at least not pride directed at him. He had almost run from the castle to greet him then taken Pinecomb's reins and offered his son an arm to steady his dismount. His face was still bright red and ruddy, although almost an hour had passed since the joust, as if he had been reliving the action in his mind and in discussion with anyone who would listen and would perhaps explode if he didn't soon get to see the man himself – Samuel Mardridge: jousting knight extraordinaire – finally the man his father hoped he would be.

'Sam, my boy!' he beamed and threw his heavy arm around his son, almost knocking him over, while he handed Pinecomb's reins over to the stable boy. Lord Mardridge towered over his son and was at least twice as wide, a fact that he often used to taunt Sam with nicknames like pigeon chest and stick man, but not today. 'I have never seen such a fine performance,' he said and pulled him even closer to him, so Sam could smell a combination of exertion and red wine. The smell took him back to his boyhood and the games his father would play with him. How long had it been since he had held him this close? The thought made Sam happy and sad at the same time.

'Thank you, Father, I have been training for some time now and did not want to disappoint you.'

'I was starting to wonder if disappointing me was exactly what you wanted to do, but I see that you are simply a late bloomer.'

'Yes, Father.' Sam's voice was quiet and hollow; such a contrast to his father's howling tones. He knew what was coming next.

'So, you are ready, son. Two weeks from today we ride out together. Those filthy Botans will not massacre themselves.'

The word 'massacre' stabbed Sam's senses. Was this what war was? A massacre? What was this war even about? It had been going on for decades and he wondered if his father even knew anymore, but he didn't dare ask.

'You will ride upfront with me – leader of men – and together we will bring victory to the Mardridge name.'

'But, Father–' Panic suddenly gripped Sam from all sides, as impossible to escape as his impending fate.

'But nothing, my boy! And to celebrate your own victory, a feast in the morrow.'

Sam looked up at his father and saw the fire in his eyes, wildly illuminating the hopes and dreams beyond, fixed forward on the castle gates, oblivious to the pigeon-chested stick man beside him, so Sam remained quiet. There was nothing he could do to make his father see who he really was – a gentle soul, a poet – so he would have to think of something else. He had the feeling that, as a result, he would be spending more time outside his bed chamber keeping lookout while his best friend got his rocks off.

Suddenly, Jennifer popped her head around the winding stairway and Sam leapt forward to intercept her. The last thing he wanted to do was expose his little sister to his friend's heavy breathing, moaning and groaning – she was not yet ten years old – so he swung his arm in front of her to block her path.

'And where is it that you are going?'

'To get a new word,' she said, wide-eyes and smiling warmly at her brother. He couldn't see it, but it was with his eyes that she looked upon him – bright, aqua pools that had the power to mesmerise.

'But now is not a good time.'

'Oh.' She looked down at her hands, gripping her doll by the waist, which was dressed the same as she was, in a long pink dress with pink bows in her hair. The doll, however, looked far tidier than the child, whose dress was covered in mud and torn at the shoulder.

'What have you been doing?' Sam asked, suddenly noticing the state of her.

'Jousting,' she said casually, looking back up to him. 'With some of the village boys.'

'On a horse?'

'No, like I said, on a boy.'

Sam didn't know what to say and eventually simply asked, 'Did you win?'

She nodded her response and beamed widely at him once again. 'So can I have my word now?'

'Well …' he debated for a moment whether or not to send her away and then realised that her company was in fact an improvement on the way he had spent the last hour of his life. She was also the first person he had encountered since his own joust that didn't want to talk to him about it and this was a definite relief. 'Okay. Sit down.'

'Why can we not go in your chamber, Sam?'

'Because some words need to be said on stairways.'

She looked intrigued and accepting of this new idea, and lowered herself silently onto the step beside him, waiting for more information. As she sat, Sam reached out and wiped a smudge of mud from her cheek.

'Has Mother seen how you look?' he asked.

'She cannot catch me,' she beamed and Sam couldn't help but laugh with her.

'So,' he began after they had calmed themselves. 'Your word for the day is ephemeral.'

'E … phem … eral,' she mouthed, testing each individual sound on her tongue.

If Sam wondered if she actually enjoyed collecting words from him, it was moments like this that confirmed it. She was a strange child: boisterous, committed to her doll and the boys from the village, heroic in her battles with both of their parents, yet intrigued by language. Even at her tender age she had worked out that each word contains, locked within it, a special power and once she had mastered the word, collected it, the power was hers. This, she had learnt from Sam.

'But what does it mean?'

'It means … well, how to describe it? You know when we lie in the grass and look for shapes in the clouds – an animal, a face –'

'Sausages!' she giggled to herself.

'If you like. Well, you know when you look away and then look back, the animal or face or sausages have vanished.'

She nodded seriously.

'It's because they are ephemeral.'

'So ephemeral means when the clouds disappear.'

'No, ephemeral means when something is only there for a short amount of time. We are ephemeral creatures,' he added and she scrunched her face up and shrugged. 'Our time on earth is ephemeral.'

Jennifer stared off into the distance for a moment before saying, 'I don't want to die.' It came out so sadly that Sam wished he had chosen a different world or at least a different way of explaining it.

'But when you die you get to go to heaven, where the flowers float and everything smells of your favourite food, they have talking unicorns and skies that are more beautiful than anything we have here and ... er, a rainbow river where you can ask for anything you want and it just pops out.'

'Is that real?' This seemed to perk her up a little.

'As real as that great clump of mud in your hair,' he said and pulled it out of her golden curls.

'It matter not anyway,' she told him, 'because I am going to live forever.' And before Sam could answer she was away, chanting, 'Ephemeral! Emepheral! Phemrelical! Smelletical!' until he could no longer hear her.

'She probably will live for ever, too,' he said and giggled to himself before remembering his own predicament and moving back up the stairs to the space outside his chamber. How he wished to go inside and relax. It had been a trying day and there was much to think about. He lowered himself onto the dusty, winding stairs and began to pick at the loose stone beside his door. When he was a child he used to worry that the castle was falling apart because of such patches, but now he knew that the castle would still be standing long after they had all been absorbed into the earth and had judgement passed upon them. The thought lingered for longer than intended; he had often allowed his mind to drift back in time to the castle's construction by his ancestors and even the days before when it was merely an idea waiting to be realised. Everything is real in the mind before materialising in the world – even something as solid and timeless as a castle. He had never really considered the future of the castle, however, and now he allowed his mind to dwell there. Who would live here when he was no longer walking the earth? His children? His children's children? And then what? He knew enough about history to know that the hands of time worked quickly and efficiently to bring change upon the world. The castle, however, would never change. It would be planted in this space, atop its picturesque hill, as fixed in the landscape as the centuries-old oak trees that spiralled down into the village.

'When the wind changes you will stay like that,' a gentle voice announced.

Sam was suddenly on his feet again with his back to the door, delivering two strong raps telling Robin to kill the noise.

'Goodness me, you are jumpy, Sammy. Are you quite well? You were making that face again, where you are away with the fairies somewhere, no doubt composing verse in your mind.'

'Er …' Sam blushed and shifted even more awkwardly in front of the door. 'You gave me a start, Mother. I did not hear you coming.'

'I imagine it is difficult to hear when your mind is in another world.'

Sam finally relaxed a little and smiled. The noise had stopped in his chamber and there was no reason to panic.

'I have a present for you, Sam, to congratulate you on your first joust, but I can only show it to you inside your chamber.'

Suddenly there was a reason to panic.

'Inside my chamber, but–'

'It will add to your collection of poetry, from the masters. I cannot give it to you out here in the stairway.' Her voice was calm and measured and her eyebrows were slightly raised, overplaying innocence that Sam could see through immediately. He knew he was rumbled.

'You are too kind, Mother. Perhaps I can come down to the hall to receive your gift.'

'No, no. I do not want your father to see it now that you are a knight.'

'I understand. Unfortunately, I was about to leave the castle, Mother, so if you would not mind …' Misguidedly, he tried to move his mother along, like an urchin begging for money, but she stood as solid as the castle itself.

'Is there some reason you would prefer me not to enter your bed chamber?' she asked, raising her eyebrows further.

'Not at all. I–'

'Well then,' she began and reached out to the iron handle. Sam tried to intervene, but his meagre strength was no match for her.

'Wait!' he suddenly announced and she released the handle and took a step back.

'Yes, son?' she said knowingly.

'I … I …'

'Quite,' she smiled then said loudly, 'That was quite a performance today.'

'Er … thank you, Mother.'

'I wasn't talking to you,' she said and waited.

A few seconds passed and beyond the door, Robin answered her, 'Thank you, m'lady.'

'Quite the double act,' she said to herself. 'And what is your plan now that your father believes you to be something a blind man can see that you are not?'

'This I have not quite worked out,' Sam replied. 'Have you really got me a present?'

Rather than replying, Lady Mardridge reached out and cuffed her son around the ear in the way she had done when he was a boy.

'Ow!' he complained and giggling was heard from beyond the chamber door.

'There is one here waiting for you also, Sir Robin,' she said and the laughter suddenly broke off.

'I can explain, Mother …'

'Save your explanations, Sam. You will need that creative brain of yours to think your way out of a battle you cannot win. In the meantime, you are both to go into the village tomorrow and help in the fields. They will be expecting you. Perhaps a day of labour will remind you that there is a price to pay for deception …'

Sam lowered his head, 'Yes, Mother.'

'… and remind your friend that he cannot spend all of his days slumbering, which I can only assume is the purpose of his extended stay in your chamber.' It was those eyebrows again, slightly raised, all-knowing, that showed Sam she knew exactly what was going on, but was too well-mannered to show the existence of such thoughts in her mind. 'They will be expecting you at first light.'

'Yes, Mother,' Sam repeated woefully.

'Both of you.'

'Yes, m'lady,' Robin called, and Lady Mardridge turned to leave, not even trying to hide the beaming smile on her face.

When enough time had passed for her to be all the way down into the hall, Robin gingerly opened the door, peered out, and when he saw the coast was clear, opened it further and stood, bare-chested in only his breeches with his hair wild around his shoulders.

'Nice work, Sam,' he groaned. 'A whole day in the fields.'

'I did not know what to say.'

'Clearly. You owe me big time now,' he said and moved to retire back into the room.

'Wait! You have been an age,' Sam complained.

'Like I said, you owe me,' he grinned and disappeared behind the door, leaving Sam sitting, pacing, pondering, keeping lookout for another two long hours.

CHAPTER FIVE

Noah sat in the back of the police car with his hands cuffed behind him watching the village slowly drift past. There was little need for the police car at all as the Sir Robin's Head was in the next road to the police station. Everything was within netting distance of everything else in Mardridge, which is one of the reasons Noah was so fond of it and had chosen to live there rather than in one of the towns closer to the uni. On this night, however, he wished for a street of miles to stretch out in front of him and postpone the moment when he would be taken into the police station. Since he met Charlotte, the only thing that he suspected would upset their relationship was getting arrested, and the chances of this happening were millions against. He was very nearly twenty years old and had managed to make it this far without so much a driving offence. Yet here he was, about to be taken in for breaking and entering – was it breaking and entering if the back door was open? And what was the sentence for such a crime? A few years inside and a lifetime without Charlotte? He would strangle Thane when he got his hands on him and he had to stop himself from thinking that this might have been deliberate. As much as Thane wanted Noah all to himself once again, and had been extremely vocal in his opinion of Charlotte, even he wouldn't go to this extreme to split them up.

Noah leaned forward and spoke to the arresting officer, a constable of around his own age, but Noah could see even through his uniform that he had the kind of muscles that he could only imagine having in an alternative universe. He also had a body builder's face, the skin taut and veiny although his body was resting. 'Any chance you could take me to a different station?' Noah asked.

'Sure,' the constable smiled, turning his head slightly on his meaty neck. 'We've got stations all over the world. Where do you fancy? Disneyland?'

Noah sat back again suddenly. He could feel his hangover forming and the sound of this guy's voice made him feel a little queasy. However, he had to try something, so he leaned forward again and said, 'I'm not from around here, you see. Maybe my case could be transferred to my neck of the woods?'

'Just sit back and shut up!' the officer answered, less humoured and more impatient this time. 'It's getting late, we're all tired. We'll get through this much quicker if you button it.'

Again, Noah sat back and looked out of the window, but he couldn't help appealing to the officer again when the police station came into view. 'Please!' he begged. 'I'll give you money not to take me in there. I'll do anything.'

'Are you attempting to bribe a police officer?'

'Yes,' Noah nodded. 'I'll do anything. Just don't take me in there.'

The officer's stern veneer suddenly dropped as he pulled into the carpark. He pulled the handbrake creaking upwards, turned off the engine and then turned to address Noah directly. 'Look, you've got nothing to be afraid of. We'll check you in, you'll spend the night and be out in the morning. It's nearly morning already.'

'You don't understand,' Noah sighed and the police officer shook his head.

'No, I really don't, but you student types are all an enigma to me.'

The door opened beside Noah and he was helped out of the car and onto his feet before being marched across the carpark and into the police station, which was a new building that was widely hated around Mardridge and had even been campaigned against when the plans were announced and the design revealed – a red-brick and coloured-glass contraption that would better fit a film set than a Tudor village.

'Right, in we go,' the officer told him, who was much taller standing up than Noah had imagined and smelt slightly of mint and curry. He opened the door for him, as Noah's hands were still cuffed, and a familiar sight awaited him on the front desk.

'Noah!'

'Charlotte! I can explain,' he said and the police officer beside him suddenly started laughing. 'I can see why you didn't want to come here now. She your missus?'

Noah ignored him and said, 'Please tell me your dad isn't on duty tonight.'

Unlike Noah and Thane, Charlotte had grown up in Mardridge and decided to stay to study music at the local university. She was a talented pianist and songwriter and the university had a good reputation within the music industry. Staying in town also meant she could remain close to her father, whom she was reluctant to leave alone. It had always been just her and her dad and she hadn't quite readied herself, or him, for the moment when she would have to say goodbye to him. She had no siblings and her mother had left them both when she was still a baby. Her father had tried to be generous about her, but even from a young age she was able to grasp the subtext: passionate and independent meant selfish and, well, a bit of a bitch. Beyond that, she had never felt the need to pursue the details. Her life was with her father and it suited her fine. Staying in Mardridge also meant that she could keep her part-time job on the front desk at the police station. Her father was the chief inspector and although he was a great big man who could easily look after himself, this was another way that she could look after him. He wasn't getting any younger after all. She wasn't an officer herself and so wasn't required to wear a uniform and Noah couldn't help noticing, despite all that was going on, how beautiful she looked as she faced the criminals of Mardridge. She was wearing a white shirt that clung to her curves and accentuated her figure, topped with a patterned silk scarf that added elegance to an already breath-taking vision. She wore modest makeup and her long, dark hair was gripped back, unfortunately for Noah, revealing her disapproval at the fact that he was standing before her in handcuffs. By contrast, Noah's face was puffy and red with booze and part of his shirt had come untucked; he too had spilt beer down his front and his hair was starting to frizz out in that way that he had been determined to keep from Charlotte.

'I can explain,' he repeated.

'What's happened? What are you doing here?' There was a trace of concern in her voice; this reflected the small hope that a major injustice had occurred or he was in fact the victim, but the handcuffs told her this wasn't the case.

'Through here,' the arresting officer interrupted and gripped his arm to lead him through to the custody officer.

'Wait! I can explain!' he said for the third time. 'Just please tell me your dad's not on tonight.'

But Charlotte didn't have the chance to answer as he was led away.

He was processed quickly by a bored-looking sergeant in her fifties, who reeked of cigarettes. She took his fingerprints, photographed him and led him down to a cell where he would remain until there was someone available to interview him in the morning. He lowered himself onto the bed and began to read the graffiti. He could gauge from its tone and language that he wasn't alone in wanting to be anywhere else in the world. He was definitely in the minority when it came to morality, though, and was actually quite shocked by the depravity and threat of some of the messages. It was like a gents toilet on acid. When he had read everything three or four times, he lay down on the rubber mattress and pulled the thin blanket over him. It was insufficient for April, but he had no intention of sleeping anyway. There was no way he could sleep. He had potentially flushed his relationship with Charlotte down the pan for a night of silliness with Thane. He probably wouldn't sleep again.

Despite himself, Noah managed to get a few hours' sleep before being rudely awakened by the heavy lock straining to open and then crashing with the force of its own momentum, and the door creaking open before slamming against the wall.

'Up! Up! Up!' a familiar voice demanded and Noah strained to peek out of eyes that didn't want to open. As the light hit his pupils, he slammed his eyes shut again. He had had hangovers before but nothing like this; it were as if a layer of his brain had been shaved away and the little people in there were spraying the raw flaps of skin with petrol, which was bad enough, before setting fire to it.

'Don't you ever go off duty?' Noah asked as the figure of the arresting officer from the night before came into focus.

'What can I say? I'm devoted. Come on now! Up!'

Noah sat up slowly, the little people in his head now bringing out the big drums and trumpets to blast him into oblivion.

'Eat this, drink this and I'll be back in fifteen,' the officer told him. Noah could now see that he wasn't particularly unfriendly, just doing his job. He dropped a tray in front of the prisoner holding a bowl of cornflakes that had been sitting so long that the milk had completely soaked the cereal to mush and a cup of brown liquid that could have been tea, coffee, gravy or hot cola. There was no way of knowing without tasting it and Noah wasn't going to go near either of them. Instead, he sat and rubbed his head then managed to get himself to his feet and tried to smarten himself up. He knew that Charlotte would have gone home by now, but there was still a chance he would see her dad and he didn't want to give him any more reason to hate him. He had only met him once and he got the distinct impression that even if he could clone himself into ten Noahs and send each one of a different quest of improvement – travelling, the best universities, learning from the masters – and then pool the brilliance of each Noah back together again, he still wouldn't be good enough for his beloved daughter. He would never be good enough for Charlotte and now that he had got himself arrested he had proven the old man right. He could only hope that today was his day off.

'Come on then, Smith,' the officer told him, returning to the cell. 'Did you sleep?'

'A bit,' Noah said pityingly. 'What happens now?'

'Now I take a statement from you and we decide what's going to happen next.' He looked down at the untouched breakfast. 'You ready?' he asked.

'As I'll ever be.'

As the officer seemed to have mellowed overnight, the experience of being interviewed wasn't as traumatic as Noah had feared. It was no different to a one-on-one tutorial he would have at university; only, this was being taped and could result in imprisonment. It took the officer no more than fifteen minutes to get all of the details and he even seemed to find some of it funny – the ignorance of the landlord getting pissed and leaving the pub open. He didn't believe for a minute that Noah acted alone, especially as two pint glasses were found at the scene, but Noah was refusing to drop his friend in it and the officer didn't seem particularly bothered whether he did or not.

'Right, so we'll get a statement made up for you, Smith, for you to sign and I just need to speak to the custody officer,' the constable told him and Noah took a deep breath that felt like the only breath he had taken that day. He had managed to get to the end of the interview and was about to be released without crossing paths with Charlotte's dad. Beyond all hope, the miracle had happened. He could speak to Charlotte, explain, smooth things out with her, but he stood no chance if her dad was involved. He would make sure that they were never allowed in the same room together ever again and he had the Mardridge connections to back him up.

'Back in a mo,' the officer smiled and left Noah alone.

Noah took another deep breath, enjoying the fact that his heartrate had returned to normal and he would be out of there in just a few minutes if the custody officer permitted it. He had even convinced himself that it was actually a little bit funny. It would be a story for him to dine out on for many years to come and he was sure he could get Charlotte to see the funny side. But then all of his optimism and relief fell away and his heart was a throbbing, jellied mess as the door swung open and nearly broke away from its hinges, revealing a terrifying figure whose frame took up almost all of the space in the doorway. Without speaking, he slowly walked into the interview room, slammed the door behind him with just as much force as his arrival and lowered himself onto the seat in front of Noah. The seat was doll house furniture beneath him and the pen he grabbed from the table made miniature as he gripped it tightly, never once taking his eyes off Noah.

'I can explain, Mr Mitchell.'

'That's Chief Inspector Mitchell, Smith, and I very much doubt you have anything to say that will interest me.' His voice was pure gravel.

Noah opened his mouth to speak then realised there really was little point. Charlotte had spoken to him often about her fears for her father and how she wanted to look after him and make sure he was okay, but to Noah's eyes he was more than capable of looking after himself. He may have been grey and the wrinkles were starting to show on his weathered face, but here was a man who was straight from the pages of the kind of book the purists at university would frown upon – the crime fiction that was all plot and thin characters with their hard-man one-liners and threatening looks that Noah always thought were simply plucked from creative authors' minds. He now knew otherwise.

'The custody officer has approved your release with a caution. Have you ever received a caution before, Smith?'

Noah shook his head.

'Have you?'

'No, sir.'

'Under these conditions I am obligated to inform you that you are officially cautioned and will be allowed to leave the police station as long as you vow not to approach the Sir Robin's Head, the landlord of the Sir Robin's Head – who is gunning for your blood, by the way – or my daughter. The caution will be kept on file for the next twelve months, after which time it will be deleted from record providing you haven't got yourself into more trouble. Do you understand?'

'I'm really sorry,' Noah said, trying a different tack, but he could hear a pathetic desperation in his voice that was never going to wash with the big man. 'I love your daughter and I made a mistake. I would never do anything to hurt her and I know you don't think I am, but I'm a good and honest person.'

'Can I just stop you there, Smith? You see, I've already told you that I have no interest in anything you have to say. Look at you with your bohemian hair and floppy shirt. I bet you're off to read a bit of Shakespeare or some such nonsense when you get out. Do you really think that's what I want for my daughter? To spend her time with a loser like you?'

All the way through the speech, he voice remained deep and deeply threatening in a way Noah would have thought impossible to maintain. His eyes were fixed and humourless and it was easy for Noah to imagine that he was growing as he spoke, right before his eyes. Noah didn't know whether to answer or not his time, so he remained still.

'So I ask you again,' Chief Inspector Mitchell began, bringing his red face even closer to Noah's across the table. 'Do you accept the conditions of the caution?'

Noah nodded slowly. There really was no point in doing otherwise. Charlotte's father had absolutely no intention of listening to him.

'Sign here,' he demanded and when he had extracted a signature from Noah he left the room with no further word and punctuated his departure with another smash of the door in the doorframe. As Noah watched the walls tremble with the impact, he decided there and then that his life was officially over.

CHAPTER SIX

Athena thought back to the moment when she had made Sam cease to exist. It was a moment that her mind returned her to often. In fact, it sometimes seemed to be the only moment that had ever existed in her life, the moment that she had slowly twisted the lid on a jar that would contain her for ... how long? Not forever. She had to believe that this was true. She had to believe that love was the strongest force in the world and Sam would succeed in finally finding Fizz and defeating the forces of death with the strength of his love. She had to believe that it would happen and she did believe it would happen, but how long it would take was another story altogether. Just how long would she be relegated to the queasy wonderland where the sky was always beautiful however much she wished for just a single drop of rain and the air was always warm however much her skin craved the sweet caress of a cool breeze.

The first few decades passed quickly, as time for Athena lacked the same potency as it would for a human, who would have no choice but to be sent insane by the solitude and monotony. After a few more decades she realised that the cycle of Sam's mission would have been played out twice and she was still imprisoned in the poetic fantasy; he had failed twice and there was no way of knowing just how many more times he would fail. Athena then slept for fifty years and cried for another fifty. And still there was no sign of release, no sign of anything, no word from another living soul to deliver her from desperation. And then one day everything changed.

She was sitting on the little finger of the hand-tree. This was the closest thing she had to interaction as she could run her own hands along the palm and feel quivering, or tickle the fingers and make them close and open. After so many years there was almost a sense of language between herself and the tree, but what any of it meant she had no idea. On this day, she was watching the beautiful horned beast, a unicorn perhaps, with a sense of boredom that she had no way of expressing other than sitting deadly still and letting the frustration figure its way out of her by itself. She could only hope that she would feel a little better in time, but she never did. Half a century of sleeping and half a century of crying had changed her somehow. Her response to most things now was to sit deadly still and let them wash over her. It was almost as if she were trying to become a part of the sickly landscape, as if disappearing into the scene was the only means of escape at her disposal. Hope had been replaced by despair and now she was moving into something far more dangerous as she almost accepted her fate and was nearly ready to buy her way into oblivion with the essence of her being. And then he appeared.

'Sam?' she asked dreamily. She had thought she had seen figures in the distance before and always been wrong. Now … could it be? 'Sam?' she called. And the figure began to move towards her, past the annoying mythical creature and its stupid, frustrating, illuminated horn, over the bridge that crossed the mucky rainbow river, through the leaves and flowers. Athena swung her body around the tree knuckle, which slowly bent and lowered her to the floor, as she had done a hundred times. She ran the short distance to the figure and couldn't decide whether to be disappointed or thrilled at the sight awaiting her.

'You're not Sam,' she told the man, but then all sign of disappointment was replaced by excitement. After almost 150 years here was an actual person before her. A real, live person had come to see her, but she had no idea who he was. His height far exceeded her own and his body was strong, chiselled from rock and determination. He was not a man who smiled easily, this much was clear, but there was something charming about the seriousness of his expression, as if he carried important news and would travel to the ends of the earth to deliver it. His hair was not dissimilar to her own, flowing languidly with as many reddened tones as waves in the sea; the only garment he wore was a thin, skirt-like wrap that clung to his waist and dropped lightly to his bare feet.

'Wait!' she said before he could say anything. 'I want to savour this. Do not say a word. Come down to the river.'

The man gave a curious nod and followed her down to the riverside where she gently sat herself amongst the emerald grasses and watched as he joined her. He opened his mouth to speak, but she stopped him again.

'Wait!' she told him and closed her eyes tightly, preparing for the most magical sound she could ever wish to hear, an actual voice communicating with her, then nodded for him to speak.

'I am Chrono,' he told her.

Her eyes suddenly flicked open. This had not been the moment she had hoped for. Disappointment once again wrinkled her face and then she started talking too quickly. 'You are the Chrono? You have to understand, sir, it was not my fault. I know I broke the rules. I know I should not have let him return. Actually, yes, I should not have intervened in the first place. But I have a chance to make it right. I mean, he has a chance to make it all right and then we can all go back to normal and forget this ever happened … Is it not so?'

Chrono simply looked at her without answering. She was still as beautiful as she always was and always would be, untouched by time, but the expression on his face told that her beauty was the last thing on his mind. 'You have brought disgrace upon yourself, Athena. And I have been forced to take time away from my vital duties to meet with you.'

'I would not think time would be a problem for you,' she replied genuinely, but Chrono's face became sterner still, mistaking her comment for petulance and ridicule. Named for the god of time, he tired of the assumption that he could actually control it. His role was far more important – fate and destiny, the product of time. He was one of a select group who delivered that which was deemed inevitable by greater powers than himself. Just as Athena had been sent to protect Sam, Chrono had been sent to destroy him.

'I didn't mean to offend,' Athena quickly added. 'I am truly sorry for what has happened, sir.' She lowered her head and after a few seconds, peeked back up to him to see if he had forgiven her. His expression hadn't changed so she continued, 'Have you come to set me free, sir? You have my promise that nothing like this will ever happen again.'

Finally Chrono smiled. 'You silly girl. You really do not understand. I have spent nearly one hundred and fifty years repairing the damage created by your ill-placed compassion.'

Athena lowered her head again. 'With respect, I cannot apologise for my compassion. It was an evil plan to take such a gifted young man, so young.'

Chrono stood up suddenly. 'I cannot listen to this,' he said and turned to leave.

'No wait! Please, do not leave me here.'

'Were you so poorly educated, Athena, that you fail to understand the bigger picture? Everything is supported by design and reason – the greater good. You think that those who work for the good of the universe are lacking in compassion?'

Athena thought for a second and then decided not to answer.

'There will always be death of all ages and it is not our place to challenge what has been written. You will never understand the damage you have caused.' He folded his arms, which should have been a hostile gesture, but Athena took solace in it as a sign at least that he wasn't leaving just yet.

'But you have solved the problems caused now?' she asked gently, desperate not to rile him again.

'This is beside the point. You are a liability, Athena. We cannot afford to retain guardian angels who act outside of the interests of the universe.'

'But it was my job to look after him.'

'While he was alive, yes, to offer the same support you would to anyone in their days on earth. You knew that he was limited.'

Athena nodded gravely.

'What would happen if you were guardian to a child destined to live not one day after their seventh birthday?'

'I have learnt!' Athena chipped in a little too quickly.

'In the last few seconds? Because it was less than a minute since that you refused to apologise for your compassion.'

Athena had no answer.

'I am afraid, Athena, that you are to remain here, out of harm's way – the harm you are likely to cause, that is.'

Athena was now on her feet, 'Please,' she begged. 'I cannot stay here. I will die here.'

'You will wish you could die here.'

This comment made Athena suddenly straighten her body and step back from him. The strength of the movement surprised them both. 'You're enjoying this aren't you?' she snapped.

'Forgive me,' Chrono bowed. 'That was an unkind thing to say. You just do not understand, Athena. This is bigger than you and bigger than me. Sam has become a mouse in a clock, running around, chewing mechanisms, destroying everything he touches. I have managed to contain him by making sure that he stays within his loop, failing in every incarnation to survive past his twentieth birthday. Is that what you wanted for him? An infinite loop of tragedy? I cannot bring him back and I cannot release you. This is fate now. It is written.'

Athena sniffed back the tears. The last time she cried she wept for fifty years and she couldn't face that again. Just as Chrono was about to turn from her again she said, 'And what of love?'

'What of it, child?' He used the word as if he were a wizened old man and she an adolescent but they were physically the same age.

'You can destroy people, you can take lives, but what about the love? That doesn't die. It cannot die. If I were not here, it would be Sam in my place.' She tried to keep her voice level, but she could hear the tone and volume rising.

'Neither of you would be here if it hadn't been for your intervention.'

'Have you ever been in love, Chrono?'

Now it was Chrono's turn to struggle for an answer.

'I didn't think so. If you had, you would dismiss anything that was "written" to keep love alive.'

Chrono thought for a moment before saying, 'You are a ridiculous creature.' He spoke the words as if they were the absolute truth and with a finality that told Athena they were to be the last in the exchange between them. All she could do was watch as he turned and walked away from her, across the meadow and bridge, past the glowing creature and into the distance, getting smaller and smaller until he finally disappeared.

Athena slowly walked to the water's edge, feeling more alone than she had ever felt, more alone even than when she sent Sam back to his many new lives, and she knew that she would replay this new moment over and over until she had worn it down to a single disappointed expression from him and the agonising feeling of loneliness from her. She moved to the bridge and folded her arms just as Chrono had done then shouted, 'Love will always prevail!' although there was no way he could hear her. Then she shouted, 'Someone, please help me!' and dropped her face into her hands. Seconds later, however, she almost fell in the smudged rainbow lake with the shock she felt at receiving a reply.

'What can I do for you?'

She looked all around her but there was no one to be seen. 'Hello!' she called out.

'Hello yourself!'

This time she traced the direction of the voice and saw that the annoying unicorn creature, who had spent the last 150 annoying years grazing and being generally useless and annoying, was now looking up at her.

'Are you talking?'

'What does it look like?'

It looked like it was talking. Its mouth was moving and its eyes had become expressive and friendly.

'You can talk?'

The unicorn nodded and then returned to its favourite pastime, grazing and eating the emerald grass.

'Why didn't you tell me?' Athena asked, skipping over the bridge to the creature's side.

'You didn't ask.'

CHAPTER SEVEN

First light was a time that often featured in Sam's poetry, when the embers of yesterday were reignited in the horizon; it was a time of silence and renewal, reflection and more and more often when he picked up a quill, romance. Nothing was beyond the reaches of romance, especially seen through the eyes of a nineteen-year-old knight-pretender, who didn't seem to be able to get any closer to a woman than standing outside his chamber door while his best friend entertained one in his bed. He could really kick himself sometimes.

'All you have to do,' Robin had told him on many occasions, usually adopting an expression from his broad collection of smug faces, 'is ask.'

Ask? Sam pondered. It couldn't be that simple. He pictured himself in the great hall of the castle, at one of his father's feasts, the aroma of fine food filling the air, music and wine fuelling the joyous dancing all around him. He would be able to see Robin either dancing with the most beautiful woman in the room or they would have found a secluded area where he would be charming her with wild gesticulations and stories of great adventure while she sat hypnotised, unable to take her eyes from his chiselled features.

Just ask? And then what? 'Excuse me?' he would say sheepishly and both words would immediately let him down, sticking in his throat, causing him to blush and shrink under the gaze of whichever fair maid he had built the courage to approach. And now in his mind she would be looking at him impatiently, hands on her hips, head tipped slightly forward, eyebrows raised. And that would be it. 'Not to worry,' he would conclude and walk away. This would be how it would surely go and so, to this day, he had never found the courage to attempt such an exchange.

'I fancy you will die a virgin,' Robin would tease and Sam always laughed this off and countered with a quick comeback – 'Which is better than dying of syphilis with a rotting member.' – but Robin's words hurt him. In fact, the situation hurt him, the fear hurt him. What if he really did die a virgin? What if he never found love? What if he was destined to remain alone forever? It was a cliché – the tortured poet, writing verse of great romance, but never experiencing it in real life – and it was not how Sam wanted his life to be. He could not prevent the poetry from forming within him and colouring his view of the world, but he was determined to have a full experience of life from which to draw, so it pleased him that first light on this day was not about poetry, but about getting up and out into the world and a new experience. Robin, however, was less enamoured by the prospect of rising with the larks and working out Lady Mardridge's punishment for the day. He arrived in the village with dark circles under his eyes and a shirt tail hanging out of his doublet. His hair had been hastily tied back and tufts were hanging over his face. He was not cut out for early mornings and this kind of labour, and he didn't have much to say as the farmer led them out to the fields with a smile on his weathered face. Sam didn't say much either through fear of stirring Robin's rage; these were the terms of their friendship. They could banter to a point, but Sam knew when to remain silent. After all, it was his fault that they were up at this hour and would spend the day on their hands and knees pulling crops from the earth with freezing fingers, as the unseasonal sun had thought better of making an appearance today and the weather had returned to a typical April gloom.

As they listened to the farmer's instructions, Sam knew immediately why he was smiling; his own black breeches and white puffed-out shirt were not particularly suitable for field work, but Lord Robin's outfit eclipsed his own: fine boots, tights and a purple doublet, slashed to reveal the vibrant red lining beneath, silk sleeves matching in colour, topped with a velvet robe and feathered cap. How the farmer restrained himself from a fit of laughter as he gave then each a basket and directions relating to cabbages, carrots and cauliflowers was beyond him.

'What even is this?' Robin asked after they had been left alone for a while and made a start on their task. He was holding a carrot in the air as if it had not only fallen from another planet, but it was a planet where all of their vegetables looked suspiciously rude.

'Imagine it sliced, cooked and in a pie with beef and other vegetables.'

'Oh,' he replied, bored by the answer before Sam had even finished saying it. 'The little orange disks?' he confirmed.

Sam nodded and they continued pulling them out of the earth in silence until Robin suddenly sat himself back away from the crops, threw a carrot into his basket and let out a massive sigh.

'No,' Sam told him.

'No what?'

'No whatever you are thinking. I know that sigh. You are bored, Robin, and you are thinking of making mischief, but I urge you. All we are to do is stay here and work for the day and Mother will be kept happy. We will have served our punishment and can go back to normal life.'

'Our punishment? She is your mother, Sam.'

'And she is your ruler.'

This silenced Robin for a moment, but when Sam looked over to him he could see that he was eying the village at a distance with intent on his face.

'Please, Robin. I do not need more trouble.'

'Tell me, Sam, would not this task be more tolerable with ale in our bellies?'

'No, Robin. Well, yes, it would be more tolerable, but no, this idea is a bad one.'

'It would take not more than an hour to sneak away into the ale house. It is too early for us to be challenged. We will leave the money and away with two mugs of ale to see us through the morning.'

Sam didn't answer.

'And is it not your twentieth birthday in little more than a week? We should celebrate.'

Sam threw the carrot he had been gripping into the basket and joined his friend, seated away from the crop. He peeked down into both of their baskets and saw that they had done quite well. Actually, Sam had done quite well and Robin had barely begun, but if they pooled their output it would look as if they had both been working hard.

'This is a bad idea,' he began, then added, 'but you are correct; it would take less than an hour and even Mother would concede that a drink is necessary for hard work.'

'Good man!' Robin said and smiled for the first time that day.

'But we bring the drink back here, and we leave the money there, so it is far from stealing.'

'Of course.'

'And you need to work harder when we return because I cannot do this alone.'

'Of course,' Robin repeated, but whether he was listening now or simply speaking the words he knew Sam would want to hear was unclear.

Down in the village, both Sam and Robin were surprised to see how much activity stirred at such an early hour. They had expected the streets to be empty, but there was clearly an early morning culture of horse-drawn commerce and the readying of trade for the day. It was far from bustling, with the average resident still in slumber, but they would have to exercise caution if they were to make it to the ale house unnoticed. And thanks to Robin's ludicrous attire they stood out like two sore toes on a ballerina.

'Down here!' Sam whispered and they both dropped behind a cart stacked with more vegetables that Robin had only previously encountered in their cooked form. They waited as words and laughter were exchanged between the only two men in this street of thatched dwellings with lead-latticed windows and swollen, overhanging upper levels that bulged out at the front and cast shadows into the dirt road. As the minutes past, Robin patted down his white tights, which were now ruined from the mud of the field and the grime of the dusty road. Sam knew him well enough to know that he would not tolerate their predicament for long, even though there was beer at the end of it and whispered, 'Listen to their words. The cart will be away soon in the direction of the ale house. If we remain crouched and move with it we will–'

'Bollocks to it!' was Robin's retort, proving Sam's assessment to be correct, and suddenly leapt back up to his finely cobbled feet. The two men turned at the sudden appearance, but said nothing, so shocked were they to see such finery in their humble streets, possibly royalty. 'Good morning, gentlemen,' Robin added authoritatively.

Both men straighten up and tipped their brown, woollen hats, but seemed too shocked to say more.

Then Robin added, 'As you were,' and they returned to their business, while Robin marched off in the direction of the ale house and Sam trotted behind him.

'What happened to being discrete?'

'These people know to keep the secrets of their betters. I should have thought of it before. We can walk freely here and probably take anything we want. No one would dare to challenge us. Can you imagine one of these wretches approaching the castle for an audience with Lord Mardridge to complain of two mugs of missing ale?'

'You are quite something else,' Sam told him and if Robin detected the sarcasm he didn't say so; he simply grinned and continued his march.

The ale house was not dissimilar in appearance to the other street dwelling, only it was slightly larger and surrounded by a noxious, beery hum. When they arrived, Robin tried the short, wooden door and found it to be locked, as they had suspected.

'Round the back,' he beamed, now warming to the challenge they faced and they both darted to the back of the building in the hope of a second entrance. In fact, Robin looked as if it was more than hope driving him. He had definitely been here before. Although Sam was no stranger to alcohol, his experiences were limited to the wine and ale served in the great hall of the castle.

'Keep lookout,' Robin mouthed to his friend as they found a second door, and Sam wandered back to the street, which was still practically empty. Just seconds later, he heard a 'Pssst!' and when he returned, the door was open and Robin was nowhere to be seen. He took one last look all around him before following inside. He found Robin behind the bar, lighting a candle.

'Is that a good–?'

'Relax, Sir Sammy. No one should ever have to work the fields sober.' He drew a mug from the shelf and began to fill it with ale. 'Actually,' he added, 'No one should have to work in the field full stop.' He spoke quietly, but there was an arrogance in him that precluded him from whispering, as if he absolutely had the right to be there helping himself to two mug of ale. He pushed a drink in Sam's direction and Sam silently acknowledged it while looking all around him. Candlelight was so strange to see at this end of the day and gave the room such a strange quality, as if it were neither morning nor evening, day nor night, but a secret pocket of time of their own invention that they would possess until the moment they set foot back out into the morning gloom and the illusion was shattered.

Sam sipped his ale. It was strong, but he didn't have the luxury of drinking it slowly, as he knew the landlord would be slumbering above them and could catch them any minute. Despite Robin's impassioned speech about their God-given right to wander freely, he didn't imagine that the landlord would quite see it that way. Halfway through the ale, he could feel the familiar softening of his bones and vibrating of his intoxicated organs, but he pushed on and soon the mug was empty. He slammed it down on the bar and motioned Robin towards the door, but Robin was already pouring more drinks. 'No!' he mouthed, but Robin simply smiled with a beer-foam moustache and started on his second mug. Again, taking the time constraints into consideration, Sam gamely ploughed into his second drink, but by the time it was finished he cared a little less about time constraints and carrots and the landlord sleeping upstairs. In fact, he now imagined him to be some kind of hilarious beer pixie whom, rather than battering them out of the establishment with any weapon he could get his hands on, would fly into the barroom and tickle them until they promised never to do it again. And now Sam was giggling. He looked over to his friend, whom, through Sam's beery eyes, now had an extra hazy outline and a smile that was far too wide to fit on his face.

'We should …' Sam tried to say, but hilarity grabbed him and he broke into a fit of laughter instead.

'Shhhh!' Robin tried, but it came out as a dribbly raspberry and made them both laugh all the more. Robin didn't even try to compose himself before pouring two more mugs of ale.

'We must not,' Sam pleaded, but the third serving found its way into his system with very little opposition and now it really didn't seem to matter if they were caught or if the vegetables got picked. In fact, it no longer mattered that his father had no time for his true personality, or that he had managed to trick his way into leading a battle that would surely result in his own death. Unless he could think of a way out of it, he had just two more weeks left on this fair planet, but even this knowledge had been purged from his system by the suspiciously speckled, dirty-brown liquid from the barrel reserved only for the hardened drinkers used to imbibing such a potent brew.

And then, after more than an hour in the ale house, as is often the way with minds addled with ale, a melancholy drifted over Sam as tangible to his mind as the sky descending and trapping him beneath its mighty shade of grey. All of his worries were still insignificant but for one and he took a deep sigh before asking, 'Am I to really die before I have sampled love?'

Robin dropped his elbows onto the bar and stared at his friend with drooping eyelids and bright red beer cheeks. 'I love you, my friend.'

'As comforting as that is, Robin, it is not exactly what I meant.' Another sigh followed.

'I know that no one deserves to be loved as much as you,' Robin said in a tone that seemed to have a layer of himself removed, as if he were talking from a deeper part of himself, which forced a seriousness to his face that Sam rarely saw.

Sam smiled in return and was about to ask Robin many more questions, about love, about physical intimacy, about death, about what on earth they could do to avert his certain death in battle, but before he could say a word, there was a noise above them. Footsteps. They were gentle and leisurely, and they should have made the boys run for the door, but instead, the two of them collapsed into yet more giggles.

'We should ...' Sam tried to say, but he just couldn't stop the laughter from flowing in him. Whatever happened with the landlord it wouldn't be as bad as his imminent death in battle. In fact, this might be just the get-out he was looking for; if the landlord beat him to a pulp there was no way he would be able to lead men in battle. He sat rigid on his stool and looked over to Robin, who had now stopped laughing and was looking up at the ceiling as if he could see through it. He also hadn't moved and it was the sight of him that stirred something resembling fear in Sam. Suddenly, the last thing he wanted to do was take a beating from the landlord and he definitely didn't want Robin to get hurt. He would have been all the more scared if he knew what the landlord was like – a mighty, ginger Scot who could rival Lord Mardridge on both stature and strength, and kept a heavy club by the stairs to take care of intruders. If he battered them to death they would not be the first; his strength and insanity were known throughout the land.

Suddenly, Sam and Robin were on their feet, tasting sobriety in the backs of their throats as they wrestled with fear and escape, but before they could make it to the back door they could hear footsteps on the stairs. They would never make it past to escape that way. Robin darted over to try the front door, but it was locked. He pulled at the handle with a panicked strength, but it wouldn't move.

'Quick …' Sam mouthed and indicated the space under a table close to them. He knew that hiding would be useless. They had already drawn attention to themselves with the mess in the bar and the noise they had made; a shambolic game of hide and seek would push the landlord over the edge, but it was the only idea Sam could think of. However, they were so drunk and poorly coordinated that before they could even organise their limbs to move in the direction of the table, the door to the barroom crashed open and thudded against the wall shaking the whole ale house and Sam and Robin to their cores.

CHAPTER EIGHT

The first person Noah wanted to see when he was released from Mardridge Police Station was Charlotte, but even he could see that this was not a good idea. He still looked and smelt like something that had been scraped off a brewery floor and her father's anger was still ringing in his ears. He so wanted to go to her and explain then curl up with her for the rest of the day, feel her cool, soft flesh on his, but he would have to exercise restraint.

The last person he wanted to see was Thane and yet there he was, waiting outside Noah's digs for him with a big smile on his face.

'I could swing for you!' Noah snapped and walked straight past him, holding his key up in the direction his front door.

'Don't be like that, mate. There was no point in both of us getting arrested.'

But Noah had let himself into his bedsit and slammed the door behind him. It was only after Thane had stood there knocking for half an hour, showing no sign that he might give up and go away, that Noah returned to him. Taking his cue from Charlotte's father, he opened the door with such force that his neighbours would have felt the building tremble. He greeted Thane with silent, wide eyes that said, 'What could you possibly have to say that I want to hear?'

'Look, I'm really sorry. I didn't know the police were going to show up and when I saw them … well, I just–'

'Completely ditched me?'

Thane looked just as rough as Noah after their adventures and was also still wearing the same beery clothes. 'I'm really sorry,' he tried again and thought he saw Noah's expression begin to soften, so he said, 'It was fun though, no?'

'No, actually!' Noah's face hardened again and Thane could see that it was too soon to laugh about the whole thing. 'How did they even know we were in there?'

'How should I know? You don't think …?' Now Thane looked hurt and this genuinely softened Noah for the first time.

'Of course not. I just don't know how they knew we were there.'

'I don't know either, mate. I know I should have come back for you, but I was trapped and I couldn't even warn you. God, I'm a shit friend!'

Noah's features softened further and then he somehow found himself comforting Thane. 'Don't say that. You're a great friend. The best. Look, it's not the end of the world.' As the words came out he wondered how Thane had defused him so quickly, but he was also pleased. He didn't want to be angry. All he really wanted was to sleep. 'I'm going to crash. You look like you could do with a few more hours yourself.'

'And we're okay?'

'You're okay. I've now got a criminal record, a ban on seeing Charlotte and apparently the landlord of the Sir Robin's Head wants to kill me.'

'I'm so sorry, mate. Anything you need and I'm there.'

'It's fine. We're okay. Just know that I am never ever agreeing to one of your hair-brained schemes ever again.'

Thane nodded weakly then gently patted his friend's arm before leaving him to rest, but the moment Noah shut the door he knew he wouldn't sleep. There was just too much going on in his head. He sat on his bed and picked up his mobile. There was a message from his mum telling him how much she loved him and was proud of him, but the words barely registered. All he gleaned from the phone check was the absence of a message from Charlotte. He brought up a blank text message and began to type. There were a million things in his head he wanted to say to Charlotte. He was used to sharing his entire internal world with her and inhabiting hers, but now all he could think to write was I love you. He pressed send and waited for a few minutes for a reply. A few minutes turned into a few more and before he knew it he had sat silently for almost an hour, turning the phone over and over in his hands. With each moment that passed the loneliness bore down on him and the walls of his tiny living space pushed in and made the room inhospitable. He had found it an oppressive space when he first moved there, with its gloomy single bed taking up most of the floor space, chipped sink, fraying green carpet and tiny window. But having Charlotte there with him turned it into a castle. It was now slowly morphing back into a soulless cell and he wanted to be anywhere else but there.

He looked at the screen again. Nothing. But then a new idea came to him. He entered the words Police, Cadets and Mardridge into his phone and waited for the results. Nothing. He wasn't sure that he realistically expected a small village like Mardridge to run a police cadet program or a police academy, but it was worth a try. He then wrote

Mardridge Gyms and waited for the results. The village was so small that this was probably also unlikely, but he was surprised to see a result for a tiny gym and boxing club just a few streets away, moving closer into town.

'That's it!' he smiled and bookmarked the page as his head filled with images of the buff policeman who had arrested him and the belittling words of Chief Inspector Mitchell. He would have Charlotte marry someone like PC Muscles if he had his way. 'Well, two can play at that game!' Noah told himself as he undressed, not quite sure of exactly what he meant by it, but as he saw flashes of his white, puny body he felt his confidence drift away. It would take him years to transform the bag of bones he carried around with him into the lean, mean fighting machine that would impress his potential father-in-law. He sighed deeply, slipped under his duvet and was soothed by the sudden knowledge that he had years and he was willing to apply himself to the task. He would scale building and endure hardships – torture even – to be with Charlotte; learning to be more of a man was a small price to pay.

Almost a month passed and there was still no word from Charlotte. Noah sent her texts every day, sometimes simply telling her he loved her, at other times trying to explain himself and ask for her forgiveness, and sometimes he sent lines from the poetry he was studying at university. He also tried to call her, but being transferred directly to her voicemail was so soul-destroying that he had stopped this. He couldn't bear the idea of her looking at her phone, seeing his name appear and rejecting the call. But Noah wasn't to be deterred. He couldn't be deterred and he couldn't imagine how she could be. His mind kept returning him to the moment of their meeting and that first kiss just minutes after their eyes had met. There was something between them that was bigger than her father's warning or his stupid behaviour that night in the Sir Robin's Head; it was bigger than they both were separately and bigger than anything Noah had experienced in his life so far. He could easily imagine that meeting Charlotte – and Thane for that matter – had been the reason he had been so drawn to Mardridge in the first place. After all, the decision to move there was the easiest decision he had ever had to make and was more of an inevitability than a choice. If it were so important for him to have met Charlotte, he had to see it through to the end and he couldn't be put off by obstacles – no matter how big they were. But even without the weight of an external force, he simply couldn't give up because he truly believed his heart would shrink and shrivel and cease to sustain him without her. There was as little choice in his love for her as there was in his decision to breathe in and out continuously throughout the day.

He checked his phone for the hundredth time that day, threw it in his gym bag and wandered out to the weights. He had joined the gym that same day, after he was released from police detention, and had been turning up almost every day for a workout and boxing tutorial. In the beginning he absolutely hated it. He hated the smell and the maleness of it all, the way people communicated in grunts rather than articulating what they really meant, the slaps and punches on the shoulder that were meant to be affectionate, the nicknames and banter that he was supposed to laugh off and the endless skipping. He had been going for a month now and unfortunately he still absolutely hated it, but he was determined and at the very least, it had got easier over the course of the month and he was beginning to see benefits. His body still looked much the same – pigeon chested, chicken boned – but he was faster and fitter and his whole sense of wellbeing had improved. He had even completely cut out the booze while he trained (much to the chagrin of Thane). Today's workout consisted mainly of weights, a bit of treadmill and cycling and then more of the dreaded skipping, which he completed without complaint. When he finished, bright red and drenched in sweat, he checked his phone again. He had expected to see the usual blank screen and almost tossed the phone in his bag without registering what was actually in front of him – a message from Charlotte: Meet me by the old well in ten minutes x.

Noah ran as fast as he could all the way to the well on the edge of the village, which he wouldn't have been able to do before he started the training, and arrived with just minutes to spare. He stopped before he reached the old relic to take in the full sight of her. How his body had continued to exist for a month without being able to drink in this sight was a mystery to him, but every part of him felt soothed just from being in her presence. He composed himself and then slowly moved towards her. She turned before he reached her, knowing instinctively that he had arrived and slowly rose to her feet. A few metres apart, they held each other in a stare that revealed little of their inner feelings and then Charlotte's façade crumbled and the tears began to fall. Noah moved in to hold her and was surprised when she fell into his arms. She sobbed uncontrollably and he gripped her tightly until the tears disappeared.

'I'm so sorry,' she said when she had composed herself and they were sitting on the wall holding hands.

'You have nothing to apologise for. This is all my fault.'

'But I shouldn't have ignored your calls and your texts.' She smiled for the first time. 'Your beautiful texts.' She was as beautiful as Noah had ever seen her, in lemon-yellow dress that welcomed the summer so joyfully and complimented the subtle lighter shades in the long, dark hair that rested on her shoulders. But he could also see the depth of her sadness, the eyes that hadn't slept, the hollowed cheeks that spoke of food left untouched. 'I tried so hard to obey my father. He is the most important thing the world to me; at least I thought he was. But I can't do this anymore, Noah. I can't be separated from you.'

Noah was yet to feel relief like this in his life and pulled her close again. 'We'll find a way through this,' he reassured her and rested her head on his chest.

'I've stopped seeing boys for my father before,' she suddenly continued. 'It's been hard, but I've done it, believing that the right person would come along and my dad would be able to see him for what he was. I tried to do it with you, but just can't.'

'It's all right,' he said soothingly. 'I understand. There's always a solution, Charlotte, and we'll find it.'

'But I feel so …' She sat up as she contemplated the right word and then began talking quietly. 'I've been having these dreams,' she confided. 'And then there's the song.'

'Hold on a minute. Back up. What dreams?'

'They're silly. It's silly. I know it is, but I can't shake them, Noah.' She looked as if she might cry again.

'Just tell me.'

'They seem so real. I can see them. They're in the village, but it's in the olden days. Everything is wooden. The poor dress in rags and the rich dress in unimaginable finery. There were two friends – and I didn't think anything of it – but then they broke into the little pub and …' Her eyes were searching for a way to continue the story, to give it more weight and show just how much the dreams had been bothering her.

'Dreams can really mess you up,' Noah told her. 'I always used to dream that I was being chased by big dogs and I'd run until my lungs exploded and I'd wake up just as they attacked me.'

'You don't understand,' Charlotte said sadly. 'It's not like that. These seem ... real.'

'You mean? ... What do you mean? I don't really understand.'

'Like I'm seeing into the past.'

Noah made the fatal mistake of smiling at this point and Charlotte jumped to her feet.

'No wait. I didn't mean to smile. It just seems a little weird.'

'I'm having them every single night!' Charlotte sobbed. 'Every night, Noah. It's like I'm in some kind of prison.' Her face was so pale and her brown eyes full of sadness.

Noah reached out to hold her, but this time she resisted.

'We'll sort this. Don't worry, Charlotte. Whatever's going on for you can be sorted. Have you thought of going to the doctor?'

Charlotte sat down sadly and nodded. 'I've already been. I got some sleeping pills, but it's the last thing I need.'

Noah suddenly turned to her with renewed excitement. 'Come to mine tonight. I'll cook, we can watch a movie, I'll even read you a bedtime story and you can fall asleep right here.' He placed his palm on his chest and she smiled weakly. 'And what's this about a song?'

'That's the other thing. It's like my brain won't turn it off. But I don't know the words. I wrote the music for my course a few weeks ago. It's so beautiful, but it's not like anything I've written before. I have no idea where it came from.' She looked down at her hands wringing in her lap as she spoke and Noah could feel her pain. 'I know what the song should be about, but I just can't find the words for the lyrics and it's haunting my every waking second.'

'What's it about?'

'It's hard to describe in words. It about making the whole world stop so that love is the only thing that exists if only for a moment. It's about the sun shining down just on that love and there being no noise but for the sound of their two names. It's stupid, I know it is.'

'It's actually really beautiful, but not if you can't get any peace from it.'

'But it's more than that. It's almost as if the song unravels halfway through and transcends words.'

Noah had no idea how to answer this. 'Hey,' he said and reached out to her chin to raise her head in his direction. It really did seem as if she was in another world, where sorrow and despair were her only allies. 'Come over tonight and we'll make everything okay.'

Again she smiled weakly before agreeing that she would tell her father she was staying with a friend and stay with him instead. And then they sat in silence, with Charlotte's head on his chest and her face moulded into something resembling peace, although her mind was clearly in turmoil before she eventually broke the silence.

'Noah.'

'Aha.'

'My cousin's coming to stay next week.'

'Okay.'

'I thought we could set her up with Thane. Kill two birds with one stone.'

'Right.'

'Thane would be so much easier to manage if he had a girlfriend and I don't want Annabel snooping around us. She's nice – she's a medical student – I just don't know her well enough to know if she can be trusted and won't go blabbing to Dad.'

'Okay. Whatever you think.'

They were silent again.

'Noah.'

'Aha.'

'What the hell are you wearing?'

Noah looked down at his baggy shorts and vest and said, 'It's a long story.'

CHAPTER NINE

Sam and Robin were nearly knocked from their feet by the force of the door slamming open as they drunkenly tried to clamour under the table and out of sight of the demonic landlord, both clawing and crashing into each other to secure their place. However, the sight awaiting them beyond the doorframe forced relieved sighs from both of them. A woman – a beautiful, young woman; they would live to see another day.

Robin immediately straightened himself to approach her, as calmly as if this were his home and he had invited her over for a bite to eat. 'You must forgive our intrusion,' he told her in his deepest, most charming voice. 'We will pay for the ale and away before we trouble the master.'

As he spoke, Sam was less able to compose himself. He stumbled further and ended up knocking over a stool and groping at the table for balance. Surprisingly, when he had gathered just a little composure, he saw a smile spread across her face and the Mediterranean sun had finally emerged over the dull village sky and lit up his entire world. He looked into those exotic, brown eyes and forgot to breathe. Her lush lips were lightly open, her long brown hair shimmering in the early morning glow like silk cascading over her shoulders. Her dress, although a dull, russet-coloured linen, fit her curves like a second skin. In Sam's entire existence, in all the castle banquets he had attended and all the queens, princesses and noblewomen he had encountered, he had never been in the presence of such an exquisite and intoxicating beauty. He felt an ache all over his body and realised it was caused by the expectation of hearing her voice. He wanted to close his eyes, to savour it, to drink it down, so that this moment would stay with him forever. However, he realised that both Robin and the girl were now looking to him to gather himself and rise to his feet. When he was firmly standing, he shyly nodded his head at the young girl and tried for a smile, but felt his cheeks burn with his own inadequacy.

'You must leave,' the young girl suddenly urged them. 'If my father finds you here he will kill you.'

'Then he is clearly unaware of who we are,' Robin said smugly, still refusing to lower his voice.

'Who you are will be less important than who you were if my father catches you here,' she told them and as she spoke, the words travelled into Sam, as if each one had a tiny pair of wings, and they flew around inside of him causing an elated feeling that could easily be confused with nausea.

'Young lady–' Lord Robin began, dusting off another from his collection of smug faces, but the girl cut him off.

'Out!' she snapped and the suddenness of the syllable seemed to wake Sam from the spell. But when he tried to open his mouth to address her, nothing came out. He wanted to say, 'We apologise, fair maiden,' and tell her how staggeringly beautiful she was, but those words suddenly didn't exist, perhaps all words had ceased to exist out of respect for the existence of such beauty – nothing could match its perfection. So instead of speaking, he looked down at the floor and waited while his face scarleted, then eventually gathered himself and tugged Robin in the direction of the door. He managed to say just one word as he passed her, and it sounded wrong in his mouth, as if he were no longer a native English speaker and was practising an inadequate vocabulary. 'Here,' he said and pressed five shillings into her palm, more than enough to cover the ale consumed. At the moment they touched, he was sure that the money was not the only thing that passed between them; it was something that Sam would try and fail to describe for the rest of his life – the essence of a poem that transcended words – but the power of the exchange was undeniable.

All at once, the space above them was filled with the thuds of an elephant going through its daily getting-up rituals and the young woman's face gently melted into concern as she rushed them through the door.

'What ye doing down there, Fizz?' a booming Scottish voice barked and the ale house trembled once again. It was definitely time to go.

'Tell your father his ale was absolutely splendid,' Robin told the girl as if he had all the time in the world and absolutely refused to be influenced by the arrival of whatever beast of a man threatened to descend upon them, but Sam, ever wiser, pulled him out of the door and they were soon out in the cool morning air. Sam turned to glimpse the woman who had stolen his heart one last time, but saw only the heavy wooden door slamming.

Back in the field, something unfamiliar and automatic was driving Sam as he pulled carrots from the ground. One after the other, he dragged them from the soil as if his life depended on it. It was the booze, he told himself. It was not yet the afternoon and he was drunker than he had ever been. The only way the carrots would get picked was if he gave himself over to the task completely, like a being not of this world, controlled by a greater farming force, but he also knew there was more to it. Every time he deviated from the task, the nausea hit him again and this he knew was not simply the ale seeking to remind him of its presence; this was the impact of the one they call Fizz. Such an unusual sound, as exotic a name as that of the most far-flung visiting royalty the castle had received. 'Fizz!' He silently mouthed the name, feeling the shape and taste of it on his tongue. 'Fizz!' he silently repeated and then something hit him on the back of the head. He turned and saw that Robin had thrown a stub of carrot in his direction from his reclined position.

'You will work yourself to an earlier grave,' he teased, the word 'earlier' adding an extra jibe, and then drew his arms up and over his head, seeking even more comfort. He looked as if he were reclining on a chaise longue rather than lolling in a vegetable field.

'You could help.'

As a reply, Robin blew another dribbly raspberry, which betrayed the fact that he was still absolutely, totally and irredeemably as drunk as a man could be. 'Why would I need to pick any when you are such an efficient farm boy?'

Sam had no answer to this, so silently turned back to the crop and continued pulling. Another ten minutes passed in this way, with Sam's maniacal pulling and Robin's relaxation, until the subject of Robin's next sentence reached his ears and he knew he would pull not one more carrot out of the ground that day.

'I fancy I shall have that bar girl after the banquet tonight,' he said casually with no idea of the gravity of the subject. 'Yes, she is very fine. And it does one well to slum it occasionally.'

'Slum it?!' The words burst out of Sam before he could control them.

'Calm down, Sammy.'

'Slum it?'

'Yes, you know, take the old chap swimming in murkier waters.'

Sam gripped a carrot tightly to restrain himself from gripping his friend's neck. He could feel his face colouring as he ground his teeth.

'Wait just one moment!' Robin smiled. 'I'm not the only one planning a stroll in slumsville, am I?'

'Can you please stop talking like that?'

'Fancy a bit of ale house strumpet too, do you, Sam?'

'If you mean did I find the girl at the ale house attractive then yes.' His whole body heaved at the understatement. 'If you mean am I going to try and get her into bed, then, no.'

'Good,' Robin beamed and rubbed his hands together. 'Tonight it is, then.'

'Hang on a minute. She is not a piece of meat.'

'No?' It was clear that Robin was now winding his friend up, but he was too drunk to notice.

'How can you speak like that? She is a real person. A really real, beautiful, magnificent ... she is the most beautiful ... and I cannot let you ... I mean I have never seen or felt ...'

'My God, Sam, you really have got it bad.'

Sam lumped down beside his friend and fell back onto his elbows. The drink inside of him gave him the feeling that although he was there, he wasn't really there. He wasn't quite floating above looking down, but he wasn't inside of his body either. 'I think I love her.'

Robin sat up suddenly and looked down at his friend. 'This is the drink inside of you. You cannot love a woman to whom you have never spoken.'

'Says who?'

'Says me, my friend. You also cannot love a woman from the shagging classes. As beautiful as she is, she can never elevate herself to the marrying classes – ladies, princesses, gentlewomen.'

'The shagging classes?' Outrage again came naturally to Sam in his drunkenness. 'Where is your respect, Robin?'

'Where is your self-respect, Sam? The girls from the village are for the night; we have ladies for the day.'

'I do not care what you think. I love her, Robin. I know this as sure as I know my own name.'

'Then I will show you, Sam. I will take her to my bed this evening and prove that she is made of the same stuff as the other village girls. A flash of a shilling and the village girls are willing.'

'And I will show you, Robin,' Sam announced and awkwardly pulled himself up and onto his feet.

'Where are you going? You can barely stand?'

'I am going to declare my love to the one they call Fizz and she will be my one true love.'

'You couldn't even speak to her when we were in the ale house. Your head is full of feathers, my friend.'

'The feathers from cupid's bow.'

'You are in no condition to go anywhere,' Robin told him, but made no move to accompany him. He simply looked on as Sam shouted, 'I'll show you!' and stumbled down through the vegetables and soil, and into the oak-laden path, where he disappeared from view.

By the time Sam arrived in the village, he had a bloody nose. He couldn't remember quite how he got it, but he knew it involved falling either into a tree or onto the ground. Either that or the sky really had fallen in and he had taken a battering. He hadn't realised at first and had simply drawn his sleeve across his nose, but then he had seen the blood on his shirt and deduced the cause. If he had a mirror he would know he looked a grimy, bloody, drunken mess, but the only thing on his mind was getting to Fizz and telling her how he felt. To his mind, it was the only thing that mattered in the entire world.

The streets were far busier now than they had been a few hours ago, with the dull-attired folk and their serious expressions either busying themselves with laborious tasks or strutting purposefully to reach the places where they could spend the day undertaking laborious tasks. Sam had never been down to the village at this time and it was all far more industrious than he could have imagined; even the children seemed full of purpose, which only served to highlight how out of place he was in the scene – a bloodied dandy in his finery; he was a mouse in the well-oiled mechanism of this village, but he had no time for the stares of the villagers. He staggered and slipped and dragged himself along the dirt road and eventually arrived outside the ale house once again. However, his bravery wavered when he heard a booming voice from within it.

'There will be blood!' It was deep, Scottish, terrifying and accompanied by the sound of breaking glass.

'Father, please, be calm,' a soft voice pleaded and the sound of it caused the alcohol to make its final encore, intoxicating Sam all over again. This was Fizz. This was his Fizz. 'I will clean the mess. No real harm has been done here.'

'No harm! No harm?'

'We have five shillings, more than enough for the ale.'

It was only then Sam realised that he was being discussed, or at least the result of their binge earlier that morning. Had there been damage? He had a vague recollection of falling over several times and there had been distinct crashing sounds from behind the bar as Robin played serving wench, but it couldn't have been that bad, could it? Maybe he should just march in there as a gentleman, apologise to the Scot and shoulder the consequences. There wasn't much the insane landlord could do if he held his hands up and did everything he could to make it right. But Sam dismissed the thought as soon as it arrived. Of course there was something the landlord could do; there were lots of things the landlord could do and they all involved the spilling of Sam's blood. Before Sam's brain had fully formed the thought, his body ducked around to the back of the ale house, protecting him from presenting himself through the front door. He could still hear the commotion inside and hid behind the stack of crates in the yard.

'I know exactly who'e are!' he heard the Scottish voice again. 'McCleod set their snivelling scrawn to work oot on the field at first light. I should rage over there noo and teach them some respect.'

'What use will hurting them do?' Fizz asked sadly and Sam loved her more and more by the minute.

'I'm'e not gannae hurt them, Fizz. I'm gannae kill them.'

Sam swallowed hard and suddenly wanted to be anywhere other than crouched behind the boxes mere feet away from a psychopath who wanted his blood, but still he remained. Fizz's voice was as inviting as her father's was repellent and Sam no longer had control over his legs.

'Fine!' he then heard, but had clearly missed the details of what the big man was conceding. 'But I want te see this place spotless by the time I get back.'

'Yes, Father.'

The fragment of conversation was followed by the heavy thud of the landlord gathering himself to leave the ale house, his legs fashioned from the oak trees that separated the castle from the village, at least that was how it sounded. And then the front door slammed and Sam was relieved that he had darted around the back, although it reeked of stale ale and excrement.

Now what? Sam didn't move. His heart had just started beating out the rhythm of an Italian dance introduced at the last of his father's banquets, which had left him breathless. He couldn't just walk in there. The thought of it increased the tempo of the dance. What would he say? He thought back to Robin's advice. Just ask. But what was he asking? Excuse me, fair maiden, but would it be within your perfect soul to lower yourself into my world and stay there for eternity? Could you furnish me with just one of your kisses and I can die a happy man? As he ran through options in his mind, he suddenly knew one thing for certain; there was more chance of him wielding a lance and defeating an enemy in battle than moving from that spot and declaring his love for Fizz. Robin was right; he didn't even have the guts to speak to her. He was a ridiculous creature.

And then the opportunity was taken from his hands when another young woman came swooping into the yard, humming gently to herself before letting herself into the ale house through the backdoor.

'Gawd!' he then heard. 'What kinda lunatic exploded in here?' Her tone was harsher than Fizz's, but there was a natural joy to her voice; everything made this young woman smile and Sam immediately liked her. If she was a friend to Fizz then he could sleep soundly in the knowledge that at least one person in this world was on her side. All of this he got from just that one sentence, but he knew he was right. Sometimes all you need is the sound of a person's voice to see into their soul. From what he had seen of the woman as she passed him, she was very similar-looking to Fizz, but of course Fizz's beauty could not bear comparison. Her hair was long, dark and loose and her linen dress was fashioned to be similarly complementary to her figure. Perhaps one of them made all of their outfits.

'You'll be all day doing it like that,' he heard her continue. ''Ere, give it to me.' And he pictured her taking whatever chore Fizz was attempting from her and the two of them labouring cheerfully, two friends together, to clean up the mess left by an hour of Sam's life that he now truly regretted. But then again, he could hear Fizz giggling in the background and it warmed his body through; without their high jinks he would not have been there experiencing this moment. He remained for a moment longer and then decided that it was time to go. His heart finally settled to its natural resting rate the moment he made the decision, knowing that he wouldn't have to face his fears and speak to her. But as he trawled back through the village, dragging the heels of his boots, an overwhelming despair caught hold of him. He was locked in a nightmare. He knew he would be haunted by Fizz; everything about her would stay with him until the moment he died – those lips, that hair, the sound of her voice, the gentle aroma, the peaceful aura – but he would never have the courage to tell her how he felt. His life, he decided on that sombre walk home, was officially over.

CHAPTER TEN

Noah was the first to arrive at the restaurant and was shown to the table by a waiter with amazing posture and a face that told all who cared to look that he adored his job. He was immaculately presented, from his slick-back hair right down his polished shoes, stopping at precision – almost military – creases on his black shirt and trousers in between. His appearance immediately made Noah straighten himself up as he followed him over to the beautifully set table for four. He had made an effort, with his checked shirt and jeans, but his hair was doing that weird frizz thing again and this guy really made him wish he had spent a little longer in front of the mirror.

Noah lowered himself into a seat looking out into the restaurant and breathed in the heady aroma of Indian cuisine. He was ravenous and the smell was a tease to his watering mouth, but he swallowed hard and tried to forget his tummy. He was permanently ravenous now that he was exercising so often and had got used to putting his hunger to the back of his mind. Looking around, the restaurant clearly had high standards and each table was draped with a crisp, white tablecloth, candles and flowers, which complemented the deep claret décor with subtle impressions of wall-length Hindi Gods cleverly integrated.

Almost every other table, however, was empty. How they managed to stay open on a quiet night like this was a mystery. He doubted that the couple in the corner, who seemed more intent on eating each other's faces than troubling the menu, would put enough in the owner's pockets to cover costs, but then he remembered just how much Thane could eat and knew there was nothing to worry about – and then there was the booze. It had been Charlotte's idea to set up the double date to matchmake Thane with her cousin, Annabel, mostly because she knew Thane wouldn't agree to it otherwise. As it was, Thane was making Noah and Charlotte foot the bill as if he were doing them a favour by attending. Noah had already made it clear that he definitely wasn't paying for the booze, too; Thane could put it away like a thirsty docker. Noah busied himself with these thoughts while watching the door. He had ordered a lime and soda, which came to him a little too tart, but he didn't like to complain, and then he saw the familiar figure of Charlotte through the glass front of the restaurant along with an unfamiliar woman who could only have been Annabel. He saw them before they spotted him and noted that there was a striking family resemblance. They had the same long, dark hair and were even wearing similar green dresses, although Charlotte's was a figure-hugging, lime affair and her cousin's was gathered into layers of an army green hue. Although they were both beautiful, Annabel's subdued charm was no match for the woman he loved. However, as they neared, he could see that Charlotte still looked tired and glazed, as if she shared her bed with ghosts that refused to let her sleep, which, in a roundabout way, she imagined she did. They had managed to snatch a few nights together since that day at the well and Noah had seen the extent to which she was troubled after dark. She either slept fitfully, tossing, turning and mumbling, or she was wide awake and obsessing about her song, tapping out silent notes onto the pillow with her dextrous fingers and digging deep into the forbidden chambers of her psyche for lyrics that would not yield. He tried to be supportive, but he really didn't know what he could do.

He rose to his feet as they entered and as the same handsome waiter showed them to the table, he wished once again that he was half as suave and well turned out. He was definitely fitter and had developed a little more muscle, but he was a gangly lit student at heart and it was difficult to disguise the fact.

'Hello, baby,' Charlotte beamed and threw her arms around him.

'What have I done to deserve this?'

As Charlotte pulled away he could see that she looked even more tired and unwell up close and he figured that this burst of energy and show of affection was her attempt to show the world that she was fine.

'Just letting you know I love you,' she smiled. 'This is Annabel.'

Annabel reached out her hand for Noah to shake. 'Pleased to meet you.' Although it had been a mild day, her hand was cold to the touch. Noah tried not to judge her on it and beckoned them both to sit. 'So,' he began broadly, beginning the conversation before he had actually thought of anything to say and hoping that one of the girls would take over from him. When they just stared at him, his brain saved him with, 'So, you're a med student, Annabel?'

'Guilty,' she smiled. 'I'm actually in the top two percent of student doctors in the country, so it would actually be extremely lucky for you if you choked on your food tonight or perhaps got a touch of food poisoning.' She didn't smile as she spoke, so it was impossible to know if she was joking or not. She was even better-spoken than Noah and had an air of unlikability to her. The arrogance and dark humour really didn't help.

'That would be lucky,' Noah answered, helping her joke along by chuckling as he spoke. 'Thane should be here soon. He's really looking forward to meeting you,' he lied. Thane had already told him that he would rather eat Noah's toenail clippings than meet Charlotte's cousin. Now that Noah had met her he knew for a fact that they wouldn't get on. The woman had only spoken one sentence and he could see she was the opposite of his best friend. Although opposites can attract, he knew that this pairing would be pushing things a little too far.

'Charlotte tells me you're studying literature?'

Noah nodded. 'Yes, and I actually can't be out too late tonight. I've got a big exam tomorrow. I shouldn't be here now really, but ...' He let the 'but' trail as it didn't look as if she was really listening anyway. She nodded distractedly without acknowledging the abrupt end of his sentence and then disappeared behind the menu.

Noah turned to Charlotte and said, 'And how are you, m'lady?'

'Don't call me that!' she snapped.

'Hey! I didn't mean anything by it.'

'It's just ... Nothing. I'm fine, thank you.'

'Are you upsetting my cousin already?' Annabel chipped in. 'I hope Uncle Robert wasn't right about you.' Now she was smiling, but Noah could see the seriousness behind her words.

'I can assure you he was not,' he answered politely, shooting a questioning glance at his girlfriend, then looked down at his watch and said, 'Where is he?'

'Well, he needs to arrive soon. I'm famished and punctuality is so important.'

'I'm sure he won't be long,' Noah assured her and they all cast their eyes down to their menus as they waited. Another ten minutes passed before Thane eventually put in an appearance and surprised everyone with the fact that he hadn't come alone. Noah jumped up and met him at the door to find out what was going on.

'Mate! I'm having a mare,' Thane told him. He was wearing his scarlet Mardridge FC football shirt, jeans and trainers, which clashed against the only accessory he had brought with him – a little girl of nine or ten years old with a shocking mop of blonde curly hair, dressed in a Spiderman costume and carrying a PSP handheld games console.

'And who's this?'

'This is my little sister, Julia.'

The little girl paid no attention as the two of them chatted. Instead, she was getting a game started on the PSP.

'Right. And you've brought her because …?'

'Mate, my mum shows up from nowhere this afternoon, tells me she's off on her jollies and I have to look after Julia for the next month.'

'That's a bit–'

'It's what she's always done, mate. She's a bit of a mess. It's just that I'm usually there to look after the kid. She's got a new boyfriend and it was going well, so I felt all right about coming away to study. God knows what's going on now, but for the time being anyway, Julia's staying with me.'

'Shit, mate, why didn't you tell me any of this before?'

'It's not the sort of thing I want to talk about all the time, mate.'

'No, of course.' Noah turned to Julia and said, 'Hey, I like your Spiderman costume. I hope you like Indian food.'

She looked up from her screen long enough to blow him a raspberry then was back in the thick of her virtual world.

'Charming! What's she playing?'

'Probably Grand Theft Auto.'

'Right.' Noah struggled to know what to say about that, so changed the subject as they made their way over to the table. 'You could have made a bit more effort, mate.'

As a reply, Thane took his sister's cue and blew him a raspberry. 'This was your idea, Noah. Not mine.'

'Actually it was Charlotte's idea and it looks as if her cousin's a nightmare, so good luck!' Noah chuckled and slapped his arm around his friend's shoulder. It was going to be an interesting evening.

The waiter brought another seat over for Julia and she troubled no one as she lowered herself into it without taking her eyes from her screen. The only person who looked truly troubled by her arrival was Charlotte; Noah could tell something was wrong straight away, although she tried to hide it with smiles. He couldn't ask her directly in this company what was troubling her, so he held her hand, stroked her knee, lowered his eyes to her and gave her every non-verbal sign he could think of to show her that he knew she was struggling with something and he was there for her.

'So what are you studying, Thane?' Annabel asked him and Noah was suddenly fascinated by the potential conversation that these two might have.

'Catering. I make a mean green scone.'

Annabel looked down her nose at him as she said, 'And that is …?'

'Well, love, it's a scone that's green.' The shrug that Thane added at the end was classic. The big surprise, however, was that his cheekiness seemed to soften Annabel. Noah had imagined a big battle of wills between these two, but she was smiling genuinely for the first time since he had met her.

'What's in it to make it green?'

'Ah now, that's the big secret.'

'Just food colouring?'

Thane made his hurt face. 'Give me some credit, love.'

'It's Annabel,' she corrected.

'Well, give me some credit, Annabel. My green scones are a culinary marvel. I spit on your green food colouring.' He made fake spitting noises and once again, to Noah's absolute disbelief, Annabel seemed delighted by him. Her cheeks had even flushed a little. She was enjoying his company and if Noah wasn't mistaken, Thane was enjoying hers. Charlotte had been right to pair them up and it really would make life easier for the two of them if Thane was occupied. He also knew that her secret motive was to find a way of stopping Thane leading her boyfriend into stupid situations, like breaking into the bar. And it was working. The food was good, the company was good, it was all going according to plan, but everything was about to change. One minute the night was a raging success and just minutes later it had turned into an absolute nightmare.

'I can't do this anymore!' This was Charlotte. She said it quietly at first, not taking her eyes off Julia, and then dropped her fork in her biriyani and repeated it so loud that even the couple on the other side of the restaurant could hear her.

Noah tried to put his arm around her to comfort her, but she shrugged him away. 'What can't you do anymore?' he asked.

'This!' she barked, and the tears that had been lying in wait throughout the whole meal broke through. Thane and Annabel both looked to her with a mutual mix of surprise and fascination; their characters were more similar that Noah had first thought.

'Just calm down, Charlotte, and tell me what's going on.'

'I'm sorry,' she said, her face now a ruin of tears, then knocked back her chair, raced across the restaurant and was out running into the night.

With no pause for thought, Noah was up, out of his seat, and after her.

'What about the bill?' he heard Thane calling after him, but the only thing on his mind was Charlotte.

'Charlotte! Wait! Please!' he called into the night, whose skies had opened while they had been eating their meals and created a dramatic, thrashing backdrop to their chase. Noah was drenched within seconds of leaving the Indian and struggled to keep Charlotte in his sights ahead of him through the darkness and dismal downpour. But he was pleased once again that he had been training and could keep pace with her easily, before closing in on her and eventually catching up with her near the old well. He held her by the shoulders and demanded she tell him what was happening.

'Don't you see?' she cried. 'It's us. They're us. I mean we're them.'

'You're not making any sense,' Noah replied, he too shouted to be heard over the powerful soundtrack the sky had conspired to deafen them with.

'That little girl, Thane's sister. She's one of them. She's your sister. He's you. I mean you're him.'

'Is this about your dreams, Charlotte? We can get you some help, sort this out.'

'Will you stop saying that? We cannot sort this out!'

For the first time ever, Noah was taken aback by the level of confrontation that he had no idea she possessed. 'I'm sorry. I just want to help you.'

'No, I'm sorry,' Charlotte replied and dropped down beside the well with her head in her hands, sobbing.

Noah dropped down beside her. 'The Pine Comb's just around the corner, Charlotte. We'll both get pneumonia if we stay out here. Let's go and sit and talk about it.'

'But you don't understand!'

'I want to understand. Come on, let's go and get a drink, warm up and I promise I won't interrupt or judge or anything else. Come on.'

Noah was relieved when Charlotte allowed herself to be led along to the other pub in the village. It was also an ancient building, but not quite as old as the Sir Robin's Head and a little more trendy. Charlotte sat shivering in the corner while Noah went to the bar and ordered two brandies, making an exception to his no-drinking rule. They both needed it. When he returned, Charlotte took a glass from him and downed hers in one. Her eyes were fixed down onto the beermats on the table and she was still breathing erratically.

'You just need to get some sleep,' Noah told her. 'You can't go on like this. I've seen it, Charlotte, and I'm worried. You're either sleeping fitfully for a few minutes or obsessing about the song.'

'I thought you were just going to listen to me,' she replied sadly. 'What makes you think you know what I need?'

'I … You're right. I'm sorry. Talk to me.'

'I went to the library,' she began, 'and it all happened, everything in my dream.'

'Really?' Noah picked up his own brandy glass and necked the contents in one. He really needed it now.

'You know about Samuel Mardridge don't you?'

Noah nodded.

'It's him I've been seeing, and his friend Robin and now his true love, her friend, his sister, father. They're all there and it's all happening the way it actually happened.' She paused and Noah remembered not to fill it with his own thoughts on the subject. 'Did you know that Robin killed Lord Samuel?'

Noah nodded. 'The day before his twentieth birthday. Apparently he was jealous of his lover and was beheaded. It's how the pub got its name. I was telling Thane about it the other day.'

'Did you know that his lover threw herself off the castle roof after he died, such was her heartbreak?'

Noah shook his head slowly. 'That's tragic.'

'Don't you see, Noah? It's us.'

'How can it be us?'

'I have no idea, but it is. Why else would I be seeing these things, endlessly, every single night, on a broken loop?'

'I have no idea, but–'

'Please don't say you can get me help again. I don't think I could stand it.'

Noah paused to think of something useful to say. 'So, let me get this right: you're dreaming of the past, but what happened in the past is happening now and we're all the same people – what? – reincarnated?'

'I have no idea,' Charlotte said sadly. 'I only know one thing for certain, that Thane is going to kill you and then it'll be me who throws herself off the roof.' She took a long, deep breath before saying, 'We're all going to die.'

CHAPTER ELEVEN

Athena circled the unicorn as it made the familiar chomping, chewing noises that had been the annoying soundtrack to the last century and a half. She looked it up and down and around as it ate, oblivious to her attention, continuing its infinite, grassy feast as if this were the only skill it possessed. Perhaps it was the only skill it possessed. Perhaps she had imagined the talking. She had been many years in Sam's heaven prototype and perhaps her mind truly was beginning to cave in around her, constructing a companion to entertain her from the only available materials, but then the truth was confirmed.

'Are you just going to stare at me?' the unicorn snapped and stared back at her with scrutiny in its eyes. 'Two can play at that game.'

'Sorry,' Athena eventually conceded and lowered her eyes.

The voice of the unicorn was firm without being unfriendly. There was definitely warmth there, but also a little impatience. In human form it would be difficult to determine if it were the voice of a gentle male or an earthy female. Perhaps a unicorn is both male and female, or maybe gender simply doesn't exist in the fantasy world of the unicorn and they are no more the product of reproduction than a spoonful of glitter or a well-told story. Athena had spent time looking at the unicorn before, many years if the hours and days were added together, and thought she knew the visual landscape of this creature as well as she knew the lines of fortune on the hand-tree's palm, but now it had spoken everything about it seemed different, as if the voice itself had emanated from its fine, white fur and left behind a kaleidoscope of colour; as if each word had fixed itself in its delicate mane, sweeping the hair in new directions; as if the glow of its horn now possessed a rhythm and intensity that her heart was easily able to decode.

'I really wish you had spoken before,' she said gently.

'You too,' said the unicorn. 'I have been lonely.'

'I have spoken before,' she snapped, suddenly affronted.

'Not to me.'

This silenced Athena and the unicorn continued to chomp the grass. This conversation was going to be difficult, so Athena gently lowered herself down onto the grass just metres away. Thankfully, the one thing she had in abundance was time. 'What's your name?' she asked.

'I have no idea.'

'Really? But everyone has a name.'

'Not me.' Suddenly the unicorn stopped its chewing and looked over to Athena with something resembling curiosity. 'How do you get one?'

'Well, usually it is given.'

'Right.' As abruptly as it had stopped, the unicorn began to chew again. Athena had tried chewing the grass once before, just to see what the attraction was, and spat it out immediately.

'I can give you a name if you like.'

'Hmmm!' This time the unicorn didn't bother looking up. 'I'm okay thanks. I've got along this long without one. It doesn't really seem to matter.'

Silence again. Talking to this unicorn was like pulling teeth. 'Do you like it here?' Athena asked, trying a different tack.

'Hmmm!' Again the unicorn didn't look up. 'It's the only place I've ever been, so I haven't really got a point of reference, but the grass is nice and you seem nice, so I think it's okay.'

The compliment gave Athena hope. 'You seem nice too. Are you stuck here?'

'I just am here,' the unicorn told her after a moment of thought, 'like the hand-tree or the river or the sky that doesn't move. We all just are, but let's cut to the chase, shall we? You asked me for help.'

'Did I?' Athena thought back and remembered her scream into the empty recesses of the fantasy sky – 'Someone, please help me!' Could it be that the unicorn was the answer to her prayers? 'You can help me get out of here?'

The unicorn sighed and said, 'The answer is right in front of you.'

Athena leapt up and looked around herself as she had done every day of her imprisonment. All that was right in front of her was hell and she had tried to exploit absolutely every aspect of it to find a way out. She had walked for miles in every direction only to find the landscape repeating itself over and over again and she had even swum the depths of the rainbow lake, which was far deeper than her lungs were spacious. There simply were no answers.

'What did you say before asking for help?' the unicorn asked.

Athena thought back through the angry blur of her discussion with Chrono. 'I said ...' She paused to make sure she had it correct in her mind. 'Love will always prevail.' She took another moment to consider the words. 'So the solution is simply to wait here until Sam succeeds. You heard Chrono. He has fixed it so Sam will never succeed. "It is written!"' she mocked. 'He will stay in his loop and I will stay here.'

'But love will prevail,' the unicorn said firmly. 'You said it yourself.'

'I know, Unicorn, but I cannot see a way forward.'

Finally, the unicorn gave her its full attention, those powerful eyes once again focusing deeply into Athena's soul. 'If love is powerful enough to change the world, might it be powerful enough to influence Chrono?'

'Chrono!? That lump of joyless fate?'

'The very same.'

'But ...' Athena tried, but then she realised that lurking in the shadows of this ridiculous idea was a glimmer of something hopeful. 'But ...' she tried again.

'But love will prevail?'

'But how can I throw him into the path of love's power? I am here and I do not even know of his dwelling or potential matches for him. All I would have is myself and you have seen, Unicorn, he cannot stand the very sight of my face. Are you suggesting that I attempt to trick him into loving me?'

'I am simply suggesting that love always prevails.'

'Is that all the help you can give me?'

'It's more than you had five minutes ago.'

'That's true. Thank you,' she said warmly and reached out to stroke the unicorn.

'I don't really like being stroked,' the creature replied and Athena withdrew her hand. 'No offence, but I'm just not much of a touchy-feely animal.'

'My apologies.' Athena couldn't help smiling. She had no idea that the unicorn would be such a complicated character. What must have been going on in its mind for the last silent century and a half? 'Okay, if I'm going to do this I need a plan. For a start, how could I get Chrono to return to this place?'

'That's no problem,' Unicorn answered. 'Leave that to me.'

'Okay, excellent. So the big problem is how on earth I would trick him into loving me. How do people get other people to love them? I always thought that it just happened and it hasn't happened for Chrono, so I have my work cut out for me.' Athena pulled out a blade of the emerald grass and felt it shatter in her fingertips, her face beautiful as her mind danced with her dilemma. 'Mirroring!' she suddenly said. 'I have heard it said. If you act as a mirror, reflecting the actions and movements of the man, he can see a sympathetic soul and falls in love. Sounds a little narcissistic to me. I fancy I would need a magic mirror anyway. What else?' She was talking as if the unicorn had ceased to exist now, in the style she had developed in nearly 150 years of solitude. 'Gifts? Cooking dinner? Meeting his desires? Interesting myself in that which interests him? Offering exactly what he needs? That's it!' she yelped. 'I will offer my services to him in the capacity of ...? This I do not know, but I will make myself useful too him – indispensable – and he will not fail to fall in love with me. And as a backup I will ...' She looked down to the grazing unicorn. 'Are you listening to me?'

'Yes, you sound like something from Cosmo Magazine, which will be available on earth in the future.'

'You can tell the future?'

'I suppose I can,' replied the unicorn as if it had just realised.

'So what happens?'

'Well,' the unicorn gave it some thought. 'In 1886 a magazine called Cosmopolitan will be launched, which will eventually mould itself around the fashion and needs of women.'

'I meant what will happen with me?'

'Oh that? No, I have no idea.'

'I've got it!' Athena suddenly beamed. 'A love potion! There is no possible way that Chrono will love me for who I am. I need a love potion. Any ideas, Unicorn?'

'Are you sure that's a good idea. You know, in light of–'

'It's a great idea. Do you know how I could make one?'

'No, but you could try asking the river.'

'The river?'

'Yup!'

'You have got to be kidding me.'

At the river's edge, Athena dropped to her hands and knees and stared into the colourful water. 'Er, hello!' she tried and again she felt somehow cheated when she received an answer. The unicorn and the river would have seen her despair over the years. Did they really need to be directly spoken to to converse with her? This time she didn't bother posing the question. Hope was slowly replacing the frustration and she had to keep the river onside.

'Hell … oooo!' the river replied in a suitably flowy voice.

'Er, hellooooo!' Athena leaned further over the edge, but saw no shift in the surface. 'Sorry to disturb you, but the unicorn said that you might be able to help me.'

'Hell … ooo!'

'Yes, hello. Can you hear me? Can you hear what I'm saying?'

'Hell … ooo!'

'This is hopeless.' She dropped back onto her bottom and could feel the familiar rising of despair.

'Just ask for what you want,' she heard in the distance and saw that the unicorn was calling out to her.

Again, Athena pushing herself forward and looked into the water, which was actually quite beautiful as long as the surface wasn't disrupted, when of course the colours would simply run into each other and it would look more like a sewer than a fantasy lake. 'Please do you think you might be able to help me with a love potion?' she asked sheepishly and waited for a reply. Initially there was nothing and then she heard, 'Hell … ooo!' She was about to huff again about how useless this was but then ripples began to appear on the water. However, these were ripples unlike any she had seen before. Instead of the colours merging, they had separated and assembled in an order dictated by the rainbow so that it truly was an astounding, magical sight. In the centre of the ripples was a bubbling and then the surface was suddenly and dramatically broken by an item rising from the depths of the water. Athena moved closer still to see that it was a potion bottle, shimmering glass with a spherical lid. She reached out to take it and the moment it was extracted from the river the water returned to its natural, resting swirls of colour. She looked down at the bottle, but then her attention returned hopefully to the water. 'River,' she began again. 'I need a table and table cloth, chairs, candles, plates, cutlery, wine glasses, and some form of romantic music.'

All at once the river began to tremble and items emerged up and down its length. As she retrieved each one in turn she was suddenly grateful for Sam's imagination. And then another thought occurred to her.

'River, I need a gateway out of this place.'

Nothing happened for a moment, and then nothing happened for another moment, and then the river said, 'Hell ... ooo!' And then all was quiet and still.

'Oh well,' Athena shrugged. 'It was worth a try.'

She assembled the collection of items under the shadow of the hand-tree, whom she was certain she could manipulate into making shadow shapes over them as they ate – animals, birds, hearts. There was no way this could fail. She would ask the river for some suitable food closer to the time. Suddenly, thoughts of food filled her head. She hadn't eaten for nearly 150 years. Of course, she didn't need to eat, but she could almost taste succulent chicken and sweet, moist cake as ideas of eating filled her mind. She would return to the river after she had set the table and ask for some tasters so she could organise the most romantic feast in history – and so she had an excuse to indulge her culinary fantasies. Before she had finished, however, the unicorn appeared at her side, or that was how it seemed. It made no sound and then it was suddenly just there, making her jump.

'Sorry, Athena,' it said softly. 'I didn't mean to frighten you. I thought you would like to know that I have organised the return of Chrono at the earliest possible opportunity.'

'Great! This is wonderful. Thank you so much, Unicorn. I must organise the food immediately.'

'He will return in exactly one hundred years.'

CHAPTER TWELVE

S am slowly opened his eyes and didn't know where he was at first. Actually, it would be more accurate to say he didn't know when he was and the confusion made his bed chamber look unfamiliar. It was dark enough for a gloomy veil to have descended, tweezing ebony shadows out from behind his dresser, chair and chest, trading their appearance for something eerie and unnatural. However, it wasn't midnight black; it could have been early morning or early evening. The time dilemma was unaided by the fact that he couldn't remember going to bed in the first place. And then he felt the throbbing headache and a few things came back to him. Number one: Fizz; she would forever be his first thought now. Number two: Fizz's father; if a man could be judged on his voice alone, this man was as tall, wide and strong as the stack of barrels in his cellar, and he wanted Sam dead. Number three … number three? No, there was no number three, just a loose thread of thought that revolved around discovering that his nose was extremely painful and had been bleeding, realising that the booze had worn off and he was now extremely hungover, pinpointing the time to about seven in the evening because he could hear merry being made in the hall below, and filling in the gaps with a reasonable hypothesis about staggering home and putting himself to bed. Number four: The banquet. It was for him and it had obviously begun downstairs without him.

He leapt out of bed, lit the lamp and summoned a servant to help him dress. Unbelievably, not more than thirty minutes later, he was completely transformed, standing before the mirror looking every bit the handsome knight. His scarlet, buckled shoes shone up at him as he inspected himself from the bottom up, past ivory tights and a strong black codpiece and doublet, slashed into scarlet to match his shoes, the cloak that hung from his shoulders and a velvet embroidered waistcoat. His ivory sleeves were magnificently full and attention had been paid to the small details: the belt, jewellery and a scarlet cap with a deep red feather atop his golden curls. Despite all of the finery, however, Sam failed to smile as he stood before the mirror. He wasn't the most confident of young men anyway and would never see the beauty that others saw in him, but on this day his head was so full of unworthiness – for Fizz, or any other woman, and for the banquet held in honour of his deception – that he wished for nothing more than to throw on his old breeches, wander out to the old animal house, look up at the clouds through the cracks on the ceiling and drift off into thought. The very last thing he felt like doing was facing whatever lay ahead in the great hall, but he really had no other choice.

Each step he took was slower than the last, delaying the moment of his arrival for as long as he could. Each step was also louder than the last as he neared what sounded like a raucous feast in the great hall, with harpsicords and viols filling the air with cheerful tunes for dancing, and the chatting, shouting and belly laughing of those in attendance who must have numbered in their hundreds. When he could delay the moment no longer, he stepped though the mighty archway and his arrival wouldn't have had greater impact had he detonated a tripwire causing heavy netting to fall on the guests, sweeping them all of their feet. The music stopped with the abruptness of a musician's heart attack, those dancing skidded to a standstill, whispers followed and then all eyes were on him. And then, all at once, with clockwork precision, faces were alight, the band recovered for an even jauntier tune, hands were slapped together and the room was filled with cheers and calls of his name. Sam may have enjoyed the attention more if his brain wasn't splitting, but he wasn't sure it would have made much difference. This was a shy man's worst nightmare. His face instantly coloured and he could manage only a thin smile.

'Here he is! Here he is!'

Again Sam's legs nearly buckled as his father threw his arm around him and dragged him over to the long table at the head of the hall, where he would be visible to every knight, nobleman, lord and lady in the room, in their immaculate dresses and doublets that spun out into a kaleidoscope of colour when the room broke into dance.

'Ladies and gentlemen – my son!' he boomed proudly, holding Sam tighter still and more cheers erupted. 'In two weeks we ride for the pride of Mardridge! We ride out men and return heroes!'

More cheers, this time deep, male, hero cheers from the army that would ride out with them and risk their lives for honour. Now Sam was seriously struggling to steady himself as the smell of cooked animal carcasses, roasted vegetables and wine collided with the last dregs of alcohol in his system and the woozy-making cheers from those who now looked to him to lead them. He couldn't lead a drunk to an ale house without some unforeseen issue arising; what chance did he have leading an army to victory in a war he did not understand, with weapons he could not use and a heart made for poetry?

'Ladies, gentlemen! Gentlemen!' Lord Mardridge repeated, attempting to regain the attention of the riotous guests, whom he had filled with the spirit of war and had broken into their chants of honour. 'If I may have your attention for just a moment longer.' Again all heads turned to Lord Mardridge who was dressed similarly to his son, in scarlet and ivory, but his fur cape hung dramatically behind him – the second skin of a warrior – and his bushy beard disguised any resemblance that may have existed between them. 'My son is not aware of this, but we have a surprise for him this evening.'

Sam's heart sank and he turned to meet his mother's eyes. He had hoped for some kind of support, a smile that said, 'Don't worry, son. Go with it and we can resolve all of this later on,' but her eyes told another story. They were narrowed and piercing and said to him, 'I know all about your abandoned duties today and getting drunk instead. Whatever happens now is your own fault.' When she was sure he had understood the look, she turned away and sunk her teeth into an impossibly massive turkey leg. She was not happy.

'My heart soared with pride when I saw this young man atop his horse yesterday and gain his first jousting victory. He is a true knight through and through and we all know what a true knight needs.'

Sam was barely listening. He was using each second to send little prayers out into the world, appealing for this ordeal to be over. However, Lord Mardridge's next words came through loud and clear.

'Yes, every true knight needs a wife.'

A great cheer from the assembled crowd and then the room began to spin. No! This couldn't be happening. Every true knight might need a wife, but Sam was not every true knight; he was a delicate soul, a devotee of true love. This could not be happening.

'May I introduce you to the future Lady Mardridge: Princess Jane of the Dales.'

Another great cheer and almost as if rehearsed, all heads turned back to the great archway and standing in the stone-brick entranceway was a slender, blonde, tall woman, smiling confidently to the crowd as if born to the stage. She looked radiant in a figure-hugging, lacy, emerald frock and golden kirtle, and a headdress that stood tall and proud on her head with jewels shimmering down onto her forehead. Lord Mardridge had picked well; she was simply breath-taking.

'The wedding is set to take place in two weeks, on the eve of the great battle. Now raise your glasses in toast to the happy couple.' As the room filled with the clinking of glasses, Lord Mardridge gave his son's shoulder a final firm squeeze before letting him go. 'Now, eat, drink and be merry! On with the music!' At his command, the room reanimated into a scene of excess, with couples dancing as if this were their last night on the planet, eating as if there would be no more food in the morrow and drinking wine like water on a sunny day. The castle was renowned throughout the country for its parties and this looked to be the best one yet. The only people not getting into the party spirit were Sam and his mother, who managed to catch him before he could even think of escaping.

It was clearly Lady Mardridge from whom Sam had inherited his looks. With her signature scarlet outfit, the colour adopted by the whole family for this occasion, and youthful looks, she could still turn heads in court, but not in the presence of Lord Mardridge if they wanted to remain on their shoulders.

'Just what do you think you were playing at today?' she asked, gritting her teeth behind a smile for anyone who happened to be watching, and dragged her son away from the table.

'I can explain,' Sam told her.

'Can you?'

'No.' Sam lowered his head.

'I'm so disappointed, Sam. You can't go on acting like this. I sent you out to work to give you a sense of responsibility and you've let me down. You can't go on floating through life. I understand that you are a gentle soul, but it doesn't preclude you from the life we all have to live.'

'I thought you understood me, Mother.'

She paused, incredulous, for a moment before saying, 'Are you listening to me at all, Sam? You can be anything you want, but we all have to exist together. I cannot help you if you do not help me.' It was during conversations such as these, when Sam was in trouble, that he recognised what a powerful woman she was. He was lucky she was his mother; to have her onside was a blessing; to have her as an enemy was to be on the losing side. However, he could see something in his mother that he hadn't been party to before – impatience, intolerance, a fraying of the bond between them and it panicked him.

'But, Mother.'

'No, Sam. This is all too much. You are leaving a trail behind you and I can no longer help to clear it. You need to appease the landlord of the ale house and the farmer and more importantly, you need to find a way of getting out of leading the army that does not break your father's heart. I can no longer protect you, Sam, unless you prove worthy.'

'But I am worth–'

'Enough! The one good thing to come today is that you are to become a man. I suggest you go and meet your bride and try not to mess that up too.'

Sam took a deep breath and said, 'I cannot marry her.' The expression on his mother's face was already terrifying, but he had to be honest. 'My heart is with another, Mother. I will not marry her.'

Lady Mardridge gripped Sam's arm and led him out of the hall. When they had reached a spot where they could no longer be overheard, she let him have it. 'Let me tell you how this is going to go, Sam, because I love you too much to allow you to traverse the path you are now choosing.' Now Sam hardly recognised her and would trade anything he owned and loved for the chance to replay the day and do things differently, not let her down and unleash her wrath. He had no idea she would be so upset. 'You are going to go back in there with a smile on your face. You are going to spend the evening talking to your new bride and you are going to thank your father for the union. Am I making myself clear, young man?'

'But–'

'Am I making myself clear?'

'Yes, Mother.' Again Sam lowered his head like a shamed adolescent and dragged his heels back into the hall. He had never felt so trapped and now his only ally in the castle had lost faith in him too. The only positive to come from the evening was the fact that he was able to speak to a beautiful woman for the first time without stuttering, reddening or making a fool of himself. However, the only reason he was able to do this was because his heart was with Fizz. He had no care for whether Princess Jane of the Dales thought him foolish or ignorant or ugly or unworthy; why would he care what she thought? Consequently, when he made his way back into the hall and joined her, he clearly made a strong impression. He wasn't rude to her, but he was hardly warm and welcoming, and the more distant and aloof he presented himself, the more interested in him she became.

He opened by asking her questions about herself, fuelled by the watchful eyes of his mother: how old was she? Eighteen. Was she having a pleasing evening? Very much so. Had she had a good day? Yes, etc., etc. He eventually ran out of empty questions and wanted to be quiet, so he simply stood beside her decoratively, trying to will the evening to an end. His future bride, however, had other ideas.

'You must be very heroic to lead your army,' she swooned.

Sam gave her a pained smile, nodded and tried to be quiet again.

'I'll wager you are a very brave man.'

Again he didn't have an answer to give her.

'You are incredibly handsome. You will make a fine husband, but I must warn you, m'lord, I am accustomed to the finer things in life.' She stood just a little taller as she told him this. 'If you are to be my husband I have certain expectations. The first is that I receive a gift every single day. This is important. If you do not lavish me with gifts I will be unsure of your love for me. And I expect to be taken around the world …'

As she continued her list of demands for her future husband, a thought suddenly struck Sam. Where was Robin? He hadn't seen his face amongst the crowds and if he were there, he wouldn't have been able to resist coming over and rubbing Sam's face in this new mess. He would know that this brash blonde was not for him, even if his father was blind to the needs of his son.

'…And I prefer gold to silver and diamonds to rubies–'

'Sorry, m'lady, could you excuse me for just one moment?' Sam interrupted as he saw Jennifer clip-clop by, neighing and galloping in a world of her own. 'Wait a moment!' he called and followed her out into the hallway where moments before his mother had opened her heart to her disappointment. Jennifer was bright red and sweating. She had been put in a scarlet, velvet dress, but had already managed to ruin it with mud. She had obviously been clip-clopping out into the grounds with her village friends. 'I fear you will be in trouble when Mother sees your dress.'

'I fear you are in trouble already,' Jennifer mocked.

'How did you know that?'

She tapped the side of her nose and giggled then became suddenly serious and said, 'Hey, Sam. Can you keep a secret?'

Sam didn't really have time for games, but he always tried to be a good brother to Jennifer and nodded conspiratorially.

'Look!' she said and pulled a razor-sharp dagger out from under her dress. It glimmered in the light, revealing the ferociousness of its teeth.

'What are you doing with that?' he snapped and she began to swing it around like a toy. 'What are you doing? You will hurt yourself, or someone else. What is wrong with you?'

Jennifer's face dropped then she said. 'I am going to be a warrior like you.'

'Where did you get it from?' Sam put his hand out to take it, but she was still swinging it and nearly hit him. 'Stop, Jennifer. This is not funny. It is dangerous. Where did you get it?'

'I borrowed it from one of the village boys. I think it is the best thing in the world ever.'

'Listen to me carefully,' Sam said, finally managing to take it from her. 'I never want to see you with this in your hand again. Do you hear me? Or any other weapon.'

'But–'

'No buts. I am going to hold onto this and you can take me to the boy who gave it to you tomorrow.'

'Sam!' she groaned.

'I love you too much to let you hurt yourself,' he said and could hear echoes of his mother's voice in his own, so he suddenly stopped himself. He then tried to lighten the mood by saying, 'I have a new word for you,' but Jennifer folded her arms and refused to be cheered.

'I have a new word for you too,' she said, 'but I do not think you will like it.'

'There is no need to be like that, Jennifer. I only followed you to see if you had seen Sir Robin on your travels. I am very glad that I did now.'

'If I tell you where he is, can I have my knife back?'

'How about if you tell me I will tell Mother and Father nothing of what you have been up to.'

Jennifer thought for a moment then nodded grudgingly. 'He is not here,' she said.

'That much I knew.'

'He has a new girlfriend and he is taking her out for cuddles tonight.'

Sam smiled – he should have known – but as quickly as it arrived, the smile dropped and panic soared through him. 'How do you know? Who told you?' he demanded and grabbed Jennifer's shoulders.

'My friends in the village told me. Ow, Sam!'

'Sorry,' he replied, realising he was perhaps holding her a little too tightly, but his mind had been taken over by a new but inevitable truth. It would be just like Robin to sneak behind his back, snake in the grass that he was. 'Please tell me, Jennifer. Do you know the name of his new girlfriend?'

Jennifer shook her head seriously. 'Are you okay, Sam? Can I go now?'

'Do you know anything about her?'

'The boys in the village said she is from the ale house,' she told him then clip-clopped her way down the hallway and back out onto the grounds as if the information she had given him wasn't the most crushing blow he had received in his entire life.

Chapter Thirteen

O ne hundred years is a long time. Whichever way you look at it, a
century is a huge chunk of time, and to be left alone in a fantasy
heaven, waiting to dine with a guardian of fate in the hope of tricking
him into romance for one hundred years, is not an experience that
many would relish. However, after waiting for forty years, sleeping for
fifty years and crying for another fifty years, Athena had become
accustomed to living life at a slower pace and this time, at least she had
hope; in just one hundred years' time she could potentially take control
of her own fate and take the first step to freedom. And this century had
additional advantages over the time that had already passed in the
heady fantasy world from hell; for a start, she now had a companion in
the unicorn. They would both concede that the word companion was
quite a strong word and would be overstating their relationship, as the
unicorn mostly just grazed and often made it painfully clear that he or
she really just wanted to be left alone. But at least there was another
living consciousness in this heaven to stop Athena from reaching the
point of absolute insanity.

The real scoop of course was the river. Although its lexicon was
restricted to one word – a flowy, sometimes haunting 'Hell … ooo!' – it

had the power to offer her anything she wanted. At first she asked for different foods; she asked for everything she loved – fresh fruit, chocolate, champagne – and then she asked for all of the foods she had never sampled before – biltong, stollen, celeriac – and then she even asked for foods that she didn't particularly like just because she could – anything involving garlic, onions or mint. This amused her for several days and then she began to ask for things to further amuse herself – a deck of cards, a chess set, puzzles, pens, paper, etc. She now had a ton to items with which to occupy herself; now she needed something resembling a home. She asked the river for this and received panels that easily slotted together, creating a tiny, yet beautiful, princessy castle with space for a bed and a few possessions. She constructed it on the banks of the river and then asked for everything she would need to fill it. The strange nature of this place meant that the moment she erected the little castle she could see more little castles in the distance – four castles, one in each direction. At first the phenomenon confused her and she ran to the eastern castle, but she really should have realised what had happened. She already knew that the landscape repeated itself in all directions. So when she reached a new castle it was exactly the same as hers – it was hers – and still there were castles in all four directions. In her more philosophical moments, she wondered if there was a facsimile her in each of the castles, mimicking her movements exactly. But of course she would never know because when she left her castle, the copies would leave theirs. Sometimes these thoughts made her head hurt, but the upshot of all of this was that time was passing.

After ninety-nine years, Athena returned her attention to the meal and Chrono. She thought back to their conversation, as she had often done over the years, and doubt gripped her. How could she make this man love her? His words rang in her head – 'You are a ridiculous creature.' Was she ridiculous? She sat by the water's edge on her chaise longue wearing a sombrero she had ordered from the river, sipping an oversized cocktail. Was it really so ridiculous to believe in the power of love? Was it really so ridiculous to want to help people and make them happy? She took a fruity, champagney gulp and smiled. If believing in love made her ridiculous then so be it. But then maybe she had changed since the last time he had seen her. Maybe she had matured or hardened or there was now something in her that would soften his heart. She wouldn't feel it, but change is often more apparent to the observer.

'River, I would like some puppets,' she suddenly asked as the idea interrupted her thoughts of Chrono. And within seconds the river had helloooed and three funny, floppy puppets were floating on the surface. She grabbed them vacantly and tossed them in the general direction of all the other stuff she had amassed, which was becoming quite a pile, and returned to her thinking. Perhaps he would have changed. Many things can happen in a century. Perhaps his own trials would have opened his mind to her plight. Or – and Athena believed this to be far more likely – what if he had hardened? He was a devout servant of the higher powers, which was not an easy position to take when he was responsible for the fate of so many of earth's creatures. The only way a guardian would be able to continue when faced with daily tragedy and injustice, such as those freely administered by higher powers, would be to fortify the self against emotion. Yes, Athena conceded, if Chrono had changed at all he would now be harder and she would have her work cut out to melt his heart. Thankfully, she had the love potion.

On the day of the meal, Athena spent many hours in front of the mirror, discovering which of her expressions she imagined would be the most captivating to Chrono and which styling of hair gave her the most alluring appearance. Eventually, she decided that simply allowing her hair to naturally cascade was the best option; it was still as vibrant and bursting with autumn shades as it had ever been and she hoped it would add to her appeal. She had no control over the clothes she would wear, as the butterflies forming her dress were as much a part of her as the nose on her face. And, of course, there was definitely something fantastical about a dress formed of fluttering butterflies and she eventually concluded that she was as ready as she would ever be. The dining table had been waiting under the hand-tree for a century, the fingers of which she had persuaded to slowly sway to and fro, giving the impression of the existence of an atmosphere in a place that had as much natural ambience as a child's drawing. The table was set with a prawn cocktail starter and a glass of champagne (spiked with the love potion). As she lowered herself onto the ornate, antique-looking chair, a waft of expensive perfume rising up in a cloud, she could just discern a figure on the horizon. It was him. After one-hundred years of waiting, he had returned. As she watched him move towards her, one by one his features came into focus: the long, infinitely toned hair tumbling down his shoulders and behind him as one long, confident stride followed another, followed another, stretching the fabric of his sarong to its limit, the smooth, chiselled chest and arms, somehow coloured from a sun that his body would not have been exposed to for years; and finally that serious expression. No, he hadn't changed, and the familiarity of him made Athena's heart leap; familiarity breeds fondness and a part of her wanted to run over to him and hug him and kiss him simply because his was a face she had seen before and here it was again after so long with only the unicorn and river to share her time.

'You sought a second audience with me?' he said in a deep, serious voice as he arrived before her. She had walked from the table to the bridge to greet him.

'Yes, Chrono, and thank you for obliging me. I realise your tasks make consuming demands on your time.'

Chrono subtly nodded his head in agreement. It was going well. Actually, it wasn't going well; he still looked as if her existence irritated him, but at least he was remaining calm and hadn't drawn attention to the fact that she was ridiculous yet.

'It was my wish to offer my sincere apologies for the inconvenience I have caused you in my handling of Sam's fate. I see my error now.' She dropped her hands onto the railing, turning slightly from Chrono and looking down into the rainbow lake. 'I have had much time to consider my actions.'

Chrono was silent for a moment before moving to her side. 'I accept your apology, Athena, and you have risen in my estimations for your strength of character. Lesser angels would insist upon begging for their freedom after such isolation and your composure is a credit to you.'

You have risen in my estimations? Love was still as distant to Chrono as freedom was to Athena. She would have to pull out the big guns.

'I have prepared a meal – a peace offering. I would be honoured if you would oblige me with your presence.'

'But we have no need of food,' Chrono said, curiosity moulding his features. Had she failed already with fanciful notions of needless eating?

Her head filled with the grand angel's voice, who had told her that the absence of those things deemed unnecessary – good food, ideas, literature, love – could be just as damaging as the absence of the essentials. Instead of telling him this, she simple said, 'Indulge me.'

Chrono tried an unconvincing smile, but if he had a watch he would have looked at it at that moment. Athena could tell he was counting the minutes in his mind until he could leave, but there was a kindness in him that precluded him from refusing her and he allowed himself to be led to the table. Athena then motioned for him to take a seat and, ever polite, he bowed courteously and lowered himself opposite her. She watched as he scrutinised the glass dish in front of him, with its salad leaves, curls of meaty prawns and pink sauce, with the expression of a man who didn't know what to do with them. Athena picked up her fork and tasted one of the prawns and now Chrono was scrutinising her – the circling movement of her jaw, the delight rising on her features, the bulging shuffle of her throat as she swallowed.

'Please, try it. It is good,' she told him and Chrono finally took the fork in his hand and poked it into a prawn and some leaves. The expression on his face when he tasted the mouthful was beyond anything Athena had imagined; a light flicked on and he was a small boy again, the years of fate and death falling off him.

'Good?' she asked and for a moment he was speechless and simply nodded before taking another bite. He then took another and another until the bowl was empty and all that remained were vague lines of sauce after he had scraped the inside with his fork. 'You haven't eaten before have you?' Athena asked.

'Don't be absurd, child. Of course I have eaten.' But she could tell he was lying. This guardian had experienced nothing that was unnecessary in the centuries of his existence; he had existed simply to serve the greater powers. Of course, she said none of this. She had waited one hundred years for this opportunity and was determined not to ruin it by deviating from her plan and upsetting him.

'Try the champagne. It is a good vintage.'

Again his eyes were aglow as they fell upon the fizz, but this time he tried to hide his excitement and show her that this was something he did all the time. He clearly had champagne for breakfast, lunch and dinner, and having it now would be commonplace. She could see right through him, but this was less important than the secrets contained within the bubbles. She had saved the love potion for a whole century, since that first day the river had said, 'Hell ... ooo!' and started to furnish her with anything her heart desired and now she finally had cause to use it.

Chrono brought the glass to his lips and his nose twitched eagerly, either the fizzy bubbles tickling him or the ripe aroma of the love potion reaching his nostrils. He flashed a glance at Athena then closed his eyes and slugged the whole glass back. When the champagne had disappeared and the glass was back on the lace-edged tablecloth, he released a mighty, 'Ahhhhh!' and had he been on his own he would probably have belched. As Athena watched, she felt a warmth for the guardian that she couldn't have imagined just five minutes before. She almost wished that she too had never tasted champagne before and was experiencing it for the first time with him, but they were exact opposites; he was disciplined and restrained; she was passionate and liked to indulge her desires. She knew she couldn't have lived without experiencing the rushing bubbles on her tongue or the feel of sand and sea over her toes, or brain-freeze from ice-cream, or the sting of nettles on a summer's day, because feeling pain was better than feeling nothing. Again, she pushed her wandering thoughts to the back of her mind; he had drunk the champagne, the potion was inside of him, now all she had to do was wait.

Chapter Fourteen

Sam gripped the reins tightly and screamed into the night for Pinecomb to run faster still as the rain powered down a deafening cacophony, drenching them both and blinding them to the treacherous road ahead, but still Sam pushed, standing rigid in the stirrups and whipping the reins furiously. He wasn't a strong horseman, but his own safety was the last thing on his mind, and it was a mind that had switched into a gear with which Sam was unfamiliar. He was stuck in a loop and the events of the last few days were playing over and over again: jousting, lying, laughing with Robin, his mother, carrots, ale, lots of ale, his mother again, this time furious with him; had he lost her love? And Fizz. Every time Fizz came back to him he yanked the reins with even more force and 'Yah'ed at Pinecomb, demanding more speed. His Fizz, his beautiful Fizz. Of course she couldn't be blamed; they hadn't even met properly, she had no allegiance to him; although she wasn't the woman he thought if she could be so easily persuaded into the sack. No, it was Robin who was at fault. He had teased Sam with threats of bedding Fizz, but Sam hadn't believed he could swoop so low.

'Yah!' he screamed again and suddenly felt the weight of the dagger tucked in his belt. He had taken it from Jennifer and ridden out without considering its presence, but now he knew exactly what he would do with it. If Robin had betrayed him, as his little sister had implied, this would be his last night on earth.

After almost half an hour of furious riding, Sam dismounted into the country darkness before Pinecomb had even ground to a complete halt and marched the remaining few steps to the dilapidated animal house in which he had shared a lifetime of adventures with Robin. He knew this would be where he would take her, even in this weather – especially in this weather; it would be atmospheric, and cold and eerie enough for a girl to warm up to him pretty quickly. As Sam marched, oblivious to the dowsing he was receiving, rain pounding his face and drenching his clothing, he could see candlelight from within and his hand instinctively reached for the dagger. His step quickened. He had never felt this way before and understood for a split second how it must feel to be a warrior, to be the kind of man his father wanted him to be. As he got closer, his fears were finally confirmed. Even over the thrash of the rain battering the rotten wood of the animal house, the howling wind and the angry screams in Sam's head, he could hear them – groaning, panting, sighing, calling out to each other as they made love. Sam gripped the dagger tightly and stopped outside the threshold. His heart was beating so furiously he could hear it over the din that man and nature had conspired to create all around him. He finally took a deep breath, stepped into the room and now there was no denying it. In what must have been the only dry corner of a structure that let in more rain than it kept out, his beloved Fizz, completely naked, was on top of his best friend, upright, straddling, grinding, groaning, her head lowered to his face before she threw it back in ecstasy. Sam had rehearsed the moment over and over as he rode through the rain and powered towards the animal house, but all he felt now was sadness and he silently withdrew before either could be alerted to his presence.

'Yah!' Before he knew it, he was back on the horse and riding painfully fast. This time there was no destination attached to the ride. His only mission was to ride as hard and fast as he could in the hope of purging what he had witnessed from his heart and somehow reassembling himself in the unforgiving night. 'Yah! Yah!' he wailed again and he could feel the power of Pinecomb's legs pushing them onwards, faster than either of them had ever ridden before. But he wanted more. He was nearing a point of transformation and although he didn't know what would happen when he hit it, he knew that he had to keep pushing towards it and he knew that everything would be different when he reached it. On and on they rode, faster and faster. Sam could almost believe that they could take off and fly together, transcending all of the troubles facing him and galloping off into another world. Either that or his head would literally explode when the transition point was reached. The rain was still relentless in its assault but it seemed to make no difference to Sam that he couldn't see the road in front of him. He had no need to see when he knew that it – whatever it was – was coming. And then the moment arrived. Pinecomb's legs stopped moving all at once, buckling and locking at the impossibly abrupt stop, but Sam couldn't contain the momentum soaring through him and his body continued to travel, over Pinecomb's head and down to the ground, cracking and smashing every bone in his body in a crippling thud. Only, for some reason, Sam didn't land. It all happened too fast for his mind to understand. He was flying, floating, gliding, soaring. Was he dead? It was only when he tried to breathe and couldn't that his mind began to grasp what had happened. The horse had pulled up sharp at the edge of a river or lake and he had been thrown into it. For a moment, he allowed his body to float under the surface and this truly did feel like the cleansing transformation he had envisaged. Such a perfect silence he had never experienced and he was in no hurry to return to the chaos of the night and his own internal carnage. The motion of his body was also soothing and he allowed himself to be guided by a greater consciousness, as the water gently pulled him this way and that. After he has been submerged for close to a minute, his lungs strained to remind him that he was a land creature and should begin to swim to the surface. He slowly began to kick his feet and sweep his arms upwards, but progress was slow. He must have been deeper than he imagined, but he remained calm. He was a strong swimmer, both on top and underneath the water, and he knew that panicking would be the signature on his death warrant. On he swam, ever upwards, his lungs now screaming at him, but he maintained his calm and his belief that he could make it. However, all of his resolve crumbled when his hands fell upon a thick, winding, green mesh that formed a layer between him and the surface. The momentum of his body had powered him through the viney weeds on his way into the depths of the water, but he had nothing of that force on the way up and would now have to fight to free himself. He dug his hands into the thick vegetation and tried to create a hole large enough to swim up through, but all he could create was a small space large enough for his arm. However, determined not to give in, he forced his arm into the space and tried to use his shoulder to lever a bigger gap. All he succeeded in doing was trapping himself amongst vines that seemed to have a life of their own, and now he could neither move up nor down and a scorching pain had reached into his head and was gripping his brain. He had felt it before when he stayed underwater too long. It was the brain's way of screaming to him, 'Get out! Breathe!' But this time he had no choice. Every time he tried to move he became even more stuck. He was no longer in control. And then, on the brink of unconsciousness, with death beating a path towards him, a hazy shape appeared before him. It was too dark to see clearly, but as it neared it brought with it a faint, unnatural glow and Sam began to discern a face. It was a woman, a beautiful woman with a beautiful face – full, voluptuous lips and the softest, gentlest eyes Sam had ever seen – untroubled by the fact that she too was stuck underwater, but her body was a blur of movement that made no sense and her hair was also impossible to fathom, with its unending, glowing shades that illuminated the waters and also seemed to form part of the weeds above. She was examining his face closely and then her own broke into a smile and Sam felt the pain in his head ease slightly. She was nodding now, smiling and nodding, telling him that everything would be okay and as if her words had reached into Sam and soothed his soul, he really did feel his body relaxing. He was still caught up in the greenery, still holding his breath with little chance of being able to take another, but peace descended over his entire body and he absorbed the perfection of her presence one last time before everything suddenly went black.

Sam sucked deeply at the air and felt its freshness fill his lungs as his senses returned to his body. He took another rich, deep breath, followed by another and another, and hardly dare open his eyes. As his awareness developed, he felt the cold of the hard ground beneath his body and was aware that he was still being ambushed by rain. He wiggled his fingers and moved his feet then began to bring movement into his legs and arms, testing their existence and solidity – they were there and they were real. He was alive. It just wasn't possible. The next thing to do was open his eyes, but he hardly dared look upon a world that had stopped making sense when a woman had appeared to him underwater. None of this was possible. He should have been dead, and he would be if he lay there in the freezing cold for much longer, so he slowly peeked out into the night and the first thing he saw was the might of the full moon overlooking everything with its knowing calm. He took another deep breath and felt that he might cry – not through sadness; euphoria was rising in him – with the overwhelming awe he was feeling. The moon and its majesty seized him with its magnificence. The finality of the darkness and the speckles of hope in the sky, twinkling around the moon, overpowered him with their brilliance. Such a scene could surely not have existed before this remarkable moment and Sam felt a monumental smile creeping across his face. He took another deep breath and closed his eyes tightly to force away the rain, but when he opened them this time the awe-inspiring view was blocked by a shape he could feel on his cheek before he could see clearly. Pinecomb was pushing his long face into Sam's and licking his cheek to rouse him.

'It's okay, boy,' Sam told him and reached out to stroke his mane. His throat was hoarse and his chest felt bruised, but other than this there was little evidence to support the fact that he was ever in the water. He was already soaking wet from the rain. There was even less evidence to support the idea that there was some kind of miraculous woman in the water with him who had appeared from nowhere with a pureness of heart and the single intention of rescuing him from a watery grave. However, in that moment, none of this mattered to Sam. He had but one thought in his mind and it was impossible to shake – he was alive. He was alive and it was the most beautiful, magical, wondrous thing to have ever happened to him. He was alive and he had his whole life ahead of him to do with whatever he chose. He was alive and the rain tasted sweet, the night smelt earthy and real, and the air gently whispered sonnets into his ear. He was alive and there was only one thing he wanted in the entire world – Fizz. It mattered not what had gone before. He could even forgive Robin now for his treacherous infidelity because he was even more certain than ever that the only reason he was on this planet was the strength of his love for this woman. It was this that had returned him to his body and he wasn't going to waste a moment of it being shy and uncertain, unworthy and self-conscious. He would never be a man who led armies, but he was determined to master his own heart and Fizz would be his.

'Good boy,' he whispered to Pinecomb. 'Everything has changed now, boy,' he told him and forced a foot into one of his stirrups. As he did so, he felt the heaviness of the dagger against his leg and couldn't quite believe he had carried such an object. Without pause for thought, he reached into his belt, dragged the dagger out into the night and tossed it into the water. 'Everything has changed.'

He rode back to the animal house at a far steadier pace. He had soothed Pinecomb with his words, but he was still spooked by the accident and everything else that Sam had put him through, forcing him to ride to his limit in terrifying conditions. Sam could now feel the calm in the horse's body and was sorry he had acted with no care for his welfare. 'We will get you some nice hay, and a good night's sleep will restore you completely, my good friend,' Sam told him gently as they trotted along.

Before long, they were outside the dilapidated animal house once again, but Sam felt none of the fury from earlier. All he felt was calm and determined: two emotions that he was unaccustomed to experiencing together, but the combination made him feel powerful beyond anything he could have imagined. Although the rain had calmed a little, the scene was unchanged from earlier, with candlelight gently emanating from the broken-down shell of the animal house. Sam dismounted Pinecomb and tied him up outside. He then slowly strolled forward, listening out for tell-tale sounds (he didn't want to disturb them in the act), before walking in.

'Sam!' Robin called out, clearly surprised to see his friend. He was bare-chested and sitting up in a makeshift bed like the cat that got the cream.

'Hang on!' Sam said as he edged even further into the room and took in the scene. 'That's not Fizz!'

Robin draped his arm around his companion, who was also naked, but had pulled a sheet up to her chest to protect her modesty. 'What are you doing here, my friend? Can you not see I am in the middle of something?'

'But I thought ...'

'You all right, duck?' the woman asked and Sam immediately recognised the voice. In that moment everything became clear. This was Fizz's friend, the woman he had seen from behind at the ale house, the woman with long dark hair very similar to Fizz's. He had been so certain that Robin had bed Fizz earlier that a simple flash of her from behind was enough to confirm it. He hadn't actually seen her face. Now that he could see her clearly, he returned to his earlier assessment of her – he liked her. There was something so down-to-earth and honest about her. She was pretty without being striking, when she smiled she showed all of her teeth and when she spoke it was with a deep, earthy voice. 'You're drenched. You should come in. You'll catch your death, love.'

'No,' Sam beamed. 'There will be no death this evening.'

'Are you okay, my friend?' Robin asked.

'I am more than okay.' Sam beamed. 'I am perfect. Life is perfect. Life is better than perfect and the very next thing I am going to do is find Fizz and tell her that I love her.'

CHAPTER FIFTEEN

Noah wanted more than anything to stay with Charlotte after the rainy night before, when she had sobbed and opened her heart to him and they had drunk brandy together and tried to make sense of it all, but the situation with her father didn't allow it. For the two of them to spend any amount of time together, they needed extreme, covert, forward planning, which they hadn't put in place. It was the night before Noah's big exam, so he had pictured himself leaving early, cramming for a few hours and then trying to get a few good hours' sleep before the dreaded hour approached. What actually happened was that he sat in The Pine Comb with Charlotte for a few hours before walking her to the end of her road and then walking himself back to his bedsit. By the time he got in it was nearly 1.00 a.m. and he was exhausted and tipsy. He fell asleep with his shoes on, without having even opened his books, and woke up with just enough time to throw on some clothes and run out of the door. This is exactly what he was doing when his phone rang.

'Noah! It's Thane.'

'I know, mate,' Noah answered, hopping close to the front door with one shoe on and one shoe off while juggling his bag and phone. 'Funny thing caller ID.'

'I just wanted to thank you.'

Noah stood up suddenly. 'Really?'

'Of course, really.'

There was a pause and Noah returned to his hopping and juggling.

'I've just ... I've just never met anyone like her,' Thane confessed.

'Me neither.'

Thane didn't notice that Noah was agreeing with him for all the wrong reasons and continued, 'She's so interesting and funny and sexy.'

'Really?'

'Yes, really. You were there. You met here. She's so dry, yet warm and a bit dark, but light at the same time.'

'My God! You have got it bad.'

'I don't know about that, but I just can't get her out of my head. It's as if we met in a former life or something.'

'What?'

'I said I just can't get her out of my head.'

'The other thing you said.'

'Oh, that it's like we met in a former life.'

'Why are you saying that?' Noah was now running down the road as he tried to investigate further.

'I dunno. It's just what people say isn't it when they're instantly attracted. I took her home, you know. First night and everything! She's a legend!'

'Look, this is lovely and all, Thane, but I've got to get moving. My exam starts in half an hour.'

'Oh yeah, I completely forgot. Are you all set?'

'As set as I'll ever be.'

'You'll be fine, mate.'

'That's easy for you to say. If I don't pass this I'm out. Things haven't been going great.'

'Really? I thought you were really clever.'

Noah couldn't help chuckling at this and then replied, 'It's not about being clever. Things have fallen apart a bit since Charlotte's dad stopped me seeing her and she's been worrying me to death and I've been putting all my time into working out. It's all been a bit mad.'

'Well, I should go,' Thane answered.

'Er … Right. Thanks. You've been really helpful.'

'It's not that, Noah. I've got to get Julia to school. She's a right pain in the morning. How's Charlotte now, by the way? I thought her head was gonna start spinning last night.'

'A bit better I think. I'll tell you about it later. I've really got to go.'

They said their final farewells and as soon as Noah pressed the End Call button, he threw his phone into his bag and quickened his pace. He had already made it halfway to the bus stop, but he couldn't relax. If he was going to make it in time he would have to move at full pelt. He sprinted the rest of the way and arrived at the bus stop just as the bus was pulling in. It was only when he had flashed his pass and found a seat at the back that he began to breathe normally again. It was a ten-minute bus ride; he would only have minutes to spare when he got to the university, but he would make it in time for his exam.

As he sat watching the world whizz past the window, the Tudor charm of the village giving way to the empty concrete oppression of the town, he tried to remember everything he could about the dystopian novel – the subject of the morning's exam. But all he had were titles of books crashing into one another without revealing their deeper meanings – Brave New World, 1984, Handmaid's Tale. All they were were titles and then they disappeared altogether and suddenly he had a head full of Charlotte. 'We're all going to die?' Did she really believe that? She had been so rational before all of this started. She was so cool and calm and easy-going; she never let life get under her skin and she definitely wouldn't have bought into the possibility of dreaming about the past or reincarnation. Funny that Thane had mentioned reincarnation, too – as if they had met in a former life. Noah had used the expression too, he seemed to remember, when he met Charlotte, and maybe even when he met Thane. The strength of the meetings had been so powerful and so completely outside of his control that there had to be something greater pulling them all together. He liked the idea of it, but if he had to scrutinise it he knew he could easily explain it away as simple attraction – powerful? Yes. Magical? No. Why couldn't Charlotte apply the same logic?

He went over everything she had told him in his mind: things that it would have been easy to find out at the library – the ultimate fate of these figures and the fact that Samuel was betrothed to a princess; and then there was everything that the history books would have no way of knowing: Robin riding Sam's joust for him and his father's disapproval, the two friends breaking into the pub, Sam catching Robin and Fizz at it and then almost drowning and then it wasn't Fizz at all. It was all so detailed, but that didn't mean it was true. She had told him about the friends breaking into the pub after she found out about Noah and

Thane's misdemeanour, and after they had both been coping with the aftermath of her own father's disapproval. Surely, it wouldn't be too much of a stretch to imagine that real life was affecting her dreams rather than the other way around. Her reaction to seeing Julia was extreme, though. Noah pushed his finger into the condensation forming on the window beside him and drew two eyes and a mouth as he thought all of this through. If she hadn't seen a little Julia from the past in her dream, why was she so shaken up by seeing Thane's sister? There was, of course, another theory. Noah rubbed out the smiley face he had drawn and was stuck by how white the sky was beyond. He sighed deeply as he began to accept that this theory might actually be reality – Charlotte was losing her mind. She had been sleep-deprived and sleep-tortured for so long now that she was losing her grip on reality. But then another thought crept in; what if what she was saying was true and he didn't believe her? What kind of boyfriend would that make him? But if it were true, he had a bigger issue. It was his twentieth birthday in a month's time. If what she was saying had any truth to it at all then he had just one month left to live.

The bus pulled into the university and the familiar, sleepy student community, comprising lacklustre figures who seemed to move just that little bit slower than people out in the real world, as if they had the rest of their lives to just hang around chatting or wander around aimlessly. Noah was a veritable hare amongst them as he pounded his way off the bus and zipped across the grass in the direction of the examination hall. It was only when he started to recognise faces from his literature group dotted around the entranceway that he could finally relax; they were huddled and chatting, showing no great urgency in making their way into the hall. He had made it with time to spare.

He slowed his jog to a walk and then heard his ringtone once again, muffled at the bottom of his bag. Keeping an eye on the bookish crowd outside the hall, he dropped to one knee and delved deep to retrieve it. The caller ID showed a number he didn't recognise. He usually didn't answer calls from withheld or unknown numbers, but this number started with the Mardridge code. It wasn't going to be someone trying to sell him something, get him to donate to charity or reclaim PPI; this had to be a real person who genuinely needed to speak to him. He looked down at his watch and then over to the assembled class by the hall door and answered.

'Hello?'

'Hello. Is that Noah Smith?'

'Yes. Who's this?'

'My name is Nurse Jackson. I'm calling from the hospital. I understand that you are Charlotte Mitchell's boyfriend.'

Noah was struck still and suddenly found himself shouting into the handset. 'What's happened? Has she had an accident? Is she okay? What's happened?'

'Please don't be alarmed, Mr Smith. She's fine. Well, she's been admitted with nervous exhaustion.'

'Oh my God!'

'She's fine. She's in the best place. She just needs to rest.'

'Right, I'm on my way.'

'Her father is here,' the nurse told him in a tone with a deep, burrowing subtext. 'She wouldn't settle until she made me promise to call you.'

'So I can't come there?'

'No, but she told me to give you a message. She said to tell you to be careful because she doesn't think that Robin did it.'

Noah didn't answer. He just didn't know what to say.

'Mr Smith.'

'Sorry, yes. I'm here. Can you give her a message from me?'

'Of course.'

'Can you tell her that I don't care if her father's there or not? I'm on my way.'

'But, Mr–' Noah cut her off before she could say more and without another glance back to his fellow students, he sprinted back off across the grass in the direction of the bus stop and stood alone at the deserted clearing with his heart banging out a deathly rhythm over the sound of the passing cars. 'Come on!' he grimaced as he looked up and down the road. 'Come on!' And then he finally looked at the timetable and saw that there wouldn't be another bus for a half an hour. Although his rational mind told him that he would get there quicker if he simply waited for the bus, his body was aching for a quicker result and propelled him into a run before he could argue. He would have to run all the way back to Mardridge and beyond, a journey that would take him over an hour, but he didn't care. The working out had paid off and he was gliding through the morning with a breeze on his face and a chain around his heart. 'It's okay, Fizz,' he kept saying to himself over and over again. 'I'm coming.'

After a little over an hour, he arrived back in Mardridge. Two buses had passed him on the way and he knew he could probably have made it all the way to the hospital if he had just waited, but he was acting on autopilot. He passed the well and a little more than five minutes later, he reached The Pine Comb, which wasn't that far away from his flat.

He slowed his pace for nothing as he reached the centre of the village and ran past the police station and then his stomach turned as he knew he would have to pass the Sir Robin's Head. Why on earth did he let Thane persuade him to go in there? He didn't have time to beat himself up again and wasn't completely sure whether the place now make him uncomfortable because he had been caught in there and was cautioned against going near the place, or because it carried the weight of history so brutally. Sir Robin's head. What if Charlotte was right? What if he didn't do it?

'Get a grip!' he whispered to himself and tried to keep up the pace, but his legs felt as tired as his brain and he had been struggling for some miles now. 'You can do it! You can do it!' he repeated, but then he was forced to pull up sharp when a tall, ginger, bearded man jumped out onto the pavement in front of him. At first, Noah couldn't tell what was happening. He didn't look at the man's face; he merely saw him as an obstacle and tried to step around him. Nothing was going to stop him getting to the hospital. When the man moved to block his path again, however, he knew he was in trouble. The man was a good foot taller than he was and at least half as wide again. As he peered down at Noah, his face was struggling to contain a battle between joy and anger – delight at the fortune of glimpsing Noah Smith jogging past his window, absolute contempt at the idea that this little shit had had the audacity to break into his beloved pub and sit drinking beer as casual as if it were a Sunday afternoon while he slept upstairs.

'Av got something fer ye!' he said in a thick Scottish accent.

'Look, I know you're pissed and I'm sorry about–' But Noah didn't get to finish his sentence. The burly landlord closed his massive fingers into a fist and launched it into the centre of Noah's face. He hit the pavement before he could even put his hands up in protest and was out cold.

CHAPTER SIXTEEN

At first there was no change in Chrono, and Athena was really scrutinising his every move. She wasn't really sure what she expected; she had never seen a man under the influence of a love potion before, but she imagined that there would be a softening, a drunkenness on love itself. His pupils would swell and alter his whole demeanour, much like those of the ferocious cat who softens into a kitten when stroked in the right place. A grin would dance across his face, forcing his cheeks to glow; even his hair would be changed, lightening, softening as he fell under love's spell. But she saw none of this as Chrono ate the rest of his prawn cocktail. All she saw was the elation he was feeling at finally sampling that which he had deprived himself of for so long, and the effort he was making to disguise it, to show her that he was a master of life's pleasure, of which this meal was one in a million and easily eclipsed.

And then a change suddenly stirred in him, just as he was beginning to explain a new policy to Athena – something about making sure all fate guardians managed their admin (Athena wasn't really listening). At first the muscles in his face contracted slightly, twitching almost unperceivably; if he had been more in control of the movement it might have looked as if he had smelt something unpleasant. He opened his mouth to continue his discourse on higher power bureaucracy, but his jaw locked before the words could come out and the fork fell out of his hand and crashed down to the table.

'Are you okay, Chrono?' Athena asked. This was not what she had been expecting. If nothing else, she had believed that experiencing love would be a positive feeling for Chrono, something he would enjoy, especially in light of the revelation that he was a stranger to many of life's pleasures, but this looked the complete opposite of pleasure. His face was colouring in a way that had to be impossible; cheeks couldn't be red and green at the same time. He tried to talk again, but it came out as a choking, gargling sound and his hands were clawing at his throat.

'You have poisoned me,' he managed to say and Athena raced around the table to support him as he dropped sideward off his chair and onto the emerald grass.

'No,' she pleaded. 'It is not poison, Chrono. I mean you no harm.' She cradled his head in her arms and the features on his serious face gathered themselves into the most pained expression she had ever seen. Blue had been added to the many hues of his face and his bare chest was burning red in her arms.

'Why have you done this?' he just managed to say, but before he could hear the answer his voice cut out, his eyelids dropped and he lost consciousness.

'Chrono?' Athena said calmly, trying to maintain her composure. 'Chrono! Wake up, Chrono. It was a love potion, not poison. Wake up.' But Chrono remained deadly still and refused to stir when she pushed her face closer to his and spoke directly into his ear. 'Please, Chrono, wake up.' And when he didn't stir this time she sat up suddenly and said, 'I'm in so much trouble.' She knew that eternity in Sam's shoddy heaven would be nothing compared to the punishment she would receive for destroying a guardian, even if it was unintentional. 'Come on now, Chrono,' she tried again, and when he absolutely refused to stir, she slid her arms out from under him and was up on her feet, pacing the grass around him. 'Give me strength, give me strength,' she repeated over and over again as her brain began furiously searching for solutions. Then, 'The bottle!' she suddenly said and raced over to her little castle, to where she had left the potion bottle. She pulled off the crystal lid, making a tiny pop, and drew the bottle to her nose. It reeked. She knew this before she gave it to Chrono and had spent time worrying over whether he would be able to smell it in the champagne, but she hadn't given the smell much thought. Seconds later, she came running out of her tiny castle, over the bridge and onto the patch of green inhabited by the unicorn.

'Smell that!' she urged and wafted the bottle under the unicorn's nose.

'What is wrong with you, my girl? Get that away from me at once.'

'But smell it.'

'I can smell it from here, thank you,' the unicorn complained, but then it characteristically continued chewing the grass as if Athena and the bottle simply didn't exist anymore.

'Can we not just have one sustained conversation ever?' Athena complained behind gritted teeth then said, 'I need your help, Unicorn. What is that smell?'

'Well,' the unicorn mused. 'It smells like a love potion that's been left to fester for a hundred years to me.'

'What?' Athena smelt the bottle again and had to agree that the smell was one of rot and decay. 'Why didn't you tell me this would happen?'

'You didn't ask.'

'Not this again, Unicorn, please, I need your help.'

'It's quite ironic really, isn't it. I thought you would have learnt.'

'Please, Unicorn.'

'Tell me, Athena, would you leave your food for a hundred years before eating it?'

'Of course not.'

'So why would you think you could leave the love potion?'

'I don't know, because it's magic.' The panic was audible in her voice as she looked back across the bridge to the figure of Chrono unconscious on the ground.

'What makes you think it's magic? It's just love, Athena.'

'Please, Unicorn, tell me what to do. He's dying.'

'Why don't you ask the river?'

'Because all it can say is "Hell … ooo."'

'No, ask it for the petals of a flowering Snapdragon. It will chase out the poison and restore him, but be prepared, Athena, he will need time to recover and you will need to nurse him back to health.'

'All I want is for him to get better,' Athena assured the unicorn and ran off in the direction of the river. 'River!' she cried out before she had reached the bank, her body now aching from the sudden reversal of a day that had held so much promise. She had to simply accept now that what little trace of freedom she had been trying to keep a hold of, as it wriggled and morphed and laughed in her face, was now slipping between her fingers; Sam's heaven had become her hell and she would be there forever, but still she pushed forward. She may not have been able to make Chrono love her, but she absolutely couldn't allow him to die. She dropped down to her knees and asked for the Snapdragon petals in a voice that sounded nothing like her own; the gravity of her mission had deepened it while blind panic ran it through with a high-shrieking register. And when she had spoken the words the river began to quake in the way that had become so familiar to her. Her chest rose and fell heavily, each breath laden with the weight of her fate, as she watched the ripples of colour swell out towards the bank and deep pink petals emerging from the water's depths and dancing up onto the surface, spreading into the distance as far as she could see. If she hadn't been so desperate she would have appreciated what a beautiful sight was set before her, but time was limited and she simply scooped up a handful of the petals and darted back to Chrono's body. She gently placed one hand beneath his head once again, her fingers swimming through his hair, and raised his head slightly, so she could administer the petals, but she was too late. She had never held a dead body in her arms before, she didn't really know that guardians could die, but she instinctively knew that there was no life force left within him; she had drained it all with her selfishness. His skin was a white so pure that she imagined the colour powdering off onto her hand if she touched his cheek. His stillness was eerie and she wanted to shake him, to reanimate him from this false death. This wasn't the death he should have had; his final expression should have been one of peace, not the twisted grimace of agony that she now saw before her. She lowered his head back to the ground and dropped her head in her hands wondering what in Sam's heaven's name she was going to do now.

CHAPTER SEVENTEEN

F ace to face in the animal house, neither Sam nor Robin moved for a moment as both absorbed the change in Sam. Was this the same man who felt terror in the company of women, now standing tall and shouldering the challenge of his heart? Was he really about to go to Fizz and tell her he loved her?

'What has happened to you, Sam? You have me worried,' Robin told his friend as he watched him trembling in the doorway, dripping into the infinite darkness of the night. 'My apologies,' he said to his bemused-looking companion, then swung his legs out from the blankets and pulled on his breeches. 'You cannot go to Fizz this evening. Look at you.'

Sam was still beaming. 'You do not understand, Robin. I have to go to her. Something has happened.'

'My friend, you look like a creature pulled from the sea. This is not a good look for a potential suitor.'

'Oh.' Sam hadn't thought of this.

'Here,' Robin offered and threw a blanket over his friend's shoulder. 'Come and sit for a moment. Come and think things through.'

'But, you don't understand, Robin,' he urged and the blanket fell to the ground.

'I understand that you have gone insane. Women do not like the lunatic look, Sam. And have you forgotten? If you go to her tonight you will have to revisit the ale house. Have you forgotten that her father wants us dead?' Robin picked up the blanket and replaced it around Sam's shoulders, but he was not to be contained.

'Okay,' said Sam, as animated as he had ever been. 'I will go to her tomorrow, but I cannot stay here. I cannot be parted from this glorious night. My apologies, m'lady,' he told Robin's companion, still nestled in the makeshift bed with the blankets pulled to her chest, and reached to his head to dip his hat before realising it was missing, which forced from her a deep, unladylike snort of laughter, which she made no attempt to conceal.

'What has happened to you?' Robin asked again, but Sam saw it as a rhetorical question and simply offered a smile by way of an answer. 'You are a lunatic. Wait for me. I will dress and escort you back to the castle.'

'No, you must stay with your beautiful companion.' He gave Fizz's friend a gentlemanly bow and she beamed a smile in return. 'The night is young. No harm can come of me, Robin.'

'Right. I fear you have been at the ale again. Promise me that you will ride straight back to the castle and take to your bed.'

'I can do no such thing, but I can assure you of my safety,' he grinned and backed out of the animal house, the blanket falling to the ground again.

Robin followed him out and watched in silence as he mounted his horse and began to trot away. 'You are a madman!' he called out into the night as he stood, bare-chested, watching his friend disappear into the distance.

The following morning, the two friends were back at the animal house. The sun had graced them with its presence and as the battered shack dried out from the night before, the stench of rot was far stronger than either the earthy moss or the aroma of early springtime flowers desperately trying to push through. They hadn't arranged to meet in the morning, but both knew that the other would be there. It was the way it had always been; something would happen and they would naturally gravitate to the old, empty animal house to debrief.

'You are looking a touch better today,' Robin told Sam as they sat side-by-side on the steps leading up to the entrance.

'Since when do you care how I look?' Sam giggled.

'I am serious, Sam. I was worried about you last night. You looked a little, well, mad.'

'Thanks.'

'Anne thought so, too.'

'Fizz's friend? Did she now?' Sam asked and raised his eyebrows. 'Since when have you started having intelligent conversations with village girls?'

Robin paused before answering, but Sam spoke first.

'Are you blushing, Sir Robin?'

'I am most definitely not blushing and I fancy you would like red cheeks of your own.'

Sam ignoring him. 'Not every woman would push you to threaten me with violence,' he smiled. 'What is going on, Robin?'

'You are changing the subject. I was concerned. Where did you away after you left here?'

'I rode for a while, but you were right, Robin. The night may have been glorious, but to lie in my bed was a thing of wonder.'

'I see you are still wearing your mad hat. What on earth happened to you last night?'

'And I see that it is you who would have us change the conversation. You were about to tell me how your union with Anne came to be.'

Robin cleared his throat, shrugged and said, 'There is nothing much to tell. I ventured into the village yesterday afternoon. I was looking for the girl from the ale house in truth.'

'I knew it. You bastard!'

'Relax. I did not find her. I found something altogether more … erm.'

'My eyes deceive me, Robin. She has you lost for words. What happened to village girls being for the night? What was it – give them a shilling and the village girls are willing?'

'I was not exactly wrong there,' Robin replied, trying for a smug look, but Sam had him on the ropes.

'She is under your skin, Robin.'

'I don't think … I mean …'

'You make me a fool for my heart, but yours is just as vulnerable as mine.'

'We are nothing alike, Sam. It is just that … It's just …'

'You are in love, my friend. Ha! I never thought the day would come. After delving into the skirts of how many hundreds of women, who would think it would be a village girl who stole your heart.'

'Okay, Sam. You have me. I am not ashamed to say that I may have accidentally and completely through no fault of my own become fond of Anne, but …'

'This is wonderful,' Sam beamed.

'No it isn't,' Robin told him. 'You have seen her, Sam. She is loud and brash, and probably takes a different bedfellow every night.'

'Like you.'

'Very funny. And I cannot begin to know her. She is strange in her habits. She was strange after you left last night and I cannot fathom the reason. And – promise me you will not laugh.'

Sam promised but was smiling already. He couldn't miss the opportunity to pay Robin back for the heavy doses of mockery he served to him on a daily basis.

'She is known in the village as a healer of some kind.'

Sam was disappointed. 'Why would that be funny?'

'People will think I have fallen for a witch.'

'A witch and a healer are not the same thing, Robin.'

'Well, it's by the by and I know I should forget her, but there is just something about her, Sam, which is why …' As his voice trailed off he looked to Sam as if he were about to ask a mighty favour and Sam was surprised when he said, 'Which is why I will help you to woo Fizz.'

'You will help me woo Fizz? Why?'

'Because she is the best friend of Anne, and if you and Fizz are a couple, Anne and I will be thrown together at every opportunity.'

'Or you could simply open your heart to her.'

Robin cuffed Sam around the ear as a father would. 'Have I taught you nothing? No, that is not the way to a woman's heart and this is not the way in which we will approach Fizz.'

'We?'

'Yes, we! I cannot trust you to get this right alone.'

'Unfortunately, you will have to trust me, as this is exactly what I will do this vary day. I have written a poem for her, confessing my undying love and I will recite it for her later today.'

'So you want to make her throw up over you. This is not the way to a woman's heart.'

'Okay then, Robin. Let me assure you, I will try my way and if I fail I will call upon your services.'

'Do you even know where you will find her today?'

'Well, no.'

'And you thought you had no use of me! She assists the pastor at the village school. Anne told me this is so. You will find her walking home from the church after school. And if you are not to be swayed from attacking her with romance, this is a picturesque place from which to jump out at her.'

'Poetry and love are things to lavish upon her not beat her about the face with.'

'Whatever, my friend. Just do not let me down. What happened to you last night anyway?'

Sam's face lit up just as it had the night before as he explained all that had happened, leaving out the part about riding out to attack Robin and catching them in the act. He told him how the horse had thrown him into the river, how he had become trapped underwater beneath treacherous reeds and then described the woman who had saved his life.

'You really are mad,' Robin told him when he had finished his story. 'Listen, you were drinking in the day. I imagine you had more wine at the banquet and then, for reasons of insanity, you risk your life atop Pinecomb. I wager you fell and hit your head. You are lucky to be alive, Sam.'

'And that is the point, Robin. We are all lucky to be alive and I have never felt so alive, whatever happened. I would have died last night without intervention from … I don't know where. And now all I know is that everything has changed. If last night hadn't happened I would have continued my life, pining after the things I want and never daring to reach out and take them. I cannot be that person anymore. Last night has shown me that life is too short. My heart will do somersaults in my chest for as long as I am alive and I will dance to its rhythm all the way to my beloved.'

'You should put that in a poem,' Robin grinned and then leaned away from his friend and narrowed his eyes as if seeing him for the first time. 'Definitely mad,' he said. 'Just don't mess things up for me with Fizz.'

True to his word, later that day, Sam was perched on the wall that ran the length of the walkway leading from the church to the centre of the village. Although he hated to admit it, Robin's tip had been invaluable and he was also right about it being a romantic spot, although he didn't plan to jump out at her. All around him, the afternoon hazed into fields, alive with the chorus of grasshoppers and the heady aroma of spring. He had chosen a spot that was a clear distance from the closest house, enabling him to walk with her, uninterrupted, and deliver his poem. As he waited for her to appear, he almost expected his resolve to disappear and his old traits to rise to the surface – uncertainty, fear and unworthiness – but they were a million miles from him now and it was all thanks to the lady in the lake – his guardian angel. The only thoughts in his mind were of his beloved: how lucky he would be to be in her presence and procure an audience from her, if only for a few minutes, and how wonderful she was to give her service to the children at the school. He imagined she was a patient, kind and gentle teacher, but as he thought this, he couldn't help laughing at himself; he had never actually spoken more than a word to this woman and had already decided exactly what kind of person she was. However, he was one hundred per cent confident that he wasn't wrong. Sometimes the heart just knows.

And then she appeared. He watched as she waved back to the church and he imagined the boys to whom she had imparted her valuable warmth and knowledge waving back at her, impatient for her to return before she had even left. And then she was making her way along the path, a gentle spring in her step announcing her vitality and zeal. In mere seconds, she would pass his wall and he couldn't wait to begin his new life by her side.

He watched as her journey continued, nearing him with every step, her fingers busy with leaves from the surrounding hedges, idly turning them in her hands before letting them fall. His heart sang at the sight of her, but screamed with impatience as she moved at such a leisurely pace. Within minutes, however, she was upon him. She made no sign of recognition as their eyes met and then she lowered them and continued her walk, but she was forced to stop when Sam addressed her.

'M'lady,' he said and now she was still and looking around herself to make sense of the interruption. She had been gently singing to herself before this, oblivious to all things around her on a path that she had walked a thousand times. 'My apologies for the interruption. I was hoping to make your avail this fair afternoon.' His cheeks had coloured gently, but not through fear or embarrassment; his spirit was warming in her presence. He took in the full sight of her and wanted only to see this vision for the rest of his life. Her dress was the same or very similar to that in which he had seen her the day before, but she had adorned it with a beautiful, embroidered shawl, which hung delicately around her shoulders. Her hair was tightly gripped behind her, in a style suitable for educating the local boys, and the open starkness of her features was mesmerising.

'I know you,' she said, almost managing a smile. 'It was you downstairs yesterday morning. And your rude friend.'

'Yes, and I apologise for our intrusion, but if I hadn't broken into the ale house I may never have had the chance to look upon such perfection.'

'You know my father wants your blood,' she said, continuing her walk, but these menacing words sounded like a gift to his ears, immaculately wrapped in her gentle, soothing tone.

'May I walk with you?'

'It is a free country,' she said, but her beaming smile betrayed her true feelings. By the time Sam had caught up with her, however, she had subdued the smile and was quite clearly going to make him work.

'I am Sir Samuel Mardridge and I am delighted to formally make your acquaintance.'

'Felicity,' she told him.

'Ah, Fizz,' he said, slotting the pieces of the puzzle together.

'No, Felicity to you.'

'My apologies.' She really was making this difficult for him, but he was determined that love would prevail. 'I understand you have been helping at the school.'

Fizz stopped suddenly. 'You have been spying on me.'

Sam shook his head. 'I did not mean to offend you, m'lady. I simply wished to find you again and it was this information that led me to you.'

'So it is no accident that I find you here today.'

'I must confess that I designed this meeting, m'lady.'

'And what would the purpose of this meeting be, Sir Samuel Mardridge?' she asked with her eyebrows raised and a distant smile. The formal nature of their exchange was both exhilarating and torturous; Fizz was exactly as he had imagined her to be – more regal and refined than any princess he had ever met – and he was prepared to earn her respect and her love, even if it took years of frustrating formalities to slip beneath her veneer.

'The purpose is simply this ...' he began and then climbed up onto the wall, held his arms aloft and more than reciting his poem, he bellowed it out into the afternoon breeze.

People,

I condemn thee to a world of darkness,

where the sun shines down on me alone,

illuminating this moment,

this beautiful moment,

when my aching heart will find its home.

All creatures vast, all creatures tiny,

traverse the world and stand before me,

bear witness to love's indestructible glory.

My heart explodes with a single story.

Owls, crickets, hold your breath.

I pray of thee the absence of noise.

Howling wind, lend me a silence,

where the only sound is my gentle voice

and the only word is her name.

Felicity.

Dear Felicity.

I am stripped before you now,

naked, bare, exposed,

poetry unravelled,

reduced to the only three words in existence.

I

Love

You

It was so much more than anything he had ever written – more forthright and passionate, more confident and direct, not to mention experimental – and when the last word had flown from his mouth, a dove delivering its declaration of love, he stepped down from the wall and was once again on terra firma, but the ground felt anything but solid. The power of the words he had freed from his soul had unsteadied him and now he was balanced on a cloud and in danger of falling through and plummeting infinitely towards oblivion. And now he really did feel naked before her; he had removed all the layers to his heart and exposed the essence of his being and his feeling for her. All he wanted now was to feel her arms around him, to feel the warmth of her body against his own, to get some sense of the Fizz that lay behind the exterior that she pushed out for the world – the aleman's daughter, the school teacher, the friend, the villager. He was desperate to see into her soul, to enter her soul and take shelter from the world inside of her. And yet she hadn't spoken. Time was passing. He was standing beside her. He had recited the poem with every fibre of emotion he could gather from within and she still hadn't said a word. And then ...

'That was beautiful, Sam, but can I let you into a secret?'

Sam's heart was pounding now. Her voice had softened and whatever she said next would change his life forever. He slowly nodded.

'Your poem was lovely, but it really wasn't necessary.'

Sam's heart sank, but she had more to say.

'I loved you from the first moment I saw you.'

Chapter Eighteen

Athena could no longer see for tears, although for whom her tears were spilling she couldn't be certain. It was sad that Chrono had died, of course it was sad, but she knew deep down that it wasn't grief that disabled her heart. She wasn't even sure she liked him very much; he had been nothing but trouble to her and at one stage she suspected him of even enjoying the power he wielded over her, leaving her to rot in the sordid wonderland. She had warmed to him a little over dinner as she watched his virgin mouthfuls of prawn cocktail and champagne, but he was hardly the love of her life. So she couldn't pretend that her tears were for him; they were for herself, for the trouble she would now be in when his loss was discovered, for the failure of her plan to make him love her, for the end of her life, which she was sure would be far worse than any death that could be inflicted upon her. She had heard of angels being bottled and kept on shelves too high for anyone to reach ever again for misdemeanours that were not nearly as bad as hers. Although she hated eternity in Sam's heaven, eternity in a bottle on a shelf would be a million times worse. And then there was the possibility of becoming a fallen angel. She didn't know the details of this fate, but she imagined a fiery pit and an eternity of pain. She let out a pained groan and when she finally dragged her face from her hands she saw that she was not alone.

'What are you doing, child?' the unicorn asked. It was now at Athena's side with its head hanging over Chrono's corpse, so close that its lips were brushing his cheek as it spoke. It then turned to Athena suddenly. 'You really are the worst angel I have ever encountered.'

'I know,' Athena said pityingly.

'Why haven't you given him the snapdragon petals?'

'He's dead, Unicorn. Snapdragon petals aren't going to restore him.'

'I realise you are a novice, but did you learn nothing in your training, Athena?'

Athena sadly dragged her hands down her cheeks and swallowed down the tears that were still forming inside her. She ignored the insults and saw a glimmer of something helpful in the unicorn's presence. 'What do you mean?'

'I mean you are all dead already, dafty. Do you remember taking a class explaining what happens when guardians and angels die?'

Athena thought for a moment and was suddenly interrupted.

'You don't remember it because it didn't happen. We are not earthly beings, you odd child.'

'But …' Now Athena didn't know what to say and simply looked down at Chrono – evidence personified in the case for the death of the dead.

'He is poisoned and will be stuck that way if you don't give him the snapdragons that I told you to give him quite some time ago now.'

'But …'

'Give him the petals, Athena. Please!'

Athena sniffed back her distress once again and began to gather the discarded petals from around her. She looked to the unicorn at intervals to make sure she was performing the task to its exacting standards as she slipped her hand beneath Chrono's head again and gently teased his lips apart. The unicorn nodded encouragement and, one by one, Athena fed the petals into his mouth.

The effect was immediate. Chrono's on-switch had been flicked and his body surged forward, coughing and spluttering as if he had emerged from the sea. His initial energy, however, was deceptive and when his lungs had gathered enough air to persuade his body that it was still alive and when his cheeks had shaken off just a little of the white powder, he collapsed once again into Athena's arms. Now she could feel his life force staggering through him, plodding, but it was very definitely there and she too felt as if she had been holding her breath for some time and could breathe freely once again. But he wasn't over the worst. He was too weak to maintain consciousness and his body looked to be somehow damaged. Athena couldn't pinpoint exactly what was different; he just seemed smaller somehow, deflated, defeated. It would be some time before he would be restored and this was all her fault, but she was committed to making him well again.

'Should I keep giving him the snapdragon petals?' she asked the unicorn.

The unicorn lightly touched Chrono's face with its own once again and then nodded. 'Give him snapdragon petals every day and wash his body with the rainbow waters of the river. Keep him warm in your funny little castle and tell him stories to strengthen his heart.'

Athena absorbed all of the information with her eyes wide open, nodding emphatically between each instruction, eager to show her commitment to fixing the situation.

'If you can hoist him onto my back I will take him to your castle.'

Athena did as she was told, then asked, 'How long do you think it will take for him to recover?'

'There is no way of knowing. Could be fifty minutes or fifty years.'

This new information stopped Athena in thought for a moment and then she reawakened to her task and began to hoist him from the emerald grass. If it took fifty years to restore him then so be it.

The inside of Athena's tiny castle was simply a room with a bed in it. It looked far grander from the outside with its tiny, ornate towers and pink stained-glass windows, but it was all smoke and mirrors, as most things were in Sam's heaven. As she didn't particularly need to sleep she didn't spend much time inside, but she had asked the river for it just so she had somewhere to call home. Over the years, however, she had come to hate it, with its cheerful exterior and gloomy, empty interior. It was more like a child's toy that a home, constructed from a material from the future that she would come to know as plastic if she lived long enough or ever managed to reclaim her freedom. As she watched Chrono sleep on the bed, his chest rising and falling peacefully, it struck her that this was the first time the tiny space had felt like anything resembling a home.

'I'm just going to …' she told him and finished the sentence by dabbing his forehead with a flannel rinsed in rainbow waters and slipping more snapdragon petals into his mouth. She then sat down on the end of the bed, leaned against the wall with her knees drawn into her chest, and watched his face as it slumbered on. She wondered for a moment what was going on behind those delicately shuttered eyes. Was he dreaming? Was he thinking? Did he know where he was and what was happening? Athena had no way of knowing, but she found that the more she looked at his face, the more she wanted to look at it. He was beautiful; she already knew this, but there was something staggeringly beautiful about his slumber. It revealed a truth that Chrono couldn't control. His layers had been stripped away to something honest and breath-taking; there was his innocence and nativity, but then there was something even deeper that Chrono kept deeply hidden; the only way Athena could describe it was as honour, but she knew the word was understating what she saw in him. His silent truth was a simple one: as a man of honour he would sacrifice his own life for the lives of those he loved; to be loved by him was to be completed.

Athena cleared her throat and whispered, 'Once upon a time ...' The unicorn had told her to tell him stories to strengthen his heart and so she sat there on that first day and told him every single story she could think of. She told him the stories that her mother had told her when she was a part of the real world and the stories that she had heard echoing in the realms of the angels for eternity. She told him stories of love and friendship, she told him funny stories about woodland creatures that wore clothes and talked and she told him stories of strength and courage. When she had exhausted her supply of stories she made them up and even began to tell him stories about her own life, and her own death, and her new life as an angel. Just before the end of that first day, she told him a sad story about a gentle, friendly, loving angel with nothing but goodness in her heart. She loved love, this angel, and had ruined her life because she believed that love would conquer all, because she wanted so badly to preserve the love between two young people, because it was such a special love and she couldn't bear to watch it die.

'But the angel has a secret,' she whispered and when she paused all that could be heard were his gentle sighs and the delicate fluttering of her butterfly dress. 'She has never been loved.' Again she paused. 'She has never kissed and been kissed. She has never felt how it would feel for love's warm arms to embrace her and inject her life with magic.' And then she sat in silence and thought her way through the life of this sad angel. She didn't say anything for some time and then she simply whispered, 'And she never will.'

Athena did not sleep; she walked around the heaven, spoke to the unicorn, asked the river for a few items that she didn't really want, but hoped would cheer her up, and finally came to rest on the hand-tree's thumb, dangling her legs above the fateful table that had played host to the dinner of doom. Their empty prawn cocktail bowls remained, waiting for an invisible waiter to bus them away. Her champagne glass was where she had left it; Chrono's had smashed on the table and shards gleamed up to her as she perused the scene. They hadn't even made it to the chicken course. She resolved to pack it all away after a few more hours of rest and she passed the rest of what she deemed night – although the sky refused to change its sickly scene – staring out into the horizon. Telling stories had left her head spinning. She hadn't heard herself speak for so long in centuries and she had forgotten that stories even existed, let alone that there were personal stories belonging to her alone. And now they seemed to be jumping inside of her, begging to be listened to, like demanding children.

Eventually, she lowered herself back down to the ground and strolled over to her little castle. She gently pushed open the door, determined not to disturb Chrono, although she wanted him to awaken more than anything in the angel realms. And when she crept inside it felt as if all of her prayers had been answered at once.

'Where am I?' His voice was weak and he was barely conscious, but he was restored enough to form a sentence. 'Athena!'

Athena stopped in the centre of the room. Chrono didn't know where he was and yet hers was the first name he called. 'I'm here, Chrono,' she told him soothingly and her presence immediately smoothed the lines on his face. 'I'm here,' she repeated and knelt beside him to stroke his hair. The moment he felt her touch, his features stilled and he drifted back to his own peaceful dream world. Athena let out a deep sigh. He was going to be all right. He would live to see another day. Additionally, it meant that Athena would spend eternity neither bottled on a shelf nor in a fiery hell, but these thoughts were not in her mind when she spent the rest of the night running her fingers through his hair.

After hours and hours of silence, a thin string of words meandered through the air. 'You have looked after me so lovingly.'

Although barely audible, the words startled Athena. She had drifted off into her own world as morning came upon them, but still she sat gently stroking his hair. She didn't know it, but he had been awake for some time, watching the colours in her hair illuminated against the glow of the yellows, oranges, reds and pinks of the perpetual sky through the stained-glass windows. When she turned to face him she saw that his layers were still away from him; he was still the innocent, vulnerable creature that she had nursed all day and night – a noble man of honour. Now that he was awake, however, it felt wrong to be stroking his hair, yet she didn't stop.

'What happened?' he asked croakily.

'You collapsed, Chrono,' Athena told him, before she had finalised the words in her mind. She had wondered if she would lie to him about what had happened when he awakened and now the words were out, she knew the answer. 'I have no idea what could be the cause, but the unicorn helped me to carry you in here.'

'You have been looking after me.'

Athena pulled her hand away from his hair and gripped it in her other hand awkwardly. Her eyes fell upon both hands as she spoke. 'You will be fully recovered in no time,' she told him and stood to leave.

'Wait!' he called hoarsely. 'How can I ever repay you?'

'There is no need to repay me, Chrono. I am just pleased that you are okay.' And she left him alone. She wondered if she should have suggested he repay her by getting her the hell out of Sam's heaven, but this would have been getting herself into even deeper hot water. She knew in her heart that he would find out about the love potion eventually – she even knew that she would be the one to tell him the truth – but she couldn't face it just yet. In these moments he looked at her in a way that no one had ever looked at her before and she couldn't be blamed for wanting to hold onto that for as long as she could.

In the weeks that followed, Chrono slowly regained his strength with Athena's help. She told him more stories and he could feel his heart strengthening; she gave him more of the snapdragon petals and he could feel his body repairing itself; and once a day she washed him all over with the rainbow water, which he found had no real medicinal effect, but gave him an all-over warmth that he had never felt before and knew he would miss when he eventually had to leave Athena's tiny castle. In addition to the stories, snapdragon petals and rainbow water, Athena brought him food and drink of all sorts – things he had seen before but never considered trying: soup, marshmallows, pork, orange juice, strawberries, curry. Even the food he found distasteful he enjoyed for the experience of eating it.

'You are ruining me,' he would joke with Athena, and he knew in part that it was true. He would be forever changed by the experience of his convalescence with Athena and now the idea of devoting himself to fate charts and guardian admin had very little appeal.

And then the day came that they both knew he would have to leave. He had been out of bed and walking for a few hours and he and Athena were sitting on the banks of the river with their feet in the cool, rainbow water.

'I cannot thank you enough, Athena,' he began and she immediately knew the direction of this conversation. She had been waiting for it. 'I have taken a vow to serve the higher powers and I must resume my responsibilities, but you have opened my eyes and–'

'Please, do not say more,' she said sadly. 'It has been my pleasure to nurse you back to health.'

Chrono reached out to his side and took her hand in his. As he turned to her he saw colours flushing in her cheeks. 'I would like to offer you a gift,' he began, 'to help you escape this place. As I have already told you, I cannot change Sam's fate, but–'

'Wait!' Athena said sadly and released her hand from his grip. She then turned away from him and was on her feet. She could not bear to have him look upon her.

'What is it, Athena? What saddens you so?'

'I cannot tell you, Chrono, but I cannot accept your gift.'

Chrono tried to confront her, but she turned from him again so he gripped her shoulders and turned her to face him. The distress in her eyes almost forced tears in his own. 'What is it, Athena? Tell me.'

'I cannot because you will hate me and I do not want you to hate me, Chrono.'

'How can I hate you? I–'

'No, don't say it, Chrono.' Now the tears were cascading down her face and she managed to break free from him and run. She wanted to run forever, but the landscape simply wouldn't allow it, so she stopped by the hand-tree and as she cried she felt the gentle, giant fingers stroking her back. And then Chrono was by her side. There was no escaping him.

'Please, Athena. What is it?'

'It was me. I made you sick. I tried to make you love me with a love potion, but I left it for a hundred years and it went rotten and I didn't think it would harm you. I wanted to trick you with love so you could see what love means and experience its strength. I wanted you to love me so that you would help me to leave this place.'

'It cannot be,' Chrono said, more to himself than to Athena, shaking his head and looking down to his feet. And then there was a stern seriousness to his face that Athena hadn't seen since before their meal. His layers had returned, fortifying him against a cruel world that laughed at him and played tricks on him for being a cold, lonely jobsworth. After a few more moments, the disbelief had left him and he was standing tall. When he spoke again his voice had an edge to it that Athena had never heard before and hoped never to hear again. He simply said, 'Goodbye, Athena.' If he had any questions to ask about the love potion, his illness, her stories, the food, the drink, their relationship, he showed no sign of wanting to ask them. He simply turned and began to walk away. For the second time, Athena watched helplessly as he became smaller and smaller and eventually disappeared from her life. When absolute silence had been restored, she threw her head back, opened her mouth and let out a piercing scream of agony that would last for two hundred years.

CHAPTER NINETEEN

It was another beautiful afternoon in which the world had forgotten its fierce ability to thrash and drown in the way Sam experienced on the night of his accident. In fact, it was easy to imagine that that night had taken place in a different world, in a different time where the elements conspired against the people, yet mirrored the violence within them. Sam wasn't even aware that violence could live in such a refined and delicate place as his soul, but flashes of that fateful night still presented themselves to him – the weight of the dagger against his thigh and the power of Pinecomb beneath him. However, he had that night to thank for so much. Without it – and his watery princess saviour – he would still be living a life of fear where anger could seize him without warning and threaten everything he held dear; where he did not know how to trust his own gentle soul to lead him to his heart's desires; he would still be living without the love of his life – without Fizz – and this was unimaginable to him now that he had spent the greatest week of his life with her. They were now sharing the beautiful afternoon and a picnic with Robin and Anne, who had spent a very different kind of week together, which began on the day of Sam's declaration of love.

'Please, tell me you were successful in your romantic attack,' Robin said when Sam returned to the animal house, after he had delivered his poem to Fizz, but he didn't need an answer. It was clear from the wide-eyed wonder on Sam's face and the pinking of his cheeks that something wonderful had seized him and it can only have been the reciprocation of his love. 'You are a dog, my friend!' Robin cheered and dropped his arm around Sam's shoulder. 'Now for the next step in our plan. You must arrange for a date of four. She will bring Anne and I will bring you.'

'Or I will bring you!'

'It matters not. We will embark upon a romantic stroll. Anne, influenced by the ease with which her friend gives over her heart, will have little choice but to fall for me.'

'It is not ease with which Fizz gives her heart,' Sam interrupted. 'It is with bravery and–'

'Save the poetic ruminating, my friend. We have pressing business ahead.'

'I fancy I am one step ahead of you, Robin. I have arranged to meet beautiful Fizz this evening at seven and she will have her friend by her side as a chaperone. I have spoken to her of you, making apologies for your rude appearance in the ale house.'

'What rude appearance?'

'And she is happy for it to be a date of four.'

'This is wonderful news,' Robin roared, with a head full of Anne, and mounted his horse. 'Wonderful!'

'Wait! Where are you going?'

'We have but three hours before our meeting. I must look my best. I am not happy to appear as if I have simply rolled out of my chamber and into my breeches in the way you do.'

This made Sam laugh, as most of Robin's insults succeeded in doing. 'I will meet you by the well at a quarter to the hour,' he told him.

'And in the meantime, my friend, I suggest you consider any one of the problems facing you. I would not trade lives with you for all the jewels in court.'

Sam was about to ask exactly what he meant when he heard, 'Yah!' and Robin rode off into the distance, leaving him alone with only thoughts of his problems for company. He lowered himself onto the front steps and was soon idly turning leaves in his hands as he had watched Fizz doing earlier. He smiled when he made the comparison in his head, but then began to explore exactly what Robin meant and it was only then that the extent of his troubles hit him. First there was his mother; he had managed to avoid her and she would be all the more annoyed with him since he left the banquet early, and he had left the castle early this morning without showing his face. Although he hadn't seen her, he could clearly imagine the look on her face – a fiery wrath of which he had received a taster at the banquet. He had always had such a good relationship with her that his brain couldn't quite cope with the shift in their relationship and so he moved on without reaching any kind of resolution. The face his mind then fell upon was Princess Jane of the Dales. He should have been delighted to have such a beautiful match, although, even if his heart were free to love another, he couldn't imagine finding union with a woman whose primary desires were treasures, jewels and other gifts with which he was supposed to adorn her. He would have paired such a materialistic creature with Robin, but now even he had surprised Sam by surrendering his heart to a woman who seemed to be an extremely genuine and earthy individual, a healer no less. Sam wouldn't have paired him with such a character in a million years, but he knew through his own experience that the heart wants what it wants. The love they had both found, however, presented yet more problems. They were noblemen, lords, knights, rulers of the land, and Fizz and Anne were village girls – an aleman's daughter and a local healer. Sam didn't have to dig very deep in his heart to realise that such unions would be forbidden. Robin could perhaps get away with maintaining a relationship with Anne, but Sam was the son of Lord Mardridge and was expected to marry well – to marry Princess Jane of the Dales – and as long as the castle stood beyond the oak-laden path, and as long as his parents walked the earth, Sam would not be able to find a way to free himself from this bond. The fact that he would probably die leading an army in just two weeks now seemed like the least of his problems.

As the hour of seven approached, Sam and Robin awaited the arrival of Fizz and Anne by the side of the well. It was far enough removed from the centre of the village for the meeting to go unnoticed and they could then walk the trail around the fields. Sam had tried to make conversation with his friend, but Robin was not forthcoming, choosing instead the company of his own thoughts. The transformation was hard to grasp; Robin was never voluntarily quiet and it was difficult to believe that a woman could be at the heart of his introspection. Sam would have been quite interested to speak to Anne and discover the qualities that had transformed his friend so dramatically, but the only woman on his mind was his own sweet Fizz.

'Look, they come,' he told Robin, and they both stood to attention, presenting themselves as tall, strong and worthy of such beauty. They had both adorned themselves in finery that they now peacocked in the direction of their mates, which would have been comical if not for the dignity and poise that they both managed to maintain.

'You are a vision, m'lady,' Sam said and bowed before fizz, who was wearing a long, lime-green dress that accentuated every curve of her body. Her hair was now long and loose, cascading down her shoulders like a darkened waterfall and the gentle shyness of her face melted Sam's heart all over again. By her side, Anne was also looking to Sam, perhaps evaluating his suitability as her best friend's suitor. She looked to be a little older than Fizz and her features were a little less refined, but she too held a certain appeal. She too was adorned in green, but a darker shade of woven fabric that hung from her frame in layers. As she stood before them, it was easy to imagine her as a healer. Her long sleeves were rolled back to the elbow and her own long, dark hair was tied back. Eventually her eyes moved from Sam when Robin addressed her similarly.

'M'lady,' he said, bowing, and she dipped her body for a chaste, almost impatient, curtsey. 'It is a beautiful evening. May I?' he asked and held out his arm for her to take. Meanwhile, Sam had offered his arm, Fizz had accepted and they had already begun their walk a few paces ahead. Anne looked to their example, shrugged, entwined her arm in Robin's and said, 'It can't hurt I s'pose.'

The look on his face told that he had never been so cheered about the actions of another in his entire life.

Just ahead of them, Sam had also felt nothing similar to the feeling of walking arm-in-arm with his beloved, but he knew he had to contain the euphoria and make conversation; he couldn't simply grin at her like a simpleton.

'So, Lady Felicity–'

'Call me Fizz, please.'

'Fizz. I want to know everything about you.'

Fizz giggled and said, 'Okay, but I fear there may not be enough pathway for such a broad topic. Is there anything in particular you would like to know?'

Sam shook his head and said, 'I simply want to know everything.'

Fizz took a deep breath and began. She was shy at first as she told him only the most basic details of a childhood spent as the child of the aleman. Her mother had passed away in the labour of her birth and the landlord had subsequently been both mother and father to her. She loved him more than anything in the world. She would play in the yard and cellar as a child, making little houses from barrels in which her dolls would play. The more she spoke, the more she warmed to her subject and she became more and more animated as she told of her progression through childhood. As soon as she was old enough to hold a tankard, her father had her working in the ale house, clearing tables. She was lucky that he was also determined for her to become a learned woman, and he taught her to read, write and manipulate numbers. Consequently, her role in life now was to look after the ale house books, as well as its general upkeep, and teach the boys to read and write in the school. She told the tale of her life with grace and restraint, shouldering the tragedy of her mother's death with dignity and sharing with him outrageous tales of drunkenness from her life at the ale house.

'And now you must tell me of your life, Sir Samuel Mardridge, although I suspect that I could tell you the details of your life just as readily.'

'Ah, so I am that easy to read.'

'Well, if I am not mistaken, you were born to Lord and Lady Mardridge, who adored you as their first and only son and lavished all your heart could desire upon you. You wanted for nothing and had riches the villagers here could not even imagine.'

For the first time since he had begun his walk with Fizz, he felt an emotion other than pure love and his smile dropped. 'There is more to me than what you imagine my spoiled life to be, Fizz. I cannot apologise for a childhood that contrasts so sharply with your own.'

'But I have not finished, m'lord. You grew up a sensitive soul, but this has escaped your father's attention and he is determined for you to lead his army. He and your mother are also determined for you to marry Princess Jane of the Dales. How am I doing?'

Sam pulled away from her and stopped walking. He wasn't thinking of Robin and Anne, but then he realised he would be blocking their path and turned to look behind him. The second couple, however, were nowhere to be seen.

'You are big news in the village, m'lord. I am not ignorant to your position. The announcement of your engagement was the only subject to be spoken in the ale house last night. Your jousting victory has been a hot topic since it happened, although my father will not hear your name spoken since your intrusion in the bar.' There was hurt in her eyes as she spoke.

'And what conclusion do you draw, m'lady?'

'What conclusion would you have me draw? My mind was screaming at me to come to my senses. "He is a lord! He is betrothed to a princess! He is about to go off in battle and may never return!" But the whisper of my heart is somehow louder and more powerful and here I am.'

Sam dropped down to his knee and took Fizz's hands in his own. 'Believe me when I say this, m'lady, that my heart speaks the same delicate language. I want for nothing but your love. I cannot marry Princess Jane, I cannot lead men in battle and I cannot make my parents happy. I would give away every comfort in the castle for a life with you and I will prove this to you, my love.'

Fizz stepped back and tugged gently on his arms, pulling him to his feet. When she stepped forward, they were chest to chest. Sam could feel the warmth of her rising up through her dress and gently brushing his face. He reached his hand to her cheek and brushed her hair behind her ear. He had never felt flesh so soft and smooth. His hands then traced the length of her, down to her hips and he felt her warm embrace around him. As their lips met, Sam closed his eyes and saw colours that hadn't existed before this moment; they were colours that he could smell and taste and feel and they surged around inside of him with a mind of their own, turning his stomach over like idle leaves in the hands of his beloved. When he opened his eyes a haze had descended around Fizz's features and when she came back into focus she was more beautiful than she had ever been.

'I love you,' he mouthed, 'and I will always love you. Together we can do anything.'

Fizz smiled weakly and kissed him again, this time quickly and tenderly, before pulling him close to her once again. They held each other, unmoved on the walkway, until the first of the night creatures began to stir beneath the most magnificent moon either of them had ever seen.

And so followed the greatest week of Sam's life. They walked every evening and embraced and kissed, and Sam met her in the morning to escort her to school. They even arranged a day away together, where they spent the entire day out in the fields, becoming further acquainted with the nature of each other's souls. They talked for hours and never tired of the sound of each other's voices. However, the issues of his parents, his position, Princess Jane of the Dales, Fizz's father and the imminent battle, silently hung over them and they were both prone to falling into silence when they could ignore their presence no longer. They didn't allow it to spoil their time together, but they were never completely free of its grip either. And now that their week had reached its end, Sam was determined to face these obstacles head-on. He had arranged the picnic to discuss his decision not only with Fizz, but with Robin and Anne also, although he had seen neither of them since the day of the walk. It was also the day before his twentieth birthday. He was used to the excesses of the castle at times of celebration, but it just didn't seem appropriate this year, so a low-key picnic was perfect. He was now sitting on a blanket in the middle of a field with Robin, waiting for the girls to arrive. They were surrounded by bowls and plates holding everything from chicken, sandwiches and potted meats to strawberries, cake and cream, all lovingly prepared by Cook, who could smell a love affair as strongly as the smell of bacon in the morning and found it just as irresistible. As he waited, Sam felt the weight of his announcement bearing down on him and desperate to lighten the mood, turned to Robin to enquire after his week, which he was sure would provide a certain entertainment.

'She is quite a woman,' Robin answered, staring off into the distance. 'I have not met another quite like her.'

'So what have you been doing? I have not seen you since the beginning of our walk last week and you simply disappeared.'

'She was very easily persuaded to join me in the bushes and we have been joining each other at every available opportunity ever since.'

'You are a dog, Sir Robin.'

'No, it is not like that, Sam. I know now that I love her, but …'

Sam waited patiently for Robin to open his heart, which was something that didn't come easy to him.

'But I think she loves another, Sam.'

'Really? So how is she finding herself in your arms with such regularity?'

'I think it is just something she does. She is insatiable. If it hadn't been with me, I feel certain that she would find another mate for the night.'

Sam smiled, incredulous; he had not heard of such behaviour from a woman other than rumours of the kind that receive payment for their efforts.

'The physical act brings her closer to her spiritual self, she tells me. I have no idea what she is talking about, other than I could be any man. I am simply relief to some kind of deep spiritual need that nestles inside of her.'

Sam helped himself to a chicken drumstick. He had promised himself he would wait for Fizz and Anne to arrive, but now he was suddenly ravenous. 'And how is she when fully clothed?' Sam asked as the chicken swirled around inside his mouth.

'If anything, she seems bored, Sam, but how can that be? My company has been sought after by women since I was old enough to walk unaided.'

'I fancy you may have met your match.'

'You are finding this funny, Sam?' He didn't wait for an answer. 'Would it be funny if Lady Felicity desired you only to scratch an itch that her fingers couldn't reach?'

The thought was a sobering one and Sam quickly began to empathise. 'Perhaps her love will develop over time.'

'This is where my hope lies, but, as I said, Sam, I suspect her heart is with another and if this is so, all is truly lost. I would die for this woman, Sam, but she would be untroubled by the gesture.'

'I will see if I can near the truth with Fizz,' Sam offered and Robin smiled his gratitude, but it was a smile that showed little consolation after a mighty defeat. He appeared before his friend as a man whose life was nearing its end.

CHAPTER TWENTY

As Noah's consciousness slowly returned, a number of things became painfully apparent all at once: his head hurt – this was an understatement – it felt as if he had saved up a year's worth of hangovers to have all at the same time. At the centre of the pain was his face, which throbbed to the rhythm of his heart as he struggled to open his eyes. He also became aware that he couldn't move his hands; however much he struggled, they remained fixed behind him at the wrist. And he was on his knees; this was the strangest realisation of all because he had never woken up on his knees before, and then everything began to slot into place: the exam; he had been running; he had run past the Sir Robin's Head and encountered the burly landlord. The smell of stale beer in the air confirmed that he was on the right track and when he finally managed to open his eyes and saw the man himself staring down at him, he knew it all to be true. But however dangerous his situation now was, the only thing on his mind was the fact that he had failed; Charlotte was in a hospital bed just a few miles away and he had managed to walk into this situation rather than making it to her bedside. Maybe he deserved any kind of justice that the landlord could deal him.

'Good kip?' the Scot asked him and the sound of another human voice helped Noah recover even more of a sense of himself and his surroundings. He was in a bathroom. It wasn't the gents of the Sir Robin's Head, so it must have been the landlord's private bathroom. He could hear the occasional car slowly driving by outside below them and could easily work out that they were on a higher floor than the main bar. In front of him was a bathtub full of water and beside that sat the oversized figure of the landlord with a contented smile on his face. He looked like a trucker on a break, with his mighty steel-capped boots, dirty jeans and sleeveless denim jacket revealing arms full of ink history, in which pin-up girls and gambling featured heavily. His face was chiselled from the same tough material as Charlotte's father and Noah wondered if they made blokes differently fifty years ago. He could imagine living to a hundred and never looking as hard and leathery as these two men.

'You have to let me go!' Noah said, surprising himself with the force in his voice.

The landlord's smile revealed a gold tooth and a message for Noah that he was in his world now and there was very little he could do about it.

'Please! My girlfriend's in hospital. I need to get to her.'

The landlord slowly rose to his feet. 'Ye'll be getting te her soon enough, lad,' he beamed and slammed his mighty palm down on the back of Noah's neck before gripping tightly. Noah was so shaken and surprised by the movement that he didn't have the presence of mind to take a deep breath before the landlord pushed his face into the freezing cold bathtub of water. He desperately tried to resist, but with his hands bound he had no way of pushing. He tried to scrabble his feet onto the ground, but every time he was near to standing he felt his legs kicked out from under him. With nothing to lever him, he tried pushing his body upwards, using the muscles of his shoulders and stomach alone, but his strength was no match for the full body weight of the landlord bearing down on him. The futility of his situation didn't stop him from struggling and he continued to wriggle and push until he felt as if his lungs would explode. He had managed to keep his mouth tightly closed to begin with, but now the meagre air that he had taken down with him was escaping his lungs and rippling past his face in fierce bubbles. What he did next was completely irrational, but he could see the end clearly, he could see himself dying right here in this bathtub, terrified, alone, humiliated. His lungs were screaming in his ears for more air and he answered by expelling everything left inside of him in a frustrated and devastated scream of his own. Thankfully, it was at this moment that he felt the hand move to the back of his head, grip his hair and drag him upwards.

'How d'ye like that, Goldilocks? Eh?'

Noah was coughing and choking too much to hear him let alone answer. The landlord had dumped him down beside the stinking toilet and he was frantically dragging in the oxygen, desperate to restore his life force.

'Good, eh?'

Noah still couldn't talk.

'What's that? Ye want te do it again? Well, if ye insist.'

Noah tried to scramble away, but there was nowhere to go and the landlord was quickly on him once again. He gripped and twisted Noah's hair around his mighty fist and pulled him back to the side of the bath.

'No, please,' Noah begged, but his voice was barely audible and the landlord was laughing too much to listen to his feeble pleading and his head was soon back under the water. He had the presence of mind to drag in as much air as he possibly could this time and he needed it because the landlord seemed to have no intention of letting him up. Noah tried not to struggle, concentrating his efforts on keeping calm and enduring the torture, but his body had other ideas and kicked out in a frenzy that he couldn't control. Once again, the air began to seep from his lungs, bubble by bubble, until he was on empty again and his head was going to explode from the pressure. And still the landlord wasn't relenting. Noah felt that he had only moments of consciousness left in his dizzied body and all he could think to do was hold Charlotte in his mind – the funny little smile she did when she was being a geek about music, the way she played with his hair when they were lying together, the sweetness of her perfume, her soft lips against his, the delicate tone of her voice. Charlotte's presence was a salve to his suffering and brought with it peace for Noah, as if the simple fact that he had had her in his life was enough for him to die a happy man. He even thought he saw her face in the water in front of him as his brain became a swirl of confusion.

'Don't ye peg out on me yet,' he then heard. He was barely conscious, but out of the water again. There was no time for relief, however, as he felt the full force of a size thirteen, steel-capped boot powering into his side. His experience in the bathtub was child's play compared to what he now felt; his lungs had been turned inside out and his brain had exploded into piercing shards. Again and again, he felt the force of the boot in his stomach, powering down onto his legs and back as the landlord shouted down at him about trespassing and how his pub was a sacred space and he wasn't welcome there. And then finally, although Noah didn't know much about it, he received a kick in the head that provided the only relief he had felt since he opened his eyes and saw the landlord – unconsciousness.

The next thing he knew he was waking up once again and this time the dawning sensations were far more tolerable – the soft cool of cotton sheets, the warmth of a bed, the relief of having neither his hands bound nor his head submerged in bath water. But the pain was immediate, although the fuzziness in his head told him that he had been given some seriously strong painkillers.

'Charlotte,' he tried to say, but his mouth wouldn't work properly and he could feel a deep cut on his lip reopened when he tried to use it.

'Just relax, Noah,' a gentle voice told him.

He tried to struggle and resist, to force himself into full consciousness and work out where he was and what was happening, but he simply didn't have the strength. And then he felt himself drift away again and the voice became distant before falling silent.

When he next became aware of himself, things were a little easier. Although painful, at least one of his eyes opened without too much encouragement and his mind didn't feel quite as addled as it had been before. His body felt just as broken and battered, but the overriding glee he felt at simply being alive made even this tolerable.

'Charlotte,' he mumbled again and tried to hoist himself up onto his elbow, but a friendly voice stopped him.

'Just relax, Noah,' it told him. 'You're safe. You're in hospital.'

Noah allowed himself to be settled back down onto the pillow and looked straight up at the ceiling, panting and frustrated.

'Do you remember what happened?'

He closed his eyes as he began to relive the ordeal in the bathroom and then opened them and focused on the nurse in front of him. She was extremely young, perhaps a trainee nurse, with a sweet, caring face that made her a natural confidante, but Noah didn't want to talk about it. 'Charlotte,' he mouthed again instead.

'Just relax and I'll get you some water.'

Relaxing was easier said than done when all he wanted to do was jump out of bed and rush to his girlfriend's side, but he took a few deep breathes and waited for the water, which would definitely be welcome. When she had returned and he had taken a few sips, he asked, 'Is anything broken?'

She smiled and shook her head. 'No. You've been extremely lucky.' She coloured a little then added, 'You know what I mean.'

He nodded slowly. 'When can I go home?'

'Let's just take things one step at a time. You're pretty well beaten up and it won't do you any harm to stay with us for a few days.'

'A few days?' There was power in his voice that surprised him. He was far stronger than he originally felt and was getting stronger all the time.

'It's lucky that you're so fit or you might have been in trouble.'

The rest of the day passed slowly with the only event of note being the moment that Noah was able to get out of bed and go to the loo. Because he had achieved this, the nurse had agreed to get a doctor to discharge him in the morning. Most of the day had been spent sighing and groaning and generally resisting the bed rest that his body needed, but a nurse had been on hand every time he made the misguided decision of trying to get out of bed and walk about. However, after the ward lights had been turned on in the evening and then turned off after dark, Noah was able to slip away unnoticed. He was on his hands and knees as he slowly progressed past the nurses' station without being spotted and then managed to move along the corridors using a Zimmer frame he had found discarded outside the next ward. He must have looked quite a sight with one eye swollen shut and purple, a slash on the bridge of his nose and a split lip, but his appearance was the last thing on his mind. All he cared about was finding Charlotte. He rightly figured that the position of her father would hold some sway at the hospital and she would have her own room. It was only a small hospital, so he was easily able to locate the private wing from the map. However, by the time he made it to the entrance, all the time ducking and dodging staff and then moving as quickly as he could without detection, he was close to collapse. The nurse had been right. He should have stayed in bed. But then he saw her name on the door – Charlotte Mitchell – and he knew that it had been worth it.

Her room was deathly quiet, especially compared to his ward, which had been in chaos for most of the day with every sound aggravating an injury somewhere on his body. The darkness and peace were a great relief to his weary bones, as was the soft chair he lowered himself into by her side. He could barely see her face in the darkness, but he knew how peaceful and beautiful she would look as she slumbered and he was pleased that she was finally able to get some rest. He reached on top of the covers and held her hand. Just as he had felt when they kissed on that first day, the essence of her crept into his body as they touched. The power of their connection clearly affected her too as he began to feel her hand stir in his.

'Noah,' she mouthed sleepily, barely conscious.

'It's okay, baby. I'm here. Don't wake up. I'm not going anywhere.'

'But Noah, you have to be careful.' She was speaking as if stuck in a dream, the words languid and stretched. 'Robin didn't do it.'

Noah squeezed her hand and wanted to simply tell her to relax and go back to sleep, but he found himself asking, 'So who did then?'

'It could have been anyone – Lord Mardridge, the aleman, Sam's mother, his little sister. Anyone could have got to him. Robin was his friend. He could trust him. He would never do anything to hurt him.' There was panic in her voice now as she mumbled sleepily.

Noah squeezed her hand tightly and said, 'It's okay. It's all going to be okay, my sweet. Rest now. It's all going to be okay.'

'But you nearly drown, Sam.'

'I–' Noah stopped abruptly as the words hit him and then the fatigue and injury of his own body became a force too strong to resist and he lowered his head slowly down to the bed, keeping her hand in his. 'Just rest now, baby,' he told her, his voice becoming just as drawn-out and dreamy as hers. 'It will all be okay in the morning.'

CHAPTER TWENTY-ONE

Fizz's face lit up when she saw the spread of food beautifully arranged on the blanket for their picnic. Her eyes perused the array of breads, pies, meats and sweets with uncontained delight and when they finally fell upon Sam she looked happier still. By contrast, Anne's reaction to Robin's presence was not one of adoration; she was pleased to see him – in fact she looked to him as if he were a far superior dish to those laid out before her and she couldn't wait to devour him – but if the eyes portray the content of the heart, it was clear that it was not a heart that beat for Robin.

'Welcome, ladies. We are so pleased you could grace us with your presence,' Sam said and both men stood to greet them before they were all were seated around the food. Again, Fizz and Anne wore the same colour dresses, but slightly different shades and styles. Fizz's figure-hugging, light, lemon, summery frock was feminine and elegant, where Anne's sunny, layered dress was heavier and more functional, and she was carrying some kind of container. As always, they both looked beautiful, but there was only one woman from whom Sam could not tear his eyes. And it was clear that Fizz felt the same, for they had very quickly found the sweet spot in each other's arms.

'Get a chamber!' Anne joked, beaming a smile, but her tone embarrassed the couple enough for them to separate, and laughter erupted between the four of them, breaking the ice on their afternoon picnic.

'I trust you are both well,' Sam began politely and both ladies responded with a gentle nod.

'It is a pleasure to see you again,' Robin told Anne, and she smiled loosely before turning to Sam.

'This is quite a feast,' she said. 'Thank you for asking me along and happy birthday for the morrow.'

'Thank you, but please do not thank me,' Sam replied and paused, adding weight to what would come next. 'Today is not about my imminent birthday. I need the support of my good friend Robin today and I feel that Fizz will need your support, Anne.'

'Why, m'lord?' Fizz asked gently, reaching over to take his hand in hers.

'First we eat,' Sam told them. 'This tantalising feast will fortify us for the task ahead.'

'You are scaring me, Sam,' Fizz whispered into his ear.

He allowed his fingertips to settle on her cheeks before bringing a finger to her lips, silencing her concern. 'First we eat,' he repeated and smiled the smile of a brave knight.

'Good!' chirped Anne. She was proving herself a master at lightening the tone. 'Because I was up half the night preparing these green scones,' she said, opening the container. 'Don't look like that,' she told the others, whose faces had all dropped at the pairing of the words green and scones. 'They are a tradition in my clan. And you must only eat as much as you need. One bite for luck, two bites for help from heaven above, three bites for money, four bites stirs the heart ready for love.'

Fizz giggled as her friend said this. She was clearly used to the quirks of the healer and happy to go along with it. Taking this as his cue, Sam also smiled, a little guardedly at first, but then he entered into the spirit of the game.

'You first, m'lord,' Anne smiled and held the container out for him to take the first of the green scones.

Sam reached out then held a scone in his hand and stared at it with wide eyes. He had never seen a scone quite like it. It was fashioned similarly to the kind of cakes he would eat for afternoon tea, but speckled through with green herbs and powder that gave the appearance that the whole thing was swamp green with extra lumps of greenery thrown in for good measure. Smeared onto the surface was a lime-coloured topping that may have been appetising adorning a moist sponge, but only added to the unpalatable appearance of this scone. 'Are you sure this is okay?' he asked.

'You will offend me, m'lord,' Anne smiled. 'This recipe has been in my family for generations and has brought luck, guidance, riches and love to both beggars and princes.'

'Well, if it's good enough for beggars and princes, it is good enough for me,' Sam smiled, and took his first bite as the others looked on expectantly, although they all knew that he would finish the scone in four bites. He already had Fizz's love, but it didn't hurt to top it up. When he had taken the final bite, the others cheered gleefully.

'May the angels look upon you gladly, Lord Samuel, and always furnish you with love. Lady Fizz,' she said and offered the container to her friend. Fizz took a scone and eyed it just as suspiciously as Sam had before her.

'What does it taste of, m'lord?'

'Erm …' Sam moved his tongue around in his mouth to test the remnants for flavour then shrugged. 'It is like nothing I have ever tasted, Fizz. It was actually delightful. My compliments to the chef.'

Anne bowed her head, playfully accepting the compliment, and they all watched as Fizz took her first bite. Her face lightened as she too was pleased by the taste. Then she took a second then a third bite and stopped eating. 'Money it is,' she said. 'To be showered in shillings for once would be no bad thing.'

'But–' Sam began, looking genuinely hurt, and before he could continue Fizz was giggling and had popped the last piece of the scone into her mouth.

'May the heavens open and rain down love upon you for ever more,' Anne told her and turned to Robin, holding the container for him to take a scone. Without a moment's hesitation he munched the scone down in four clear bites, all the time maintaining eye contact with his beloved Anne.

'May the Gods deliver amore and a mate for your soul.'

Robin smiled at this, seemingly pleased with his lot, before Anne took out the final scone and held it in her hands. She held it above the picnic feast theatrically and all four eyes fell upon it like a chalice of miracles. When she had held them rapt for as long as she could get away with, she slowly moved the remaining scone to her own mouth and pushed the whole thing in without taking a single bite. She laboured at her chewing, her mouth bulging, before swallowing it down in one.

'And what does taking no bites mean?' asked Sam.

'It means I am hungry,' she beamed. 'Let's eat!'

With the ice well and truly broken, the four ate and laughed and played and joked as if they had known each other all their lives. They told stories and poked fun at each other, and made light work of the substantial picnic. Their merriment was only interrupted when Sam spotted a slight, familiar figure in the distance, hiding in the long grass.

'Do my eyes deceive me, Robin, or is that Jennifer over yonder?'

Robin turned behind to where his friend was pointing and saw Jennifer in the distance, oblivious to their picnic, clearly playing a game of cat and mouse with the boys from the village. He smiled widely. 'She is a wild one, that sister of yours. She is more of a warrior than you are, Sam.'

'Very funny! But she is going to get hurt, Robin,' Sam replied and was soon on his feet and marching towards his sister. When he eventually made it over to her hiding place, he scared her so much that her instinct was to draw her weapon on the intruder.

'It is me! It is Sam,' he assured her, and she lowered what was another fierce-looking dagger.

'You should not creep up on people, Sam,' she complained and settled back into her lookout role as if their conversation was over. Again, she had been put in a dress that she had ruined. Sam wondered if their mother might not have noticed by now and dressed her more appropriately, but what was the alternative? It wasn't as if she could dress her little girl in breeches.

'What are you doing?' Sam asked.

'I am playing war and you will get me killed if you don't bop down.'

Sam crouched by her side and could see the village boys way out in the distance trying to find her.

'But this is not a toy,' Sam said and took the dagger from her.

'Hey! That is mine!'

'No, I do not know where you got this one from, but it is not yours.'

'You are such a loser, Sammy. Just because you faint at the idea of war does not mean that the rest of us do.'

'Why do you speak this way, Jennifer? Are we no longer friends?'

'Friends spend time together, Sam. I have not seen you this past week. You have given me no new words. You forget you have a sister when you fall in love.'

'How did you …? It matters not. I could never forget you, Jennifer. I love you.'

'I do not care anyway,' she snapped. 'I have other friends. I do not need you.'

Sam was too stunned to speak for a few moments and then said, 'I will always be your friend, Jennifer.'

'If you were my friend you would give me back my knife.' The words sounded so strange coming from the soft and delicate lips of a child with her blonde curls mirroring Sam's own.

'I will not give you back your knife and I am going to speak to Mother about this. I am worried for you, Jennifer.'

Jennifer was suddenly on her feet and snatched the dagger from Sam's hands before he could ready himself for the offensive. It would seem he couldn't even lead a battle against a nine-year-old girl.

'You're not going to tell Mother,' she yelled and the sound of her raised voice signalled shouting in the distance. She had blown her cover and the village boys were racing towards her, shouting her name amidst their deadly war cries. Jennifer readied herself to run, but faced her brother and said, 'You won't tell Mother because I will stop you, Sam.'

'And what is that supposed to mean?' Sam was also on his feet, moving towards her, but there was something wild in her eyes that persuaded him to keep his distance.

'I will stop you!' she repeated at the top of her voice and then ran away from the village boys as fast as she could and disappeared into the surrounding bushes. Sam was too stunned to move to begin with and was almost sent flying by the stampede of village boys that tumbled past him, determined to sniff her out. He watched the bushes with his hands on his hips and when all was finally quiet, he re-joined his picnic.

'I told you she was a wild one,' Robin laughed. Even at a distance he had heard her shouts and seen the way she handled the dagger.

'Wild? I fear she is a lunatic.'

'She is just a child,' Robin told him. 'Do not take her so seriously, my friend. She likes to have fun like the boys. This is not so unusual.'

'But I will still tell Mother. She will hurt herself eventually with the weaponry she wields.'

'Women were always traditionally warriors,' Anne added, also smiling.

'Urgh! Can you imagine it?' Fizz answered. 'How awful it would be to dress in metal, straddle a horse and ride apace with the intention of killing.'

'My thoughts exactly,' Sam said.

'But you really are a girl,' Robin quipped and laughter abound once again. 'Do not worry, my friend,' Robin added. 'Would it sooth you if I sought her out and spoke to her, tried to teach her a little more about the dangerous nature of weapons? You may not be able to stop her games, but you can at least appease your mind with her safety.'

'That might actually work,' Sam answered.

'I will return shortly,' Robin smiled, gathering himself to his feet.

'You are going now?'

'There is no time like the present. I should easily catch her on the other side of the river. I will be no more than a half hour, Sam.'

Sam watched as Robin sprinted off to catch his sister. He knew that Robin couldn't resist a weapon-related challenge, even if it was simply taming his little sister.

True to his word, he returned a little under thirty minutes later, out of breath and beaming. 'Success!' he was saying, seemingly to Anne, who didn't look particularly interested. 'I got it,' he said, and swung the dagger in front of them. It may have been a threatening gesture in the hands of another, but his control and skill turned it into yet another display to impress Anne. 'She's a ferocious-looking creature,' he added. 'The dagger, that is, not Jennifer,' he smiled and slipped the dagger into his belt. 'I exchanged it for the promise of combat lessons in the morrow.'

'Thank you, my friend. This means more than you could ever know.'

'I will ensure her safety and you never know; your father might yet have a knight to lead his army in the future.'

This caused an eruption of laughter all around and even Sam saw the funny side, but just as the subject of the imminent battle was raised, the sun disappeared behind a miserable-looking cloud and Sam's heart sunk. The beginning of the afternoon had gone exactly as he had planned – with merriment and dining, laughter, love and friendship – the second part had also been formulated in his mind and its content was far less joyous.

'My friends,' he began solemnly and each of the faces around the blanket knew that this was the moment they had been waiting for, for which all that came before had led. 'This week has been sheer bliss. I have never known the happiness I have experienced with my dear Fizz and I want for nothing more when I am in her arms.' He took hold of Fizz's hand as he spoke, and Robin and Anne's smiles were similar in their admiration of the moment. 'But we all know that such a sweet union is currently balanced precariously on a fantasy island, which is sinking under the weight of responsibility, to lead an army, to be a worthy son, to be a worthy suitor to this beautiful woman in the eyes of her terrifying father. The stars are crossed in our union and I have turned my face from both problem and solution for too long. This past week I have managed to avoid my mother, father and his army, my betrothed and the ale house, but I propose to alter this.' He paused to let this sink in and all faces remained silently upon him. 'This very afternoon, when the last of our feast has been devoured, I will march into the castle and confess my heart to my mother and father. I will tell them that my loves are of this woman and a peaceful existence where poetry prevails ahead of war.'

'Are you sure, my friend? You have much to lose.'

'The only thing I have to lose is my precious Fizz and I would be no kind of man if I did not stand up and declare the contents of my heart.'

'But your father might ... he could kill you, Sam. He is such an unpredictable man.'

'I do not believe that a man could kill his son no matter how deeply his disappointment fires his vengeance. I am ready to do this and would feel stronger with you all beside me. What say you?'

Fizz gripped his hands tightly. 'I have only fear for you, m'lord. I would die without you. My life would simply cease to exist and I would see no reason to drag my soulless body from empty moment to empty moment.'

'You must not speak like this, Fizz. Have faith. We do not know the outcome. I will stand tall and brave before my parents and they will have no choice but to respect my decisions as a man. After we have visited the castle I will beg the mercy of your father for my unforgivable behaviour in the ale house and throw myself upon his mercy to prove my worthiness as a suitor to his daughter.'

'Now, he really will kill you,' Robin told him, and although there was an element of jest to his tone, they all knew that this was a possibility. Fizz's father had once thrown a man through the ale house window for looking at his beloved daughter the wrong way when she was clearing tables; he would do whatever it took to protect her.

'I ask again,' Sam said, sitting upright and noble in the face of the task ahead. 'What say you?'

'You're so much braver than any of your old man's knights,' Anne told him. 'If you need my support, you've got it.'

Sam bowed his acceptance and turned to Robin.

'You know I always have your back,' he said, which left only Fizz.

'M'lord, I would follow you to the ends of the earth and back.'

'Then it is settled. Today is the day I will finally seize control of my own destiny and become a man.' And of course Sam had no way of knowing that today would also be the day that he breathed his last breath.

CHAPTER TWENTY-TWO

Noah began to stir as a lazy sun started to appear through the thin hospital curtains. He had fallen asleep just where he had sat talking to Charlotte, with his hand in hers and his head resting on the bed. As he wrestled to keep his good eye open, fighting the desire to go straight back to sleep, he saw that she hadn't changed position either and was still sleeping soundly, which made him smile. It was exactly what she needed and he hadn't seen her so peaceful for weeks. He slowly levered his hand from hers and quietly stretched out his body, which felt a different kind of terrible now that his injuries had had the time to settle in; rather than acute pain, his body was now seized by aches and stiffness, and he knew he would need the Zimmer frame he had borrowed to make it back to his own ward. He so wanted to stay, but above all else Charlotte needed to rest and he didn't need any more trouble.

Judging by the strength of the sun, it couldn't have been much later than 7.00 a.m. and if he left now he could be away without alerting anyone to his absence from his own bed or presence at the side of hers. He swung his legs to the side and reached for the solid railing at the bottom of her bed to hoist himself up onto his feet. When he had made it he simply stood there for a few seconds, waiting for the head-rush to pass and for his legs to strengthen into a set of something useful and strong enough to carry him back into his ward. He took a few deep breaths in and out and then slowly began to put one foot in front of the other with his head down, as if his legs wouldn't work unless he scrutinised their every movement. He managed to shuffle away from the bed in this way, with his head down, but when he looked up again he saw that he wasn't alone in the room. Charlotte's dad was standing in the doorway in his police uniform, taking up almost all of the space, his face configured into terrifying disbelief and his body edged slightly forward as if he could launch at any moment.

'Shit!' Noah couldn't stop the word escaping him.

'I'll give you "shit"!' Mitchell told him and reached out to grab his gown.

'Wait! Please! I can explain!'

But Charlotte's father clearly wasn't in the mood for explanations as he yanked Noah out of the room, with no regard for his injuries and dragged him through one corridor after another. Noah tried to find purchase on the walls and railings he passed and desperately tried to dig his bare feet into the shiny, tiled flooring, but he was a ragdoll in the big man's arms. More than one nurse tried to stop him as he dragged Noah out, but he was a man possessed, and when he finally reached the exit, the security guard took one look at the superior status of his uniform and left him to it.

Charlotte's dad pushed the exit door open and the cool morning air hit Noah hard, but not as hard as the cold concrete ground, which came up on him far too quickly for him to prevent more injury. This time he cut his knee wide open as he landed, with no shoes or jeans to protect his prone body. Strangely, in that moment, Noah almost felt grateful to the landlord who had attacked him. He had been thumped in the street, kicked, punched and nearly killed in a bath of water – But you nearly drown, Sam. As far as attacks went, this one paled in comparison; his body had already been pushed so far beyond its limits that he had very little left to give in terms of surprise, fear and pain. He had felt it all before and twice as bad, but this attack had an added dimension: Charlotte's dad had the power to take away the one thing that he cared about more than anything else in the world.

'I told you to stay away from her!'

'But I love her!'

'If you love her you'll leave her alone to find someone who deserves her, a real man.'

'And if you loved her you would give her the freedom to spend her life with whomever she chooses.' Noah surprised himself with the force in his voice.

'Are you back-chatting me, boy?' Mitchell demanded and marched the few steps across to where Noah was helplessly propping himself up by the side of a Vauxhall Corsa.

Noah slammed his eyes shut and awaited the inevitable blow, but it never came. Instead, he heard a familiar voice.

'No, Dad! Stop!' She could barely be heard for fatigue, but it was very definitely Charlotte.

Mitchell softened on sight of his daughter, raced to her side and was suddenly like a different person, but as he tried to support Charlotte, she shrugged him off.

'I can't believe you would do that!' she cried weakly and now there were nurses at her side, encouraging her back into the warm and two more had raced through the doors to scrape Noah off the concrete and get him into a wheelchair.

'Sweetheart, he's no good for you.'

He really was a Jekyll and Hyde character and Noah couldn't believe the change in him now that his precious daughter could view him. No wonder she loved him so much and wanted to look after him.

'I'm not buying it, Dad, not this time. I've never seen you like that. I didn't even know you were capable of behaving like that.' She also allowed herself to be helped into a wheelchair and took a deep breath before speaking again. She was as pale as it was possible to be and barely had the strength to hold her own head up, but her determination was fierce. 'To think of all the boys I ditched because you told me they were wrong. But it's you; you're the one who's wrong.'

One of the nurses tried to wheel Noah away, but he made her stay; he wasn't going to miss this for the world.

'Sweetheart, I only want the best for you.' He was crouching beside her now, using soft, fragrant words that were a million miles from his earlier display.

'I'm sorry, Dad, but I have to take control of this, of my whole life.'

'That's what I'm here for, love.'

'No, Dad, it's not. You're here to love me and support me, not run my life.'

Noah could see the cracks in his veneer starting to show as he straightened himself up and cast his imposing shadow over her. 'I'm not to be made a fool of, Charlotte.'

'I'm not making a fool of you, Dad.'

'You're welcome to see whoever you want. Just don't expect a bed under my roof while you're doing it.'

The agony on Charlotte's face was clear and Noah desperately tried to pull himself up out of the wheelchair to be by her side, but he felt a heavy hand on his shoulder and turned to see a nurse shaking her head. He wasn't sure whether she was stopping him for his health or because going over would only make things worse, but he was glad she did, because after the hurt had passed, charlotte looked to her father with a strength that far exceeded anything he could add to the occasion.

'Then I guess I won't be living you anymore,' she said and turned away, indicating to the nurse that she was ready to be wheeled back to her bed.

Noah was wheeled away moments later, past the big man who hadn't moved since his confrontation with his daughter. His world had clearly crashed down around him and Noah could almost feel sorry for him, but not quite.

Noah and Charlotte spent the next couple of days in hospital, where they decided that she would move in with him. This decision was further cemented by the fact that her father had packed up all of her possessions and dumped them on the street outside Noah's bedsit. They had learnt this from Thane, who had taken them to his house. They had also learnt that Annabel was also refusing to stay in the house because of her uncle's actions and was currently staying with Thane. It was all such a mess, but at the same time these were exciting times. Noah and Charlotte loved each other so very much that the idea of living together outweighed the trauma they had both suffered. For Charlotte, moving in with Noah almost made up for the pain she felt at losing her dad – but not quite. Every time she thought about him her stomach still sank and she prayed for things to be different, but she ultimately knew she would just have to make the best of this new situation.

Noah recovered well from his injuries and Charlotte's nervous exhaustion had been soothed by the nights of uninterrupted sleep. The dreams had stopped and she had managed to write the lyrics to her song, which slotted beautifully into the music. They came to her one night, as if delivered by divine intervention and then she was suddenly at peace. All the weeks of obsession and dreams wearing her down seemed a distant memory and they both put it down to the fact that she was under more pressure from her dad than even she had realised. He had done such a good job of manipulating her that she had internalised her distress, which had created the dreams. It wasn't uncommon in the face of stress.

They adapted to living together well, with Noah taking any opportunity to spoil her, from bringing her breakfast in bed to massaging her feet, while Charlotte would sing to him and play with his hair as they held each other close. And every time he caught Charlotte in a distant fug, thinking about the loss of her father, he would comfort her and tell her that a lifetime is a long time. He would eventually see that they were happy and come back into their lives.

On a sunny Sunday, almost a month after they were released from the hospital, a knock at the door stirred the couple. Standing on the doorstep of the bedsit were Thane and Annabel with a picnic hamper and blanket. A little further down the walkway, little Julia was propping herself up on the gate playing her PSP.

'Surprise!' They both shouted when Noah came down to open the door. It was late morning, but he stood before them in just his boxer shorts and a bad case of bed-head. Charlotte joined him moments later with a robe wrapped around her and a matching just-got-out-of-bed look.

'Interrupting something mucky are we?' Thane giggled and Noah stretched his arm out around Charlotte, pulled her close and kissed her. 'Urgh! Get a room!'

'We've got one thanks and we'd like to get back to it if you don't mind.'

'But we're here to surprise you, take you out. We've got a picnic and everything.'

'And what's the occasion?'

'Well, if I'm not mistaken, it's someone's twentieth birthday tomorrow.'

Noah flushed and beamed a smile down at Charlotte. 'Did you know about this?'

She shook her head.

'We cooked,' Annabel added.

'No, I cooked. Annabel here burns ice-cream.'

'No I don't!' Her mock outrage turned into laughter and the other couple were soon also kissing and fooling around on the doorstep.

When they had finished, Noah said, 'That's really sweet, the picnic and all, but we might need an hour or so to get ready.'

'You've got thirty minutes,' Thane told them, already backing away from the house. 'We've chosen a lovely spot just before the oaks leading up to the castle. Come and find us.'

'And if you can't see us just follow the incessant beeping of Julia's video games,' Annabel smiled, as Julia jumped down to walk with them without taking her eyes off her game, but the smile hid a grimace and her true feelings about her boyfriend's little sister. Annabel was not the maternal type and Julia was a tough child to love.

Half an hour later, the five of them were sitting around Thane's tartan blanket and the feast he had laid out for them all – chicken, ham, eggs, salad, savoury rice, coleslaw and a sweet selection of cakes and pastries. Charlotte and Annabel were both settled back against the legs of their men and Julia was idly munching on a chicken drumstick as she maintained her gameplay with one hand.

'So have you heard anything more from the university?' Thane asked.

Noah shook his head gravely, but then smiled, determined that the day wouldn't be about his woes. 'They said they'll consider my appeal, but they're right really; I was failing and I didn't turn up to my exam. They had every right to kick me out.'

'What you gonna do now?'

'Well, I really was considering joining the police. It's funny. I only did all that training to impress Charlotte's dad, but I've never felt better. I think I'd make a decent cop.'

'Ha! You? Bacon? Do me a favour. You're too soft for that. Na, mate. We need to get you back to the books.'

'Maybe you're right,' he sighed and looked to Charlotte to see if she had anything to say on the subject, but her face had fallen still. 'Charlotte, what is it?' The colour had drained from her in a way that he hadn't seen since her nervous exhaustion.

'It's nothing,' she said weakly. 'It's just–' She struggled for the right words and then was struck dumb by Julia's PSP, which came flying past her head and was mere inches from smashing her in the face.

'Fucking thing!' Julia shouted, surprising them all.

Annabel sat up suddenly with her hands on her hips and turned to Thane with a look on her face that said, 'You need to sort this child out or you can kiss me goodbye.'

'What's wrong?' Thane asked.

'Fucking battery's fucked!'

Noah and Thane burst into laughter – the contrast between her sweet voice and filthy tongue was too much to bear – but Annabel was not amused and Charlotte wasn't reacting to anything around her at all.

'Julia, you can't talk like that. At least not out in public,' Thane told her, still laughing at her at the same time, but Julia was already up on her feet.

'Get fucked!' she told him and then ran away into the long grass shouting all the swear words she could think of. 'I don't want to be here with you anyway.'

'Great kid,' Noah smiled. 'You must be really proud.'

'Don't! Mum's supposed to be back by now. This is doing my head in.'

When Julia was out of sight, Noah suddenly remembered where he was before the interruption, trying to find out what was wrong with Charlotte. He reached down and took her hand then stood up and pulled her to her feet. 'Walk with me,' he whispered in her ear then nodded to Thane to tell him they were taking a walk. When they were out of earshot, Noah asked her again what was going on for her.

'It really is nothing,' she assured him. 'I know everything that happened before was stress related and all in my head. But I've got a weird feeling about today. There's just something about us all being out in the field, the picnic, that psycho kid again.'

'Is this because it's the day before my twentieth birthday?'

Charlotte looked down to the ground, 'I didn't think you would remember.'

'I remember everything you told me.'

'Look, I know none of it's true – or rather it is true, but it's got nothing to do with us – but it all just seemed so real. It's hard not to carry it around with me, especially as today is just one déjà vu after another.'

Noah placed his hands on her hips and pulled her close. Although she was upset her emotional state didn't compare to the lows she had hit before she was taken to hospital and he felt confident that they were over the worst. 'I've got an idea,' he whispered in her ear. 'Let's put this to bed once and for all.'

'How do you mean?' she asked, unable to hide her concern.

'It's the day before my twentieth birthday and what better way to spend it that up on the castle roof, where it all happened. And we can laugh in the face of all of your dreams and move on with the rest of our lives.'

Charlotte slowly shook her head, unable at first to find the words to describe how she felt. 'I have to be honest with you, Noah. It's a terrible idea. What if–?'

'There is no "What if", Charlotte. Nothing bad is ever going to happen to us and I'm going to prove it to you.'

'But aren't we tempting fate just a little bit? Wouldn't we all be a lot safer if we just stayed here and enjoyed the picnic?'

'But you're not enjoying the picnic. I can see it in your eyes. I know the dreams seem real and I know you know they weren't, but I understand how powerful they can be and I want to prove to you that they were just dreams, for your own peace of mind. Does that make sense?'

'Yes, but I still don't like it.'

'Well too bad,' he grinned and nibbled the end of her nose until she couldn't help laughing. 'We're going and that's settled.'

CHAPTER TWENTY-THREE

T he picnic had started off so well and now they ate in silence, a last
 supper, less a birthday celebration than a wake. The chicken, so
succulent and tasty at the opening of the meal, was now dust and
feathers, but on they ate, knowing that every strained bite brought them
closer to Sam's moment of reckoning, which each of them sensed would
somehow change the world as they knew it. The pies had turned to
stone, the cream had curdled and imaginary worms burrowed in the
meats; such a sombre and laborious meal they had never experienced,
especially as the very same food had bought them so much joy just
moments before Sam's announcement. The sun, which had favoured
Sam and Fizz's courtship and smiled down merrily on their picnic, had
now had a change of heart and threatened to send in the rains; the pale,
smoky-blue sky brought with it an unusual stillness. Could it be that
the world was also holding its breath waiting for the outcome of Sam's
announcement to his parents?

Sam looked to each of his companions in turn. He could see that
each bite of food Fizz took stuck in her throat and he was sure that the
activity was stopping her from crying. Her words sang in his mind – 'I
would die without you, m'lord.' Such a sorry and devastating

sentiment, but it warmed him through and made him all the more determined to face his parents. No one had ever felt for him this strongly nor had the bravery and openness of heart to express it. He would die without her too, he knew this, and he couldn't waste another moment of his life in the falsehoods of his castle existence. If he had to live the life of a pauper for the rest of his life then so be it.

He then looked to Anne and Robin. Robin had changed so much over the last few days, such was the power of love, especially that which is unrequited. Sam could see that his desire to impress and attract Anne was taking over his concern for his friend as he tried to catch her eye and start conversations to no real avail. Anne really was difficult to work out. She rebuked all of his efforts, but they had been enjoying the physical pleasures of each other all week. Sam had seen evidence of this in the animal house on that fateful night. And here she was seemingly bored and frustrated by his existence. Sam glimpsed her again; perhaps it wasn't boredom and frustration. Her eyes met his and he could see a deep sympathy for his plight. Perhaps it was focus and empathy for Sam that was keeping her from acknowledging Robin's advances at this moment; she was a healer after all. She was clearly feeling the intensity of the afternoon deeply and she gave him a supportive smile and encouraging nod. All around him, it was amazing how much could be said in silence.

And then it was time. The imposing figure of the castle loomed over them even at this distance and Sam couldn't keep his eyes from it as he gathered the plates, bowls and cups and cleared them into the basket. Robin threw the blanket over his shoulder and the intensity of the expressions all around him told Sam that this was it. It was time to go and make history.

At first their pace was slow and then Sam led them in a march through the bridleways, around the village and eventually through the giant oaks that sheltered the rising pathway to the castle. He now appeared as a man who knew that destiny was knocking for him and had decided to accept the calling sooner rather than later.

When they arrived at the castle, they were able to wander straight through to the great hall, unhindered by sentries, who were busying themselves in preparation for the battle that lay ahead, many miles from the castle gates. The atmosphere in the hall couldn't have been more different from the vibrancy Sam experienced at the banquet. It now appeared cold and empty. His parents were sitting at either ends of the dining table enjoying a meal together, their every need served by the servants around them. But Lord Mardridge leapt to his feet as soon as he saw his son and marched towards him.

'My boy! I have not seen you. Preparations abound. We must talk strategy, training. We must ready the horses and the weaponry. Where is it that you have been to keep you from such essential enterprise? And your betrothed awaits your company. We have not seen you, my boy. Your mother and I deserve an explanation.' He stood before Sam, towering above him with his hands on his hips, his stomach and bushy beard puffing out with every word he cried. Sam hardly dared reply, but the presence of Fizz beside him and those words – 'I would die without you, m'lord' – spurred him on.

'Father, please, be seated with Mother. It is with you both I need to speak.'

'But we have no time for this.' Lord Mardridge's voice was louder still.

'Please, Father.' Sam held his glare and eventually his father relented and moved to Lady Mardridge's side. Sam's mother wore the same expression Sam had seen at the banquet. He had hoped she would calm a little, but the passing week looked to have fuelled her impatience with her son.

'Mother, Father,' he began, but then Lord Mardridge interrupted.

'Wait just one moment. What is this you have brought over our threshold? A witch!'

'What? No. I–'

'She will jinx us all and the imminent battle,' Lord Mardridge continued, pointing his finger at Anne.

In her defence, Robin stepped in. 'She is a healer not a witch.'

'And you are an imbecile not an idiot.'

'Please, Father.'

'I want her out! We will have no witchcraft in the castle. Her only use here is to fuel the fire and if she remains this is where she will end up.'

'Father!'

'Out!' he screamed.

Robin and Fizz took a step back, almost blown back by the force of his wrath, but Anne remained and then Sam surprised everyone by shouting. 'I will not do as you say. Anne is our friend. I will not marry Princess Jane and I will not fight in your stupid battle. It was Robin who fought and won the joust on my behalf. I am not a knight. I love this woman.' He reached back, grabbed Fizz's hand and pulled her to his side. 'She is my true love. She is the aleman's daughter and a teacher of young boys and I am ready to sacrifice all I own in the world to be with her.'

And then there was silence.

The shock of the outburst had knocked Lord Mardridge back into his chair, but he was clearly composing himself for his own offensive. The four friends remained standing in the middle of hall, ready to shoulder whatever came next and Lady Mardridge's face was completely unreadable. She appeared calm, but she had coloured slightly and her eyes were wide, taking in the sight of the couple in front of her who had dared to bring their forbidden love into the castle, along with the witch and Robin, who appeared as a lovesick puppy if ever she had seen one. Lord Mardridge's face had been gradually purpling in the lull, and now he was slowly rising, as if in slow motion, to instigate his attack and throw either words, food, chairs or a dagger at his son and the band of misfits he had brought with him. But before he could gather his arsenal, the heavy door to the hall swung open and a voice even greater and fiercer than Lord Mardridge's filled the space.

'Where is he? I will kill him!' The Scottish accent was instantly recognisable and the four friends turned to see the terrifying, ginger figure of the aleman commanding almost all of the space in the vast archway with his mighty presence. His brown, linen rags barely covered his portly shape, but there was a dignity in his poverty and he stood tall and proud, with a beard to rival Lord Mardridge's. 'Fizz! Get ye home! I will deal with ye later!'

Sam squeezed Fizz's hand even tighter and tucked her behind him.

'Take ye filthy, drunken hands off ma daughter, Mardridge. I give ye to the count-e ten, Fizz, and then I will come for ye.'

'What is the meaning of this?' Lord Mardridge demanded and marched out from around the table. 'How did you get in here?'

'Ye sentries are distracted by war, and I fear ye will be a soldier down, m'lord. Your son is under the charge of breaking into ma ale house, stealing ma ale and ma daughter.' As he said the word 'daughter' he pulled a sword from his belt and wielded it menacingly. 'I have come for no less than blood.'

'And you think you can march in here and attack my son?'

'Attack him? I will kill him.'

At the mention of the word 'kill', Lord Mardridge pulled his own sword from his belt and boomed, 'No one kills my son but me!'

Their furious declarations were then overtaken by the furious clinks and clanks as their swords met each other in battle. Neither man was fast on his feet, but both showed surprising agility with a sword and provided an even match of strength and zeal. All Sam and his friends could do was watch from a distance as the fight overtook the hall, the men gravitating from one end of the room to the other as each battled for supremacy, knocking food from the table, furniture to the floor and adornments from the walls as they utilised every scrap of space in the hall. The insults flew as each desperately tried to overpower the other in vain, and then Sam felt a tap on his shoulder. He turned suddenly to see his mother behind him.

'Come with me,' she mouthed and led them all out into the hallway before the fathers could notice their absence.

Sam leaned against the wall, breathing heavily. 'I fear they will kill each other.'

'You have no time for this, Sam. Stand tall and strong as you did before your father and me.' Her face had softened into something warm that Sam recognised once again.

'Do you forgive me, Mother?'

'There is nothing to forgive, Sam. I want the best for you. This is all I have ever wanted. I asked you to deal with your issues and it looks as if this is exactly what you have done. Your young lady is beautiful.'

Sam beamed a smile and placed his arm around Fizz.

'You have no time to waste. They will spot your absence before you know and realise they are on the same side. You cannot escape before them. Go up to the roof and form a barricade. I will sooth your father and attempt some kind of resolution.'

'But, Mother.'

'I love you, Sam. Now go.'

Sam released Fizz to pull his mother close to him. 'I love you, too,' he said before letting her go and leading the other three up the stairs, past his own chamber and out onto the roof. They had no need of a barricade; the heavy door slammed shut behind them and was held in place by a wooden beam that would keep a rhino from breaking through. The sky welcomed them with the same misery they had left behind before arriving at the castle, only at this height a fierce wind was added to its arsenal and shivers abound from the moment they walked out into the open air.

The roof was a vast and barren space with steps leading down to a centre clearing and vacant sentry posts dotted around the perimeter, facing out in all directions. Both girls found a vantage point at the roof's edge and were looking out over the village – a magnificent view that they had never experienced at such a great height. Sam and Robin had gravitated towards the clearing.

'What now?' asked Robin as Sam lowered himself onto the stone steps. But Sam didn't answer. 'Hey, Lord Samuel!' Robin said and still Sam didn't answer. It was only when he asked a third time and got no answer that Robin realised something was wrong. He sprinted over to his friend's side and saw that Sam's breathlessness was overtaking him. The colour had drained from his face and he was now slumped, unable to hold himself up. 'Sam, what's wrong? What's going on?'

Sam remained silent.

'Anne!' Robin called. 'Something is wrong!'

Anne bound forward across the roof, followed by Fizz and both dropped by his side.

'What has happened?' cried Fizz. 'What is happening to him?' She looked to Anne for answers, but her friend looked to have fallen into a state of shock. 'Help him, Anne, please.' But Anne was frozen. 'Sam! Can you hear me?'

Sam's eyelids had fallen, but he was just managing to keep a thin sliver open. He could see fizz in front of him, but she seemed a million miles away. He could not hear her, but he could see her face slowly exploding into screaming tears and he knew as well as she did that he was about to breathe his last breath. He tried to move his lips to appease her silent hysteria, but they would not be persuaded to move. He felt her hand in his and squeezed as hard as he could, which barely made an impression on her and then his eyes closed completely. His final thought was a wish for his guardian angel to appear as she had done before, with her face close enough to his for him to feel her breath and smell the sweet fragrance of her flesh. And he would lose consciousness and wake up once again, saved from whatever this death had been, from whatever fate had befallen him. But this time it wasn't to be. He took a final breath, his heart stopped beating and there was nothing that he or anyone could do about it.

'No!' Fizz screamed and collapsed onto Sam's emptied chest.

'Come now, my friend,' Robin told him. 'This is no time for jokes. Reveal yourself. Come back to us.' But Robin's smile gradually faded as he spoke and realised that this was no joke. His friend wasn't going to move and suddenly come back to life. He was dead.

He looked on as Fizz soaked Sam's cold heart in tears while Anne simply sat back on her heels with wide eyes, hypnotised by the scene, too shocked to move from the spot. 'Why has this happened?' he said to himself and then screamed it into the dull, imposing sky. 'Why has this happened?' and he too could not hold back the tears. He lowered himself beside Sam and Fizz and took his friend's hand. 'What had happened to you?' he sobbed and his distress danced with fury as he shouted once again into the afternoon breeze. When his tears overtook him, he too lowered his head to Sam's chest and as he did so Fizz was stirred into motion. She was suddenly sitting rigid and upright as if she had been visited upon by a new strength, although her face was a battlefield of devastation. And then she was on her feet, still moving mechanically, operated by a force greater than herself, backing away from the dead body of the love of her life. One step followed another, followed another, until her back had reached the stone boundary of the roof's edge. 'I will not live without you!' she screamed and it was only at this point Robin noticed that she had moved at all.

'No, Fizz!' he shouted and he too was now on his feet. 'Don't do this, please. I cannot lose you both.'

'I cannot and I will not live without him,' she shouted across to Robin and then they were simultaneously stirred into action. Fizz began to climb the three feet of stone separating her from a death drop while Robin sprinted with every bit of energy he had left to reach her in time, but he was too late. A split second sooner and he may have been able to catch her, but as he arrived at the edge all he could do was watch as her body plummeted to the ground.

'No!' he screamed and slammed his fists down on the stone. 'No! No! No!' He looked like a man defeated, a man who would lie down and cry or die, or follow Fizz over the wall and plummet to his own death, but then he was seized by a new resolve; a new idea or direction had taken him over and he slowly walked back to Sam. He dropped on his knees beside his friend and gripped him by the sleeves. 'Wake up, Sam! Wake up! Don't do this to us.' But there was nothing left of his friend. He even felt lighter and his face was an unearthly shade of white. 'Wake up, Sam, please! Come back to us!' Eventually, he released Sam and turned to Anne, who hadn't moved from the spot. 'Say something, Anne, please. You are a healer. Why is it that you did not help him? What has caused this tragedy? Talk to me, please.'

Anne didn't answer and simply maintained her vacant stare.

'Please, Anne! Say something!'

Finally, Anne turned her head in Robin's direction. She tried to speak, but her mouth had dried. She moved her tongue through her lips, blinked back tears that were now forming in her eyes and said. 'It was me, Robin. I killed him.'

Neither spoke for what seemed like hours. Robin had fallen back against the steps and words had failed him. Words had ceased to exist in his mind. Anne, however, had managed to rouse herself from her shock and was holding Sam's hand to her forehead and lips and heart, whispering to him and wiping away the tears that now freely flowed. 'I'm so sorry,' Robin eventually heard her say and the inadequacy of the words brought him back to the moment. However, although he now knew something of the truth, his heart refused to harden against the woman he loved.

'Tell me how this has happened,' he said softly and when Anne didn't respond he repeated himself with a sterner edge to the sentence.

'I ... I ...'

'Please. I need to know.'

'It was he I loved,' she sobbed.

Robin nodded solemnly. Suddenly it all made sense. All of the looks he had seen her deliver to his friend; he had thought she was offering deference and support in his plight, but it was he who held her heart. In that moment he could almost sympathise; he knew what it felt like to have his feeling unrequited.

'I loved him from the first day I saw him, hiding from Fizz's old man in the ale house yard. I watched him in secret and found I couldn't move – his beautiful face in turmoil as he listened to Fizz and her father's argument. He was the most beautiful creature I had ever seen.' She paused. 'It was the green scone. I slipped a love potion into Lord Samuel's. It should have made him love me. It shouldn't have killed him. Perhaps I used too much. Perhaps he is allergic to it. I did not see that it would harm him.'

'You used a love potion on him?'

Anne nodded slowly.

'What about me? I was here. Was I not good enough for you?'

'You do not understand, Robin.'

'I understand well enough that I am good enough for your bed but not for your hand.' Is that not the way you have always treated village girls?'

'Why was it that you troubled my heart at all?'

239

'It was the only way to be close to Lord Samuel,' she responded and for a moment they were away from Sam's dead body and the memory of Fizz's suicide and into the realms of sexual politics, each desperate to defend their position. Then Robin seemed to feel the gravity of the situation all over again and sobbed into Sam's chest. Anne also broke into tears and they remained there until they heard banging at the door.

'Open this door, young man!'

'Open up! Ye Cannae run forever!'

The voices were easily recognisable as both Fizz and Sam's fathers. Whatever had occurred downstairs it would appear that they were both now single-minded in their quest to drag Sam from his hiding place and made him accountable for his actions.

Anne sat up suddenly. 'I must confess,' she told Robin. 'I have caused so much pain and now I must atone.' She struggled to her feet, but Robin caught her hand before she made it to the door.

'They will kill you,' he urged. 'Lord Mardridge already thinks you a witch. He will have you hung, drawn, quartered. I cannot let you do it.'

'It was me!' she shouted and Robin now jumped up beside her and forced his hand over her mouth to silence her.

'They will kill you!' he repeated.

'You can't stop me!' she told him and was crying uncontrollably. 'My life is not worth living now that he is dead anyway.'

'I still cannot let you do it. You may not love me, but my heart would wither and die without you, Anne.'

'You cannot stop me!' she repeated then shouted, 'It was me!' once again and Robin struggled to contain her calls. He held her in his arms, praying that her rigid body would soften to his touch and melt into him, but she fought him off and refused to be contained. She squirmed and wriggled and eventually broke free of his grip and ran towards the door. 'It was me!' she screamed again, possessed by a force of integrity, and began to wrestle the wooden bar, first pulling it upwards and then forcing her shoulder beneath to wrench it out, free herself from the roof, confess her sins and face the consequences. All the time she could hear Robin shouting, 'I can't let you do this. It was an accident. I love you, Anne!' But her focus was beyond him now as she finally managed to lever the bar from its hooks. And then the roof was overrun with the larger-than-life presence of both Lord Mardridge and the aleman, followed behind by Sam's mother and a handful of servants. 'It was me! I did it!' she said one last time, but was pushed aside by the new arrivals who were all now running over to Sam and Robin. When she recovered her balance she turned to see them crowded around an unfamiliar death scene. Sam's throat had been slashed open and his shirt was stained red with blood. Sitting beside him with Jennifer's dagger in his hand, his own hands and face bloodied, was Robin. His eyes were fixed firmly on Anne and he just managed to mouth the words 'I love you' before the angry weight of justice crashed down upon him.

CHAPTER TWENTY-FOUR

N oah had lied to Charlotte. Actually, lying was too strong a word to use; he had hidden his true feelings. He had acted surprised that she was full of trepidation because of what day it was – the day before his twentieth birthday; the day in Lord Samuel's life that he had breathed his last breath – but it had been on his mind for some days. How could it not be? He hadn't told Charlotte, but he too had been to the library to read more about Samuel Mardridge, and the resemblance between them was definitely striking, although he could only find one weathered portrait of him and their biggest similarity was their golden curls. He had put so much energy into allaying Charlotte's fears, about a past determined to creep up on them and snatch them from their lives and about her own sanity, but if he had to confess his true feelings he would say that the whole episode had churned him up a little. He was far from a believer of anything Charlotte had dreamt, but he knew there were unexplainable things in the world and wasn't naïve enough to believe he couldn't be touched by them. On the whole, he dismissed parallels as coincidences – the biggest one being Charlotte's whispers that night in the hospital: 'But you nearly drowned, Sam.' But he sometimes allowed doubt to creep in along with the 'what if?' questions.

What if he was really Sam's reincarnation? What if he was also destined to suffer the same fate as Sam? But he always came back to the same answer – there was nothing special about him, he was just an ordinary lad with an ordinary life. If this kind of thing were truly possible it would be happening to someone else. He couldn't deny, though, that he had faced more danger in the last few months than he had in his entire lifetime, but unlike Sam, he had managed to survive. And he was determined to continue doing so, so as he walked along the pathway leading up to the castle, shaded under a canopy of oak trees, their strong arms and pale-green leaves, he did so with strength in his body, determination in his heels and with his head held high. He held Charlotte's hand tightly and demanded the same pace from her. Although he had told her that they were doing this to lay her demons to rest, it was as much for him and it was for her. He needed this final proof and then they could move on with their lives and truly put the last few months behind them.

'Hey! Wait up!' Thane called out from the bottom of the oak path, struggling with the picnic hamper and blanket. 'Where's the fire? We haven't all been in training for the bloody Mr Iron Balls competition.'

Annabel was marching beside him, but wasn't helping with his load. Instead, she wore the same look of fascination that she had displayed that night at the Indian restaurant when it looked as if Charlotte was losing her grip on reality. It was unclear whether it was professional interest, or a simple morbid fascination, but she was desperate to catch up with Noah and Charlotte and see how all of this was going to play out. All they had told Thane and Annabel was that it would be a great end to their picnic to visit the castle, but the seriousness that neither of them was able to hide gave them away. Something was going down.

'Seriously,' Thane called again, 'If you didn't want us to come you should have said.'

Noah and Charlotte finally stopped, allowing Thane and Annabel to catch them up.

'I'm sorry, mate. Let me give you a hand.' Noah took the blanket and tossed it over his shoulder, but it didn't make that much difference to Thane's load.

'What's the hurry anyway?'

They were on the move again.

'And why does Charlotte look like she's seen a ghost?'

'Shh!' Noah urged and hung back while Annabel and Charlotte continued ahead, chatting to each other. When they were out of earshot, he said, 'It would have been today.' He lowered his eyes to Thane to force understanding on him. When he saw none, he said, 'It's the day before my twentieth birthday.'

'I know, mate. I just did you a picnic,' but then the realisation dawned on him and he interrupted himself with. 'Ohhh! It's the day I'm supposed to kill you!'

'Keep your voice down.'

'It's okay, I've spoken to Charlotte about it loads. It's quite funny really and I'm glad she can see the funny side now she's better and all. She's okay, you know. Not as much of a cow as I first thought.'

'That means a lot, Thane,' Noah smiled.

'So why go up to the roof of the castle where it all happened? It's tempting fate a bit isn't it.'

'That's what Charlotte said.'

'You should try listening to her, mate.'

'Does Annabel know all about it, too?'

'I imagine so. They're probably talking about it now,' Thane answered and as they watched the intensity of the conversation going on ahead of them it was perfectly clear that they all now knew the exact nature of their expedition to the castle.

They reached the castle gates with a little less than thirty minutes left until it closed for the day. Thane and Noah had visited the castle when they first moved to Mardridge, but Annabel had never been and Charlotte hadn't been since she was a child. The castle itself hadn't changed at all since then, but she didn't remember the entranceway being so touristy, with its little gift shop selling tiny jousting knights perched in the top of pencils and soft-toy Tudor men in tights and doublets, with their puffy sleeves and feathered caps, and women in their long flowy gowns and kirtles, with ornate headdresses resting on top. There were signs everywhere encouraging tourists to support the National Trust and pick up a headphone pack from the front desk to bring the experience to life with an audio tour. Charlotte also couldn't remember it being so expensive, but Noah paid for all four of them and they were soon alone in the open of the banquet hall. It was difficult now to imagine this cold space alive and full of banqueting reverie, although there were paintings on the walls and reconstructed photos attesting to the life that had once existed here, when it had been filled with singing and dancing, while a whole suckling pig rotated over an open fire and wine splashed from the goblets of burly, animated men as they gesticulated fierce tales of battle and slaughter.

'I don't like it here,' Charlotte told them and her face had fallen grave and pale once again.

'Let's get this over with,' Noah told her and squeezed her hand tightly then led the group through the arch and into the hallway that led to the stone stairs.

'Can you imagine living here?' Thane said cheerfully. 'You'd have to get a few carpets down, few radiators, wi-fi.' But no one answered so he kept the rest of his thoughts to himself.

The staircase spiralled around the castle, passing smaller arch and doorways, behind which had slept centuries of the castle's inhabitants, including Samuel Mardridge. And then they finally reached the door leading them out onto the roof. It was propped wide open with a heavy iron relic of some kind and the four of them slowly stepped past and out into the open. True to form, it was Thane who opened his mouth to state the obvious.

'Well, there's no danger of you throwing yourself off this roof,' he chuckled and turned to Charlotte who was also laughing. In fact, the moment they had stepped onto the roof the colour returned to her cheeks and she seemed lighter than she had been in days. She slowly moved over to the roof's edge to take in the view and giggled as she held onto the high fencing that had been constructed with the sole purpose of stopping people from throwing themselves off the castle roof. The barbed wire on top was the razor-sharp icing on the cake; even if her whole world crumbled around her in the next few minutes she would be physically incapable of jumping.

Annabel joined her and they both stood overlooking the view while Noah and Thane moved to the centre, in which stone steps led down to a clearing. It was incredibly windy on the roof and Noah wondered if the centre area was designed with this in mind, to protect them from the elements.

'What now?' asked Thane as Sam lowered himself onto the stone steps. But Noah didn't answer. 'Hey, Noah!' Thane said and still Noah didn't answer. It was only when he asked a third time that Noah heard him over the wind.

'Sorry, mate. What?'

'I said what now?' He lowered himself beside his friend and they both watched their girlfriends laughing and messing about next to one of the sentry posts.

'I'm not sure to be honest.'

'What did her dreams tell her happened on the roof?'

'She didn't ever dream about what happened on the roof. I think that was one of the things that left her so frustrated. All she has is the history books to go by.' Noah shook his head suddenly. 'What am I talking about? It almost sounds as if I'm buying into all of this.'

'I think it's all awesome.'

'You would. Anyway, she looks happy enough. I guess we just wait until she's happy to leave.'

'The things we do for women,' Thane sighed, sounding like a fifty-year old man and Noah laughed far harder than the comment deserved. It was the relief pouring out of him. Perhaps he had been more stressed about Charlotte's dreams than he had admitted even to himself, because as he sat there with his friend, safe, sound and out of harm's way, and watched his playful girlfriend enjoying the first day of the rest of her life, he felt a gentle release inside of himself – his insides had been gripped by anxiety and he hadn't even noticed it until this moment of release – and now he felt like dancing. He turned to Thane, but now it was his friend's turn to look as if he had seen a ghost. 'Thane? What's up?' he asked, but when he followed his friend's eye line to the entranceway he saw exactly what was up. Chief Inspector Mitchell had taken his first steps onto the roof and was standing staring at his daughter with his hands on his hips.

Without pause for thought, Noah was up on his feet and by his girlfriend's side. As soon as she noticed her father her face lit up, but then sunk again when the memory of all that had passed between them brought her back to the reality of their current relationship. Noah placed his arm around her shoulder and pulled her close. At the same time, Thane arrived at his side and he and Annabel stood tall beside the couple in a show of solidarity. After a few moments of eying each other without moving, Charlotte's dad began to walk towards the four friends. Noah could feel Charlotte's body tensing and he pulled her even closer to him.

'I want a word with you,' Mitchell growled and now Noah's body tensed. He was surprised, however, when Thane stepped forward to block his path, but Mitchell spoke before he could say a word.

'I've got something belonging to you, lad. A set of fingerprints on a pint glass seized from the Sir Robin's Head the night Smith here let himself in for a midnight drink.'

Thane opened his mouth to reply but for once he was speechless.

'I'd step back, lad, if I were you.'

Thane's mouth snapped shut and he did as instructed.

Annabel then surprised Noah even more by stepping in on their behalf. 'Why can't you just leave them alone, Uncle Robert? Noah's not too bad when you get to know him.'

As far as compliments went it was a little backhanded, but Noah would take it.

The biggest surprise of all then came when Mitchell relied with, 'Would you all please just relax. I'm not here to cause trouble.' He then took a deep breath before saying, 'I'm sorry. I saw you walking into the castle and I knew I would lose my nerve if I didn't seize the moment and speak to you now. I behaved terribly and I'm so sorry.' He looked as if he might cry and Noah felt Charlotte's body relax. She had forgiven him already. 'I heard about how you left your exam and ran all the way to the hospital. I would never have dragged you out of her room if I knew ... or maybe I would. I don't know. I've been doing a lot of thinking though and I know I behaved terribly. I also know that I am nothing without my daughter by my side and you were right that day, Charlotte, it is your life to live and I just have to accept it even if you do decide to date ...' he indicated Noah with something resembling disgust and struggled for a word to describe him then said, 'whoever you chose to date.'

'Oh, Dad!' Charlotte cried and ran into her father's open arms. They held each other tightly and both sobbed as the others looked on, smiling and full of relief.

Mitchell then held his daughter to his side with his arm around her shoulder and stretched his arm out to Noah. At first Noah was reluctant to move towards him, but he could see the sincerity in his teary eyes and slowly took the few paces over to shake his hand. It was a hairy, concrete hand, but thanks to Noah's fitness regime, he held his own and Mitchell even nodded his approval at the strength of the shake.

'I've spoken to the university,' Mitchell said, his voice now much softer than Noah had ever heard it and his eyes far kinder. He was starting to see Charlotte's dad rather than the policeman who had terrorised him in the interview room and thrown him out of the hospital. This man was far more preferable. 'I've submitted a statement vouching for your character and explaining why you were unable to attend your exam. As I understand it you have a lot of catching up to do, but you're back on the course.'

'Are you serious?' Noah beamed.

'I don't joke, lad.'

Noah moved close to hug him, but then thought better of it and stopped himself just in time, instead opting to pat his shoulder, which also seemed a little too affectionate judging by the expression on Mitchell's face. However, he then pushed out a weak smile and shook Noah's hand again.

'Thank you for looking after her through all of her troubles. She looks a lot better and I know this is in part down to her happiness. I know we will need to take things slowly, but you are both welcome at the house whenever you want. In fact, I'm making a chilli on Thursday and you're both invited.'

'I would like that very much, sir.'

'Me too?' asked Thane.

Mitchell took one look at him before saying, 'You've got to be joking,' then patting Noah on the shoulder. He then made his way back to the entrance. 'It will be on the table at seven. Don't be late,' he called back and was gone. As if he had never existed, Thane had already moved onto the next thing on his mind and was trying to persuade Annabel to climb onto his back. When she was up, he ran around the roof wielding an imaginary joust and shouting at the top of his voice. Noah and Charlotte settled back against the roof's edge and laughed at their friends as they held hands.

'I love you, m'lady,' he mouthed.

'I love you, too.'

CHAPTER TWENTY-FIVE

A thena's lowered her eyes to the water's rainbow surface for what must have been the tenth time that minute. 'Erm …' she said.

'Hell … ooo!'

'Erm … I would like a whistle,' she answered. She had stopped acknowledging the river's drawn-out greeting many years before. She had also stopped watching the magical shift in the rainbow waters, as each colour separated and rippled outwards. And when the whistle came bobbing up to the surface – a shiny, long instrument, the kind a Bobby might use – she was equally disinterested. She reached out and grabbed it, turned it in her hands a few times and threw in behind her without even drawing it to her lips. She needed a whistle as much as she needed a globe, a hammer, a rocking horse, a set of knives, a book shelf, a set of goal posts and football, a collection of encyclopedias and a hamster cage, but these things had also made their way from her imagination and the magical depths of the rainbow river onto the enormous piles of things all around her.

'Erm …' she repeated and this time closed her eyes to think. She was running out of ideas for things to ask the river for. 'Could I have …?'

'Please, Athena,' she heard beside her, but didn't even bother opening her eyes.

'I would like a flask please, River, to keep my tea in,' she continued, ignoring the voice, and only then she opened her eyes, just in time to retrieve the second metallic item to come floating up to the surface.

'This has to stop, Athena.'

'Erm ...'

'Athena!'

Athena eventually turned to the unicorn and should have responded to its serious concern with something other than a smile, but she had heard it all before and wanted to be left alone. 'What? Would you like me to order something for you, Unicorn?'

'No ... I–'

'River?'

'Hell ... ooo!'

'I would like a saddle and some horse shoes.'

'What are you doing, Athena?'

'I thought I could start riding you.'

'What is wrong with you?'

As they discussed the prospect of this shift in their relationship, the waters stuttered into separate shapes and suddenly a saddle and four horse shoes floated up to the surface. Athena looked to them with as much interest as she had the whistle and the flask and then leaned in to collect them. When they were in her arms, she simply tossed them onto her pile of things and said, 'Relax, Unicorn. I would not ride you. It was ...' Perhaps she was going to say a joke, but she stopped before the word came out. It didn't really feel funny, even she could tell that, and instead she let out a deep sigh and lay back onto the emerald grass. In the clouds above her she saw the same shapes as she always saw – a small boy's face, a window, a bear – and wished more than anything else that the sky would move just an inch and give her something else to look at. Actually, it was untrue that she wished this more than anything else, but that which her heart truly desired was too painful to contemplate. She had only just recovered from her two-hundred-year scream and could not allow her mind to draw her back into her heart's longing.

'This has to stop!' Unicorn said sternly and when Athena refused to stir, it butted its long face into her hair.

'Aw!' she said and suddenly sat forward, rubbing her head. 'Why can't you just leave me alone?'

'Because I don't like what is happening.'

Athena softened and said, 'It is nice of you to care, Unicorn, but you mustn't worry. I will be okay.'

'You are not my concern, Athena. Look at this place. Look what you have done.'

Athena slowly moved her head to the left and to the right, taking in the full panoramic of Sam's heaven and the extent of the growth of her piles of things, which had completely taken over. She had asked the river for so much that there were things everywhere. At best, there were areas where the emerald grass was simply covered with bits and bobs that would reach Athena's knees if she tried to wade through. At worst, there were mountains of rubbish that nobody would ever want. And because the landscape repeated itself in all directions, heaven now looked like an infinite landfill. Her little castle and the hand-tree had now completely disappeared under the mess and the unicorn had had to fight to keep possession of a clear grazing spot on the other side of the bridge.

'Why do you need so much stuff?' The unicorn asked and it could see in Athena's eyes that she didn't have an answer. And because she didn't have an answer, or because she was just sad, the unicorn couldn't be sure, those eyes began to fill with tears. 'Oh no, Athena. You're not going to scream again are you? I do not think I could handle it.'

Athena smiled despite the pain she was feeling. 'No, Unicorn. My screaming days are over,' she said warmly. As much as she tried to be cold and distant, she knew that talking to the unicorn always helped her and she didn't really want to alienate her only living companion.

'So, why, then?'

'I do not know. Getting things from the river used to make me smile, sometimes at least, and now I get nothing from it. I keep getting more things to see if my smile will one day emerge also, but I fear it will be forever submerged in the depths of the rainbow waters.'

The unicorn moved closer to her and brushed its face against her cheek. She recognised that it was a rare sign of affection and reached out to stroke its mane.

'I just do not know what to do,' she said.

'Is this about the poisoning?' the unicorn asked. 'You made Chrono better again, Athena. Yes, you ballsed things up, but you have nothing to feel bad about.'

'It is not that, Unicorn.'

'Is it that you are stuck here infinitely and have no possibility of escape?'

'I wasn't actually thinking of that, Unicorn, but thank you for reminding me.' A weak smile tickled her features, but disappeared when she said, 'I miss him, Unicorn.'

'Who? Chrono? Really?'

'Yes. I had read about love and seen it in other people. I have nurtured and protected love, believing it to be the most powerful force in the universe and now I know that this is so, because only something as powerful as love could hold me in its hands and grip with such intensity for so long.'

'Chrono who was here a few centuries ago?' the unicorn asked, ignoring her outpouring of emotion.

'Yes, Unicorn, there haven't been any other Chronos here.'

'He's coming back tomorrow.'

'What? How do you know? Why is he coming back? When? What's going on, Unicorn?'

'He has requested an audience with you but his earliest convenience was a one-hundred-and-fifty-year wait.'

'He's coming to see me, to speak to me? What could he want? What will I wear? What if it's bad?' She paused. 'Wait a moment. A hundred and fifty years? He told you he was coming a hundred and fifty years ago.'

The unicorn nodded as if it were perfectly reasonable that it had kept the information from her.

'Why didn't you tell me?'

'You didn't ask.'

Athena spent the next day getting ready. This meant trying to return her landfill to the river, but she soon released that this was not the way it worked. Anything she threw back simply floated on the surface and the rainbow waters grew splurgy and murky around it. 'What have I done?' she repeated over and over, but eventually had to just accept that there was nothing she could do to prepare Sam's heaven for the imminent arrival. Chrono would think her a pig and there was nothing she could do about it. So she turned her attention to herself. She had asked for many mirrors over the years and perused herself for the hundredth time in the moments before his arrival. As expected, she had not aged a day since she arrived in Sam's heaven centuries before. The butterflies were as elegant as they had ever been and her hair was almost as alive as the creatures of her dress, but even she could see that there was something missing. She tried a smile, but it looked weak and unconvincing. The moment that Chrono left he had taken her light with him, the light that residing inside of her and glowed out through her eyes. She was now nothing without him.

Just as Athena was thinking this, she felt a churning in her stomach. He was here. She could feel it. She looked out over the horizon and saw his tall, strong silhouette striding into Sam's heaven. As she had done before, she watched his form as it came into focus, but this time it was through eyes of adoration. However, when his face was clear to her, she could see the sternness that still existed. If she had hoped he had returned to declare his undying love then she had been mistaken. As he slowly approached, she tried to manage her own expression, to find a steady neutral that betrayed none of the intensity of her feeling, but he was upon her all too soon.

'Hello, Athena.' There was an awkwardness to his voice; her name was a forced pleasantry and Athena couldn't work out what true feelings he was masking – hate, fear, contempt?

'I am pleased to see you, Chrono,' Athena told him and could feel herself blushing.

'I like what you have done with the place,' Chrono replied. He tried for a smile as he joked with her, but again it came across as disingenuous.

'I was going for the rubbish tip look. It is the height of fashion,' she joked, but she too couldn't manage a genuine smile and looked to him with curiosity and shame before swallowing deeply and saying, 'Why have you returned, Chrono?'

'I …' He stopped himself from finishing the sentence and turned from her. 'You will think me very strange, Athena.'

'Try me.'

'I did not want to return but the matter is outside of my hands.'

Athena's heart sank. He was there on official business.

'I confess that I was disappointed when I left this place two hundred years ago.' His face showed Athena the extent of this understatement. 'Your deception was unforgivable. I had planned to relegate the matter to the back of my mind and continue with my life as a guardian, but you have ruined me.'

Athena said nothing.

'I told you that this was so and it has become my reality.'

'But I do not understand, Chrono.'

'I should never have tasted the first prawn. I have been dreaming of the taste of it for two hundred years.' He was salivating as he spoke, his mind drifting to the succulent taste and texture. 'I have been dreaming too of ice-cream and champagne and strawberries and chicken and avocado.'

'But these things are readily available to you, Chrono. You did not need to return for them.'

'May I?' he asked, indicating a dining chair poking out of the mountain of rubbish. When she nodded he pulled it out and lowered himself onto it. Athena sat herself onto a nearby box and waited for him to continue. 'I cannot stand what you have done to me, Athena. The love potion must have poisoned my soul.'

'But it didn't work, Chrono. It was too old. It poisoned your body, but there was no love left inside of it.'

'All the same, I cannot forgive you for your deception, but there is something in the food here that sustains my heart. The moment I left here I felt as if … as if …'

'As if a light had gone out inside of you.'

Chrono nodded slowly. 'All I ask of you is that you bring me a meal and then I can be away.'

Athena opened her mouth to challenge his request or ask a question or tell him that he was being ridiculous, but none of it came out. 'As you wish,' she finally said, sadly, then bowed her head and walked down to the river. She returned moments later holding a hot plate and a knife and fork. When she presented it to Chrono he closed his eyes and inhaled the flavours deeply – steak, potatoes, vegetables, gravy. He slowly opened his eyes and began to eat.

'I will leave you with your meal,' Athena told him and walked away. She wished she could wade through to the hand-tree, but there was just too much mess. She missed the comfort it had given her over the years and now knew that the touch of the giant fingers against her flesh would ease the sense of solitude she felt, if only slightly. Because it was true that she felt even lonelier with Chrono in Sam's heaven in this way, with his layers of defence hardened against her and his empty words, handpicked to keep her at arm's length. She had dreamt about his return for two hundred years and now she wanted nothing more than for him to leave. She would not throw herself at his mercy with the honest content of her heart; his heart was clearly not a match for hers. This she could see now. All she could do was wait for him to leave and then wait for her heart to heal. She had all of eternity for this to happen and suddenly the endless time spread before her was a comfort. Just as she was thinking this, she saw Chrono emerge from behind a pile of guitars that she had collected one lazy afternoon when she couldn't think of anything else to order.

'Athena, could I trouble you for a sweet course, please?' he asked and then disappeared, returning to his meal.

Athena couldn't answer for a few moments and simply stared at him, then she obliged, all the time rehearsing what she wanted to say to him in her mind – 'Just go, Chrono. My heart hurts when you are so near but so far.' She returned to his side minutes later with a slice of black forest gateaux and watched as he made a start on it. This time, however, instead of savouring the taste, there was nothing but confusion on his face.

'Does it not taste as you imagined?' Athena asked.

'I ...' He paused to consider what it was he wanted to convey and then seemed to think better of explaining his feelings. 'Curry,' he eventually said. 'I would appreciate it if you could bring me a chicken curry.'

As before, Athena disappeared and returned moments later with a fresh plate of food. She watched as Chrono ate, neither speaking a word, but his confusion still obvious. When he had finished the curry he asked for soup; when the soup had been eaten he asked for shortbread, then some gammon and then a plate of chips. He finally asked her for a block of ice-cream and some orange juice and when he had finished this, he slumped back into his chair and stared out into the distance.

'You eat in the same way I order my things from the river. They do not reignite my fires either,' she said, but he wasn't listening. His face had grown pale and grave and he actually looked as if he might cry.

'But I don't understand it. The food still tastes the same. I had imagined it so differently. My heart was warm, my soul was content. I was at peace, Athena. Why is this not working?' The tears were trying to push through and he was just able to hold them back, but his distress was obvious. 'My life is over. I have an itch that can never be scratched. I will be forever in this limbo.'

Athena took a deep breath. It was now or never. Either she could let him leave – empty, destroyed, alone – or she could try the most brave and extraordinary thing she had attempted in all her years in heaven and the centuries in the angel realms before that and in the years of her short life on earth. 'Close your eyes,' she whispered.

'No, Athena. I do not have time for this. The only thing I have now is my work and I need to–'

'Trust me, Chrono. Close your eyes.'

He tried to protest once again, this time with his expression alone, but Athena held his glare and he eventually shrugged and gave in.

'Keep them closed,' she whispered and gathered all of her courage to move towards him. A thousand stories were dancing in her heart, told and untold, loaning her their strength for this pivotal moment as she moved so close to him that she could smell the early aroma of his body and feel the heat rising from him. When their faces were mere inches apart she closed her eyes and moved closer still. And then it happened.

'What was that?' Chrono was suddenly on his feet, leaping out of his chair as if a thousand volts had been delivered to his lips. 'What did you do to me? What is this? I feel … I feel …'

Athena looked on as he struggled once again with words. She felt melty and bendy and hazy and nebulous, as if she had eaten the best meal in the world and been a part of the best and most amazing dance, or climbed the highest mountain, drunk but sober, asleep but awake. She couldn't begin to put it into words and she could see from Chrono's face that he felt exactly the same. Although he was stunned and full of questions, and desperate to explain the feelings in his body, Athena could see that he was her Chrono again. His layers had been shattered by the kiss and he stood before her exposed, vulnerable, beautiful and totally, completely, madly and deeply in love.

'Would you like to do it again?' Athena asked and a sudden smile came over Chrono's face. All of his worries and fears for the intensity of his feeling dropped away in that moment and he was free.

'There is nothing in the universe I would like more,' he told her and slowly moved towards her. He took her in his strong arms, stared lovingly into her eyes, tenderly placed his lips on hers and they were both in heaven.

'I cannot stay,' Chrono said sadly. Several hours had passed and they were curled up together with the fabric of Chrono's sarong thrown over them, watching the butterflies that formed Athena's dress flutter in the sky above them. Finally Athena had something new and different to look at.

'I know,' Athena said sadly.

'It would seem that your plan worked all along, to make me love you.'

'Believe me, my love, none of this has been my design. I am as surprised by our love as you are.'

'Charming.'

'You know what I mean.'

'I do,' Chrono told her and she could hear the smile in his voice as he pulled her even closer.

'You wanted me to love you so you could escape and now I cannot leave you here, especially now this place is unfit even for rodents.'

Athena shuffled up onto her elbow to see his face and force him to look into her eyes as she said, 'I understand that you have no control over Sam's fate now, Chrono. I do not blame you for the position in which you find yourself and I love and respect you too much to ask that you act on my behalf.'

'But I truly cannot leave you here. I can visit you, but not very often, and I fear that my heart will corrode in every minute that we are separated. I am surprised I survived the last two hundred years, although I had no idea of my own yearning.'

'But we have no options, Chrono. I am stuck here and you are free.'

'But remember, Athena, I had planned to offer you a gift to help you escape and it is still within my power to make it so. Although I cannot change Sam's fate, I can enable him to see his past in visions, in dreams. As he sleeps at night I will give him the power to see the stories of his own past life. If he can see the cause of his original death all those years ago, he may be able to avert tragedy this time.'

'But, Chrono, will this not alter the universe or cause fate issues or some other consequence?'

'No, I have chained him up in time for centuries, locked him in a cycle that I can no longer access. All I can do is dangle a key in front of him and hope that he will take it. I have dealt with the consequences of his impact on fate before and I will do so again. I will do so gladly now I know the power of love and that this is the only way we can be together.'

'And Sam and Fizz will finally get to spend a lifetime together,' Athena said warmly and settled down onto his chest again.

Chrono held her tight and said, 'I love you so much.'

Chapter Twenty-Six

A lmost six months had passed since that day on the castle roof, when Charlotte's father had held out the olive branch to his daughter and it had been gratefully accepted. In that time a new relationship had been established whereby he would still try to tell her what to do, but she would remind him that this was not the way things were going to be anymore and he would reluctantly take a backseat. Eventually, he would learn that the decisions in her life were exclusively hers to make, but it would take some time. If Charlotte was completely honest, she loved that her father cared enough to try to interfere and was patient with him as he learnt to give her more space. She even moved back in with him and things went back to how they had been before Noah was arrested; except that now she was allowed to have Noah over to spend the night and her father tried not to question her when she stayed out all night. Although they had enjoyed living together in Noah's bedsit, they both agreed that it wasn't the right time in their lives to be living like an old married couple.

In terms of Charlotte's state of mind, she had had no more Tudor dreams and was eternally grateful to Noah for forcing her up onto the castle roof. It gave her the finality she needed to draw a line under the whole episode. She wasn't ashamed – everyone hits lows in their lives and she was no exception – but she couldn't believe how readily she had believed the stories woven by her mind. She was just glad that it was all behind them and they had so much to look forward to. It wouldn't be long before they graduated and she and Noah had already decided that they would travel the world together.

The long, hot summer had given way to a nasty winter and enforced nights indoors in front of the fire, but on this particular night Noah and Charlotte were layering up and getting ready to go out.

'I can't see why we can't just stay in,' Charlotte grumbled as she pushed her hands into gloves that were still wet and cold from earlier in the day.

'Because I'm taking you out is why,' Noah told her and pulled her woolly hat down over her eyes.

'You're not funny.'

'I am actually,'

'Well, you're not.'

'Yeah, I am actually.'

They went on like this for quite some time and then Noah stopped and looked down at his watch. 'We need to get a move on. Come on.'

'What's the hurry? The Pine Comb's not going to explode if we don't make it there in the next five minutes.'

'But I might,' Noah joked and pulled the front door open. The cacophony beyond almost knocked him back into the bedsit – filthy, whistling wind and thrashing snow. They could barely see the gate at the end of the path.

'Are you kidding me?'

'What?' Noah beamed, making a pantomime of basking in the imaginary heat blustering in from outside. 'It's fine. It won't look quite so bad when we're outside anyway.'

'You couldn't pay me to go out in that,' Charlotte told him and pulled off her hat, leaving her long, dark hair standing on end. She then slumped down onto Noah's bed and pulled at her gloves.

'No, wait!' Noah urged. 'You have to come.'

'To the pub, for a drink? I don't think so.' She managed to undo the top two buttons on her coat when Noah grabbed her hands to stop her.

'No! Stop! We're going out.'

'We're really not.'

'We are.'

'No, Noah. You've got rocks in your head. We can't go out in that.'

'But, we have to,' Noah told her and immediately regretted it. He had said too much.

'Why do we have to?'

'Erm …'

'Noah, what are you hiding?'

'Nothing … erm.'

'Tell me or you won't be able to move me from this spot for the rest of the night.'

Noah sighed deeply and groaned, 'It was supposed to be a surprise.'

'What was? Tell me.'

'For your birthday tomorrow. It's just a few friends, and Thane's doing a bit of food–'

'I knew it!'

'No you didn't'

'Alright I didn't, but … really? You've planned a surprise party for me.'

'Yes, but don't get too excited. It's nothing too big. I'm saving all of my big ideas for your twenty-first next year.'

Charlotte jumped up and wrapped her arms around her boyfriend. 'Shouldn't we get going then?' she beamed. 'We don't want to be late.'

The ten-minute walk to The Pine Comb was actually more like a twenty-minute walk in such dire conditions and they were both coated in white before they had reached the end of the path. The force of the icy wind on their faces and its incessant screaming in their ears prevented any kind of conversation, so they leaned into it and ploughed their feet into the thick snow, making slow progress. With The Pine Comb in view, Noah released Charlotte's hand and ran a few steps ahead of her. He leaned down to the snow at his feet, scooped up a handful and began to mould it into a ball.

'Don't you dare!' Charlotte wailed and just managed to dodge out of the way as the snowball came flying past her head. 'You're in trouble now,' she shouted and squatted to grab a claw-full of snow for her own projectile. She clearly had her old man's sporting arm and hit him clean in the face.

'Right!' Noah bellowed and dodged down behind a car, where he began creating an arsenal of snowy missiles. Taking his lead, Charlotte lowered herself into a crouch on the other side of the car and began to create the biggest snowball she could muster. When she was satisfied and could only manage to hold the massive ball with two gloved hands, she leapt up, but as quickly as she had risen she was down again. The ice beneath her feet had flipped her up and thrown her down onto the hard concrete. When Noah had finally finished messing about with his own snowballs he stood to confront her in warfare and found her out cold in the road.

'Holy shit!' he mouthed and leapt down beside her. 'Charlotte, sweetheart, talk to me. Baby?'

At first there was no movement and then he could see her eyes twitching before slowly opening.

'Sweetheart, are you okay?'

Charlotte was trying to blink away her confused expression, but failing. She looked as if she had been dropped from another planet and had no idea who she was or where she had come from.

'Speak to me, Charlotte. Say something.'

Very slowly, she opened her mouth. 'It was me all along,' she said, staring out into the darkened road. 'It wasn't you at all. I'm Sam.'

Noah helped Charlotte onto her feet, but her legs began to buckle and he knew he had to get her somewhere warm where she could sit down. The Pine Comb was just in front of them, where all of their friends would be waiting for them. It also had a separate saloon bar and Noah felt confident that they could slip in unnoticed and she could recover before having to face anyone. He held the door open for her, guided her through to the tiny side bar and the relief from the cold was instant, but Charlotte looked far from soothed.

'Two brandies,' he told the barman and went on to explain what had happened and that he would appreciate it if he stopped any of their friends coming through. He took the drinks over to Charlotte and couldn't help noting that they were sitting at the exact same table they had occupied that night by the well, when she had started to unravel.

'Here,' he told her and prayed that this time it would be different, but the way she grabbed the glass and downed the contents gave him a bad feeling of déjà vu. 'Are you feeling better?' he asked, careful not to ask her about this 'I am Sam' nonsense. 'Shall we go in? We can go outside and then back in through the other door for the surprise. How's your head.'

'Didn't you hear what I said, Noah? My God, it all makes so much sense now. I dreamt it all, Noah, just then in the road. It's like my brain has been holding onto the final part of the jigsaw. And do you know why?' she was scarily animated as she spoke.

Noah shook his head and said, 'Are you okay?' but she ignored him.

'Because my brain was protecting me, making sure I had all of the information when I needed it. And if I'm Sam then it was never going to be Thane because Thane was never Robin. I should have seen it sooner. Thane is nothing like Robin. He's more like–'

'You sound a bit mad,' Noah ventured, but was ignored again and downed his own brandy in one gulp.

'Robin didn't kill Sam, Noah. It was Anne, Fizz's best friend.'

'The one Robin was shagging?' Noah was being drawn into the story despite himself.

Charlotte nodded frantically. Her cheeks had coloured fast with the change in temperature and the effects of the brandy.

'She poisoned him. She didn't mean to, but she did. Don't you see? If I'm Sam and this is the day before my twentieth birthday then it was always going to be today.'

'Slow down, Charlotte, please. I really wish I hadn't started throwing snowballs.'

'And if you hadn't I would die without standing a chance against destiny.'

'What? And you think Anne is going to kill you tonight?'

'Of course not. Anne is Robin. It's Thane who's going to kill me.' Far from irrational panic, she looked calm and composed as she imparted this new knowledge.

'And who am I then?'

'You're Fizz.'

Noah stood up suddenly, pulled off his woolly hat and dropped it down on the table. He was about to talk to her about doctors and making an appointment to see her counsellor for the morning, but as if pre-empting his reaction she said, 'I know what you're thinking, but before you have me carted off to the funny farm I have to tell you something. Anne killed Sam with a green scone. Sound familiar?'

Noah shook his head. 'So you dreamt about a green scone. It's not as if Thane's never mentioned his green scones before.'

'But he hasn't mentioned them for months. I bet–' she began, but she didn't get a chance to finish her sentence as the doors burst open and the bar was flooded with her friends and family.

'Happy birthday! Happy birthday!' they all sang and crowded around the table.

Charlotte's dad, who had grown a full, unruly, white beard in the last six months, threw his arm around Noah, who was still on his feet, and asked why he had changed the plan, and Noah gave him a grave look that revealed some of his concerns for his daughter. Then the lights suddenly went off and they were plunged into darkness before the light of a single candle glided through the crowd down to Charlotte.

'Happy birthday!' Thane beamed. 'I've made you one of my legendary green scones,' he told her. 'Make a wish.'

Charlotte shot Noah a look that said, 'Now do you believe me,' before blowing out the candle. Cheers went up all around her and Thane led them all in a round of 'For she's a jolly good fellow.'

'Okay, everyone back to the party,' Noah announced when the singing was done. 'And we'll be through shortly.' He then herded his friends back into the other room like the worst party host in the world and shut the door on them, leaving just Charlotte, Thane and himself in the room. The sudden change in atmosphere was made all the more noticeable when Noah demanded Thane join them at the table.

'Hang on!' he half-smiled. 'What's all this about?'

'I think you know,' Noah told him and pointed down to the green scone. It was an ugly looking pastry with unattractive chunks of a leafy green substance protruding from its crust and a thin layer of bogey-green icing on the top.

Noah shrugged.

'He doesn't know anything,' Charlotte told Noah.

'I really don't,' Thane agreed.

'Thane,' Charlotte said slowly and calmly, leaning across the table and maintaining eye contact to show him how serious she was. 'I need you to tell me what's in that scone.'

'Ha! No way! All this just to get me to reveal my secret ingredient!'

'For God's sake!' Noah snapped impatiently, but Charlotte was able to handle Thane more sensitively.

'If I eat this I'm going to die,' she told him, lingering on the word 'die' so he could absorb the magnitude of it.

'Don't talk shit! My scones are legendary. No one's ever died from eating them yet.'

'I need you to tell me what's in them. Have you put anything in them that you wouldn't usually use?'

He shook his head and they could both see from his eyes that he was starting to get upset. He looked so boyish all of the sudden. He had tried to do something so nice by preparing food for them and now he was in the middle of the Spanish Inquisition.

'Just tell us what's in them!' Noah demanded and his tone made Thane suddenly defiant. He shook his head again and then reached out to take the scone away.

'I'm going,' he told them. 'I don't have to stand for this.'

'Please, just tell us what's in it,' Charlotte tried again.

'It's a secret recipe,' Thane told her again and sat back in his chair with his arms folded. Nothing was said for a heartbeat and then he suddenly sat forward again. 'Nothing's happened to anyone else, but what if you were allergic to something that's in them?'

'Well, what's in them?'

'I can't tell you that.'

'I swear, Thane …' Noah raged and let the threat hang in the air.

'Are you allergic to dairy?' he asked.

'No,' she said and shook her head.

'Oh well, there's nothing dairy in them anyway.'

'Would you please take this seriously!' Noah demanded.

'Nuts!' he offered. 'Peanuts?'

Charlotte sat forward again suddenly. 'Are there peanuts in the scone?'

'There might be.'

'Please, Thane. I'm seriously allergic to peanuts. If there's even a trace of a nut in there it will probably kill me before I can make it to the hospital.'

'Would you be happier if I had or hadn't used peanuts to make the scone?'

Noah cuffed his ear as a father would a son and Thane held his hands up in front of him. 'Yes, he finally conceded. It contains peanuts.' He was about to add the proviso that they shouldn't tell anyone because it's top secret, when Charlotte jumped up out of her seat, practically leapt across the table and planted a kiss on his lips. She pulled out the candle, tossed it out onto the table, picked up the scone and held it aloft on the saucer away from her body as if the merest touch of it would burn her skin. She then ran out of the pub door, gripped it firmly and threw it with all her might. She watched as it landed in a green splat on the other side of carpark.

'Charming!' Thane smiled, as he and Noah arrived beside her, and they all laughed uncontrollably as they watched a car run the green splodge over and drive away with icing going round and round on its back wheel. They laughed so hard that the icy wind and snowfall barely troubled them. But Charlotte's laughter suddenly subsided when she saw shapes forming in the falling snow. She blinked away at the flakes that had fallen on her eyelashes, but the shapes in front of her remained.

'Can you see that?' she asked the boys and looked at them both in turn. Their stunned expressions confirmed that she wasn't imagining it; the snow was no longer falling to the ground, but hovering before it could land and then fluttering around their heads with silken wings – a million tiny, beautiful butterflies. Charlotte, Noah and Thane were unable to move as they watched the night magically fill with butterflies. They were equally dumbstruck as the butterflies began to move closer together, first creating a fluttering wall of movement before refining their shape until a figure emerged.

'Are you seeing this?' Thane managed to ask, but neither of the others was able to reply as the butterflies took the form of a woman's dress, long and flowy, and the woman beneath slowly began to glide towards them.

'I know you,' Charlotte mouthed and could say no more as the woman stood just inches away from her and radiated her warmth over the three of them. She was the most beautiful creature that any of them had ever seen, although she was snow-blanched and nebulous. Her hair cascaded down the shoulders of her butterfly dress and her open, honest features told a hundred love stories that all three of them felt in their hearts at the same time. She remained in front of them for no more than thirty seconds then opened her mouth and simply said, 'Thank you,' with her eyes fixed on Charlotte. The word radiated around the entire carpark and sounded like a calling from heaven itself. Her message delivered, she smiled warmly then the butterflies took to the air once again before returning to their original form, gently snowing down onto the ground and leaving Charlotte, Noah and Thane standing alone in the silent car park.

Epilogue

E xactly a year to the day later, the day before Charlotte's twenty-first birthday, she was standing out the front of the Sir Robin's Head with her father on one side of her, Noah on the other and an audience and camera crew in front of her. The old landlord was serving time for an assault on some other poor soul and the new landlord was a much kinder man who had welcomed Charlotte's interest – or obsession, as her father called it. It was early evening and the weather was shocking, but not as bad as it had been that night – the night that marked the beginning of the rest of Charlotte's life. In her hand she held a pulley attached a curtain, which had been hung just below the roof of the pub.

'As many of you know,' Charlotte announced, 'I have been immersed in research for the last year, to prove the innocence of Sir Robin, whose eponymous head was removed when he was accused of murdering his best friend. Although I have been unable to uncover new evidence, I have managed to wear Mr Reynolds, the new landlord here, down and he agrees with me that a public house should not celebrate the death of a man potentially wrongly accused. And so, ladies and gentleman, I give you …' She pulled the cord and the curtain opened, revealing the new name of the pub, 'The Brave Sir Robin's Arms.'

The small assembled crowd gave a supportive cheer and then a more enthusiastic one when Mr Reynolds said, 'First drinks are on the house,' and everyone raced inside to take advantage of the offer, including Noah and Charlotte, whose days of standing around in the freezing cold were over.

Printed in Great Britain
by Amazon.co.uk, Ltd.,
Marston Gate.